SINFULLY SHAMELESS CHEF

THE FURY FAMILY SERIES
BOOK 3

GWYN MCNAMEE

Sinfully Shameless Chef
by
Gwyn McNamee © 2021 © 2023 (previously published as Shameless Chef)

Cover Design: Tiffany Black at TE Black Designs
Cover Model: Andrew Biernat
Photographer: Wander Aguiar
Editor: Stephie Walls

1

JAMESON

The only thing that could make this moment any better would be having my dick sucked while I stand here in this beautiful building. Since that isn't an option—at least, not without things getting *really* awkward with Grant watching—I'll have to settle for having my ego stroked.

Thankfully, this blond real estate agent showing us the space is a super fan. She hasn't stopped batting her long, fake eyelashes and practically offering herself up to me on a silver platter since the minute we met outside. She even brought the damn edition of *Foodie Magazine* with my picture on the cover for me to sign.

Who the hell does that? A total psycho.

People always say the crazy ones are the best in bed, though, in my experience, they're far more trouble than they're worth. So even though having her pretty red lips wrapped around my cock would be an enjoyable way to spend the day, there's no way I'd touch her with a ten-foot pole.

No matter how badly I might need a little stress relief right now.

She beams at me and holds out her arms as she spins in her sky-high stilettos. "So, what do you think?"

I don't even need time to consider my response. I knew the second I walked in. "It's fucking perfect. I'll take it."

"*You'll* take it?" Grant snorts and pushes off the wall by the door where he's been scrolling through his phone and clicking away at it for the past few minutes. "*You* are not taking anything. In case you don't remember, *you* don't have any goddamn money."

I toss him a dirty look. "Yeah, yeah, yeah. Thanks for reminding me that I need you, asshole."

And I do have *some* money—though only because I was smart about my winnings from *Prime Chef*. It wasn't much, but being willing to put up my own money convinced Grant to let me retain forty-nine percent of our venture to his fifty-one percent.

He chuckles and shrugs, his perfectly tailored suit that likely costs twice what I made last month moving fluidly with him, undoubtedly made to custom fit his lean frame.

Always so fucking arrogant.

Though, I guess he has reason to be. He clawed his way up from the bottom on his own and is a force to be reckoned with. His name means something in New York. It's why he's the perfect partner, even though I would prefer to be doing this on my own.

"But"—I tap my temple—"I seem to remember you telling me I could have the final decision on the location."

He sighs and rolls his eyes. "I did, Jamo, but this is only the second place we've looked at, and we have seven or eight other potential locations lined up to check out next week. Don't you want to see what the other options are before you make this decision?" He glances around and motions toward the street outside. "I mean, this place is kind of a shitty location. It's all residential. There isn't very much foot traffic. It isn't exactly the best place to put the restaurant, is it?"

Normally, I would agree that he has a point, but there are a few things he's not considering. The fact that there are no other restaurants around this area of Bushwick is a *good* thing. It means we'll be at the top of the list of options. This is also an up-and-coming neighborhood. Lots of yuppies making their way over from Manhattan, which is exactly the type of clientele I'm looking for—people with loads of expendable income.

This building is also perfect. The exposed brick, high-lofted ceilings with massive steel beams, the raw, scratched-up wood floors. I couldn't have designed it better myself, and it comes like this. It's the kind of location restaurateurs kill for. We're lucky to have seen it before someone else snatched it out from under us.

I shake my head at him. "I don't need to look at anything else. This is the place. Trust me. It's perfect."

It's exactly what I've been busting my ass and working so hard for—some place that will be *mine*.

Grant sighs and turns back to the real estate agent.

Betsy? Barbara? Whatever...it doesn't matter.

He scowls at her. "How much is this place going to set me back?"

She plasters on that saccharin sweet smile. "It's listed at $875,000."

"Jesus Christ." Grant whirls and looks around at the interior of the old warehouse. "For this piece of shit?"

Her smile doesn't waiver. "This is an up-and-coming neighborhood, Mr. Mason. There's a lot of demand for real estate in this area, especially for commercial and business properties. I just sold a residential unit across the street the other day for almost $700,000 that would have sold for half that two years ago."

His jaw drops. "You've gotta be shitting me. Maybe this is where I should've been investing the last couple of years."

She laughs, a high, tinkling sound that's almost as fake as that smile of hers. "That might've been wise, Mr. Mason. The building you share a wall with sold several months ago to a group of investors. I'm actually surprised they didn't come back to scoop up this side, too."

Grant raises a dark eyebrow. "Any idea what they plan to do with it?"

She shrugs. "Who the hell knows. None of my business."

He turns back to me, his eyes narrowing. "$875,000, Jameson. Just for the building. What's it going to cost me to put in a full kitchen?"

I inwardly cringe at his question but try not to show my concern outwardly. He has no idea how expensive it is to put together a professional kitchen. The range alone will cost around twenty grand.

When he agreed to back my restaurant venture, I told him it would not be cheap, but I held off on giving him specifics, mostly because I couldn't afford to have him back out. He's the only one I know who has this kind of money and the right amount of faith in me. For the amount of cash I could bring to the table compared to what will be needed to get us up and running and in the long-term, any other backer would have demanded *far* more than the fifty-one percent Grant took.

It wasn't a great business move, to be honest, and at times, I still wonder how I managed to convince him to take this gamble. But my whole life has felt like one giant risk— ignoring my natural ability, even as a child, in the "family business" and ultimately going to culinary school was viewed by some as a major mistake. And the other investors I approached saw me as way too big a risk to take on.

Grant doesn't see me that way, though. If I hadn't met him at that event at the Met, and if he hadn't tasted my food there and loved it, we wouldn't even be here today. I'd still be stuck cooking in someone else's kitchen while they raked in all the dough and got all the publicity.

After winning *Prime Chef* and getting the magazine cover, this is the time to strike while the iron is hot. We need to leverage my name and Grant's connections while I'm still on the rise. Before I do something to fuck it all up.

I clear my throat and try to sound casual when laying out the costs he's going to be looking at when it comes to the kitchen. "You're probably looking at another two hundred grand, at least, to get all the new kitchen equipment and have it installed."

Whoever saw the potential in this place years ago left behind bits and pieces of low-end stuff I will never be able to use, but at least they did some of the major renovations needed to make this place a functioning restaurant. It will save us a lot of time and money.

He shoves a hand back through his dark hair. "Jesus. Then, we have to add any remodeling and building-out."

I glance around and grin at him. "That's one of the reasons I like this place. We're not going to have to do a whole lot. Seal the floors. Erect a partition or two. Décor. The only major thing I wonder about would be any issues with the roof or any wood rot."

Betsy/Barbara steps up to us. "We had the place inspected. As far as we can tell, there isn't any major damage anywhere despite the building's age. And since someone already started building it out as a restaurant years ago before they abandoned the project, the kitchen is already laid out in the back, and some of the permits are already in place. It shouldn't be too much of a project."

Grant holds his hand over his mouth and brushes his thumb across his lips as he ponders the situation. "Which means we might be able to open sooner than anticipated?"

Ding. Ding. Ding.

It's no surprise a suggestion we can make money faster would get him on board. The man is nothing if not predictable when it comes to cash.

Opening a restaurant from the ground up can take a year, eighteen months sometimes, but with this location mostly built-out and permitted, and with Grant's resources, we can fast-track things and hopefully cut it down to a few months.

I wander over to him and elbow him in the side. "What do you think?"

He drops his hand and scowls at me. "I think you're trying to bankrupt me."

I smirk and shake my head. "You have more money than God. This project isn't going to bankrupt you. Nice try, though."

He frowns at me, and his phone rings. He pulls it from his pocket and glances at the screen. "I need to take this. If this is really the place you want, have the papers sent over to my office and I'll get everything taken care of."

Fuck yes.

It's the first step of many to finally attain the dream I've had since I was five and helping Mom in the kitchen back home in Michigan. After all the hard days in culinary school and long nights working in sweltering restaurants under chefs who treated me like a fucking child, I'm going to have a restaurant. A place of my own.

Jameson Fury—owner and executive chef.

It has a nice ring to it.

Grant disappears out the front door, and the blonde turns back to me.

"So, do we have a deal?" That saccharine-sweet smile returns as Betsy/Barbara bats her lashes in a way that makes it look like she has some dust in her eye.

Definitely going to pass, sweetheart.

"We do. When can you get the paperwork together?"

"I can have them over to Grant's office this afternoon."

"Perfect."

She places her hand on my forearm. "So, Mr. Fury, do you know what you're going to call the place?"

I pull my arm away from her and survey the building that will become the home of my first solo venture—well, solo aside from the whole Grant owning fifty-one percent thing.

A thousand different names have bounced around in my head since I first decided to take this step, but only one has stuck.

"I'm going to call it *FURY*."

———

IZZY

There isn't any use fighting the tears like I've had to so many other times. It would be a failing battle. They trickle down my cheeks unrestrained, the salty taste hitting my lips—so familiar after so many wept over my lifetime. Over Mom. Over my situation. Over losing Grams...

I brush them away as fast as possible, but it isn't quick enough to keep Rochelle from seeing them and frowning with concern.

Shit.

Not only is this embarrassing, but I fucking *hate* that

look from people. *Pity.* I'm so sick of people seeing me as weak and in need of constant help and support. Grams always knew how strong I am. She understood I would never give up, never stop pushing to ensure I got what I want.

She always said she admired my drive, that it would do me well in life, especially when she was gone and I was on my own. I never believed that day would come, though. Despite witnessing death and knowing it was inevitable for everyone, Grams always seemed so invincible. So full of life and brightness. The kind of person who truly lives forever.

I should have known better. Deep down, I *did*. Yet, her death still hit me harder than even Mom's did.

But I shouldn't be crying right now.

Not for her.

This is a *happy* thing. A day I've always fantasized about the way most little girls do their wedding. While some imagined white puffy dresses and a man waiting for them at the altar, I was dreaming of gleaming stainless-steel appliances, the smiles of customers I've just served delicious food to, and my name listed as executive chef.

And now, it's all finally coming true, despite all the things standing in my way. Years of pain and struggle are *finally* paying off. But even with my heart full of hope for the future, it can't mask the hole there left by the fact that Grams isn't here to share this with me.

She'll never get to see what the money she left me is going to allow me to do with this space. She won't see the name of the restaurant on a sign over the door. She won't be here opening night to celebrate and enjoy the dishes inspired by her recipes. I won't get to see her eyes light up or that wide smile she always wore when she tasted my cooking.

Rochelle squeezes my arm. "You okay?"

Get it together, Iz. You look like a blubbering idiot.

I nod and swipe under my eyes again to remove the evidence of my meltdown. It's a good thing I don't really wear makeup, or I'd look like a drowned hooker right now. "I'm good."

She dangles a set of keys in front of me. "Here they are. This place is all yours. At least, for the next five years under the lease."

We share a laugh, and it helps loosen some of the tightness in my chest. Taking the keys from her and clutching them in my fist feels almost surreal. A dream I'll wake up from and get snapped right back into my painful reality. Like this can't really be happening—not to me.

Things like *this* don't happen for me. Nothing is ever easy. I've had to *make* things happen and fight tooth and nail against all the ways life and the world try to beat me down.

And it's only the beginning. It's going to take a lot of work to turn this place into what I've imagined in my head all these years, but I'm not afraid of hard work or a little adversity. Hell, I put myself through culinary school while working two jobs and taking care of Grams, despite everything else going on in my own life.

If I can do that, I can do this.

Rochelle pushes me forward. "Let's go in."

I step up to entrance to the old building, insert the key into the ancient lock, and twist. It clicks open, and I push the door in to what will hopefully become a beautiful restaurant in the not-too-distant future.

My breath catches in my throat the same way it did the first time I stepped inside this place a week ago. "It's gorgeous."

The perfect rustic, industrial style I was looking for. With the right furniture and décor, this place will be quaint and homey—exactly how I want it to feel for any customer who steps through the door.

Rochelle's heels click across the hardwood floors as she makes her way to the center of the massive place. "You're very lucky to get a lease for this place. If you had waited a few more months, our prices probably would've doubled. The whole area is really starting to boom. You can't even imagine what the owners paid for this space."

"Oh, I believe it." I twirl around and take it all in like it's the first time. "It's beautiful *and* a great location."

I've never wanted a restaurant in the hustle and bustle of Manhattan. That just isn't me or my vision. I want somewhere locals can gather. A place the neighborhood can think of as their own. A welcoming hub.

Rochelle raises a brow. "You have any ideas about interior yet?"

I grin and walk over to the far side of the space where a basic kitchen is already set up with appliances that look almost as old as me. "I'll keep the kitchen over here, obviously, since it's already built out somewhat. I still can't believe someone had a restaurant here at one time and abandoned it."

She nods her agreement as I walk the perimeter of the room. "That was well before my time, but I imagine this neighborhood twenty or thirty years ago was a lot different than it is today."

No doubt.

While it saddens me to think someone tried and failed here, it also makes this start-up a little bit easier and faster. Time isn't exactly on my side, and I want to get as much done as possible before anything gets in the way.

Looking around, a vision takes shape, crystal clear in my head, almost like I'm viewing it on a movie screen in front of me. "I think I'm going to have about twenty-five tables.

Varying sizes. I want to do some long community tables, some round tables so everyone engages in conversation with each other, and then some smaller, more intimate ones for couples."

Rochelle smiles, her dark pink lips curling up naturally. "Wow, you've really been thinking about this a lot."

I grin at her and clutch the keys tightly in my hand. "My entire life."

Literally.

"I grew up in my grandmother's kitchen and always wanted to share her recipes and what she taught me with the world." Emotion tightens my chest, and I rub at it absently. "When I graduated from culinary school, I thought it would take me decades to have the money to open my own place, but my grandmother's passing brought me an unexpected small inheritance."

Barely enough to afford a year's worth of rent on this place and not nearly what I'll need to open a restaurant. The small personal loan I managed to secure using Grams' house as collateral is the only reason I'm holding these keys.

Her death almost broke me emotionally, but it offered me an opportunity for something she always wanted for me. I just have to keep reminding myself of that as I go through the steps of getting this place ready.

Rochelle's eyes soften, and she offers me a sympathetic look. "I'm so sorry about your grandmother."

I smile at her through the unshed tears blurring my vision. "It's okay. She was ninety-three years old. She lived a good, long life full of happiness and family and friends. It's all anyone can ask for."

"True." She glances around the space. "Well, you know under the terms of the lease that you're permitted to make any changes you need to convert this to a functioning restaurant, but the owners don't want any work done on the exterior or any changes to the interior architectural elements."

"No worries. It's perfect. I'm not going to change anything that I don't have to."

"Excellent." She claps her hands. "I'll leave you to it, then. I have another meeting downtown in an hour."

I glance at my watch. "An hour? Do you have enough time with traffic to get down there?"

She chuckles and shakes her head. "Probably not, but they can wait."

Not exactly the attitude I would use for clients, but I guess when you work for such a wealthy investment firm that owns properties all over the city, you can kind of do what you want and treat people like they aren't worth your time.

It's the same thing they do at all the fancy restaurants. Those arrogant chefs who think their shit doesn't stink serve fancy food you can't even recognize and use ingredients most people can't even pronounce.

Those places are stuffy and cold. My place will be different. I'll create a community here. Another home where I can make the people of the neighborhood my family and share all the love Grams bestowed on me through her food with them.

Rochelle makes her way toward the door. "Have you figured out what you're going to name it?"

I shake my head. "Something will come to me eventually."

"I'm sure it will. Good luck."

"Thank you."

She ducks out the door, and I'm left standing alone...but I don't *feel* alone. Not when I'm finally *here.* I can almost feel Grandma's presence with me, guiding me and helping me stay strong when I have no doubt this entire process is going to break me down mentally *and* physically.

"Thank you so much for helping me get here, Grams."

Tears roll down my cheeks, and I reach up to brush them away. She wouldn't want me to cry for her. So, I won't. I'll just create the best restaurant I can and totally kick ass in her name.

And there's one more thing I can do in her honor. Something I should have thought of a long time ago, long before she took her final breath in this world. Something that just feels *right* and makes my heart swell.

Every day, I'll stand outside on the cracked sidewalk and stare up at the name above the door and be reminded of why I'm here, of who brought me to this point and everything she sacrificed and taught me.

I'm going to call it *Grandma's Kitchen.*

2

IZZY

What started out as a light drizzle has become a torrential rainstorm. Buckets of water fall from the sky, and my windshield wipers just can't keep up. Even at full speed, I can barely see out of the glass to the street directly in front of me.

I might as well be driving under water, and the fog building around the edges of the windshield doesn't help, either.

Shit.

Not exactly the best day to be meeting with the contractor about starting work on the restaurant.

I hope he isn't delayed by this weather.

People drive like idiots when it's like this, and it took me twice as long to get here as it should have this morning. It's only amped up the tension in my shoulders at finally starting the dream I've had for so damn long. The slow progress would have been even more agonizing if I didn't have Ashley with me today to keep me company and prevent me from getting road-ragey.

But with her attention focused on her phone screen, she doesn't seem to be interested in the distress the weather is causing me or my nerves about meeting with person who will be in charge of making my dream a reality.

Two blocks from the building, I start scanning for parking spots. Technically, the road directly in front of the building is a loading zone, but Rochelle said I could park there during the construction to make it easier to get in and out and reserve the area for any unloading of supplies. Which is good because the streets around here are just as bad as everywhere else in greater New York, with so many cars parked on them that sometimes I can drive around for an hour, trying to find a spot.

I approach the cross-street, checking both ways to see if anything is open near the corners. A big black SUV rolls through a stop sign to my right, turns in front of me, and flies down the street, spraying water off the tires back onto my car.

"Shit!" I slam on my brakes, both to give myself a little distance from the monster vehicle and because the water completely blinds me momentarily.

Ashley huffs, the abrupt stop finally dragging her from whatever has her face glued to her phone screen. "What a jerk!"

"I know!" I glance her way, then refocus on the road. "The asshole could have waited at the stop sign for me to pass before they pulled out."

It seems it's going to be one of *those* days.

I can barely see the building through the driving rain, but at least it looks like I can pull right up front and avoid getting drenched to start my day. Nothing sucks worse than being wet and cold, and if I had to sit in soaked clothes all day, I would be fucking miserable.

As soon as I flip on my blinker, the brake lights of the

SUV driven by the douchebag in front of me flare, and it pulls into the spot directly in front of the building.

My building.

My fucking spot!

"What the hell?"

With a frustrated scream, I slam on my brakes next to the offending vehicle and roll down the passenger window.

Rain pelts Ashley through the opening, and she cringes and shifts as close to me and away from it as she can. "Oh, my God! What are you doing? Close the damn window!"

Not a fucking chance.

The driver's door of the SUV opens, and a dark head of hair appears, followed by a far too handsome man who I might actually appreciate if I weren't so furious at him. He steps out into the rain, instantly soaked by the downpour.

I lean over Ashley and glare at him. "What the hell are you doing parking in my spot?"

He bends down and peers into my car. His dark eyebrows rise, and amber eyes shimmer back at me. Water soaks his black hair and trickles down his cheeks, only accentuating how perfect and angular they are.

A smirk pulls at his picture-perfect lips. "*Your* spot? Nice try, sweetheart."

He winks at me, slams his door, and jogs around the side of the SUV and into the building I share a wall with.

"Shit."

Is that jerk renting the place next door?

Ashley's jaw drops. "Oh, my God. Do you know who that is?"

I shift back into my seat and hit the button to raise Ashley's window so she doesn't end up looking like a drowned rat. "No, what the hell does it matter who he is? The asshole just took my parking spot!"

"That's Jameson Fury—"

A car horn blaring behind me has me jerking my head to look in the rearview mirror at a vehicle waiting on the street, unable to get around me to pass with cars parked on both sides.

"Shit." I take my foot off the brake and make my way farther down the block, scanning for somewhere to park now that *my* space has been occupied by that prick.

Ashley digs around the back of my car through all the junk and grabs something from the floorboard behind me. "You know who Jameson Fury is, right? Winner of *Prime Chef* on Webflix last year? Voted *Hottest Chef in New York*?"

She waves something around, and I turn the corner and pull over illegally in front of a fire hydrant just to see what it is.

Foodie Magazine.

An issue I remember very well. The one with a shirtless, dark-haired, smoking-hot guy on a blue apron crossing his arms over his chest on the cover. The look he gives the camera is so dirty, it's almost a promise he's going to tear off your panties and fuck you on the table he stands behind.

A shiver rolls through me looking into those same eyes that locked with mine only a minute ago through the rain. "That was Jameson Fury back there?"

She nods, and I glance up and down the street.

No available spots.

I could be parked and inside and working already if it weren't for him. Now I'll waste half my morning driving around and then get there soaked. "Well, I don't care who the fuck he is. He's a *dick*. We're going to be looking for a spot forever."

Ash's lips twist. "I think you have a bigger problem than that..."

"Oh, yeah, what's that?" I pull back out onto the street and continue scanning for a spot. "Because right now, this seems like a big problem when I'm supposed to be meeting with the contractor."

"Iz, he parked in front of *your* building and went into the door right next to yours. What do you think Jameson Fury, the hottest chef in New York, is doing there?"

A heavy sense of dread wraps around my spine. "Oh, shit. You don't think he's opening a restaurant, do you?"

I catch her shrug out of the corner of my eye as I turn down the next block.

"I don't know, Iz, but it's definitely a possibility." She leans forward and points. "Look! There's a spot."

Thank God!

But of course, it's tiny, and I need to parallel park to get into it.

Of fucking course.

I throw on my blinker, pull past the spot, and throw my arm across the back of Ashley's seat so I can turn and see what I'm doing. The move sends a tiny twinge through my side that I brush to the back of my mind so I can focus on the task at hand. Ashley knows better than to try to talk to me while I'm doing this. I'm a decent parallel parker—a skill I had to learn to master young growing up in Brooklyn—but this is a tight spot, and with my adrenaline running this high already, I don't need any interruptions.

After a minute of finagling, I finally put the car into park and drop my forehead against the steering wheel, giving myself a moment to process what she just said.

"Great, so now we can get soaked running a block and a half back to the building where this douchebag might be opening a competing restaurant right next door?"

Ashley squeezes my shoulder gently, and I force myself to drag up my head and look at her.

She grins at me. "Look at the silver lining. He is the

hottest chef in New York, and he's right next door. At least you'll have something nice to look at every day."

Maybe that's a bonus for her, but I'm not in any place in my life to enjoy gawking at a handsome man—even if he weren't an asshole, which he *clearly* is. There are too many other things going on, things that need my attention constantly. Things that I can't let get out of control.

Any distractions are dangerous to my plans and goals.

Ashley can come to ogle Jameson Fury. I have my priorities straight.

———

JAMESON

I *almost* feel bad for the blonde who wanted the parking spot. Almost. But I'm not about to give it up to walk a couple blocks in this rain—not when I got here first, fair and square. I'm already wet enough just from stopping to talk to her for a second.

Nothing like wet clothes to make your day shit.

Drops roll down my neck and back, and I run my hand through my hair to squeegee out some water. That only pushes it down my thoroughly soaked white T-shirt, making it even wetter—which I didn't think was possible. It clings to my chest and abs like it's painted on me. Even my jeans are soaked just from getting out of the car and running in.

This is going to be a long day if I'm cold and miserable, but I don't have much choice. No time to run home and grab a change of clothes. If we have *any* chance of getting this place opened quickly, there isn't any time to waste getting things rolling.

I'll just suffer today thanks to Miss Blondie.

I glance around the building to take in all the work that

needs to be done. Danny should be here any minute to start sketching out the final plans for my dream restaurant and take the measurements. His preliminary layout looked great, but we need to get all the specifics before ordering the equipment and furniture and really getting to down to business.

With Grant's money on the line, any delays aren't just costing me; they're costing *him*. Owing anyone anything rubs me the wrong way, but none of this would be possible at all without him. That means I'll do whatever it takes to ensure *Fury* is a success as soon as possible.

This place needs to be up and running in two months... three months...tops. Which means, the list of things to do is endless. I pull the folded sheet containing the checklist out of my pocket and try to peel the wet paper apart.

The ink spreads out across the pages in blobs.

Shit. At least it's still legible.

> *Order sign for outside.*
> *Order kitchen appliances.*
> *Order tables, chairs, and other furniture.*
> *Order plates, glasses, other décor.*
> *Hire manager, waitstaff, kitchen staff.*
> *Have Danny schedule inspections.*

It goes on, and on, and on...

But until Danny gets here, I can start on some calls and trying to make some headway on this shit.

I wander over to the windowsill and lower myself down on it since it's the only real place to sit right now to search for the number of the sign maker Grant recommended— somebody he used on another project—and hit send.

"Hello, Waters and Sons Signs"—the woman's perky

tone this early in the morning when I'm sitting here cold and wet grates on my nerves—"how can I help you?"

"Hi, yes, I need to order a sign for a restaurant."

"Oh, okay, do you have any idea what size and style?"

I grin to myself, picturing it hung on the brick outside. It's something I've been giving a lot of thought, but one vision has been clear in my head since the moment I first decided to go to culinary school. "Red neon with flames around it."

"Ooooh!" the woman practically coos. "That does sound fun. I can have somebody come out there tomorrow to figure out what type would work, take measurements, and figure out the placement. Just give me the address and your contact information."

I rattle off the address and my phone number and end the call.

One thing to check off the list.

My phone screen barely goes black before the door flies open. A very angry and wet blonde stands in the doorway, her hands fisted at her sides—the chick from the car, with her friend right behind her.

What the hell?

She storms in, green eyes blazing and dark T-shirt clinging to her body under the soaked jacket she wears open over it. Her nipples pebble through her bra, something I doubt she's even noticed, given how all of her wrath seems to be directed straight at me.

But even the twist of rage on her lips, the hint of mascara running under her eyes, and her hair plastered around her face can't hide how beautiful she is.

She points back toward the door. "I just had to walk two blocks in the pouring rain because of you."

I shove off the ledge and meet her halfway across the

room, the squish of my wet shoes on the floor in my ears. "Sorry." I shrug. "Not my problem, though."

The woman opens and closes her hands at her sides. "Didn't your mother teach you any manners?"

I snort. "I don't think that includes having to give up a parking spot that I got to first in the middle of a rainstorm."

She scowls at me, her perfect pink-bow lips twisting up. The move makes her appear far younger than she probably actually is, and while it should be annoying or even make me angry, it's almost comical to see such a cute woman so angry about something so asinine.

Her eyes dart around the empty space. "What are you doing here, anyway?"

I smirk and cross my arms over my chest. "How is that any of your business?"

She glances back at her friend, who waves her hand, urging the blonde to continue. "Because I'm leasing the space next door."

Well, hell...

That does make me feel slightly bad about taking the parking spot, but I'm not going to let her know that. This woman is hot as hell when she's pissed off. Changing that would be a real shame.

I raise an eyebrow at her. "And who might you be?"

She glowers at me, looking determined not to give me any information, but her friend steps forward and pushes her way up between us.

The friend flashes me a smile. "Her name is Isabella Baldwin, and she's opening her first restaurant next door."

"Oh, hell." I sigh and rub at my jaw. "You're fucking kidding me."

The friend shakes her head and opens something rolled in her hand. A magazine...my cover. "And I know who you

23

are...Jameson Fury. Which is why we want to know what you're doing here."

Isabella narrows her eyes at me. "I sure as hell hope you're not opening a restaurant here."

Things just got a whole fuck of a lot more complicated for my business plan.

One reason I chose this location was that the immediate neighborhood lacks any restaurants. Bushwick is blowing up and revitalizing at a tremendous rate. Setting up here would have made me unique in an underserved area and in the perfect place when things do explode here. "So what if I am?"

Isabella nudges her friend out of the way with her shoulder. "Well, that's going to create quite a problem for me."

"Is it?"

Her mouth drops open incredulously. "It's a big-shot celebrity chef competing with my restaurant when I have zero name recognition and probably a quarter of the budget you do. Of course, it's a problem!"

I shrug and fight a grin at the fact that she called me a "big-shot celebrity chef." Though, she definitely didn't mean it as a compliment the way *she* said it. The woman does have a point, though. It will be hard for her, but I don't want to make her day any worse than it already is. "Maybe it won't be so bad after all."

That's a lie.

She's right. I have no idea who this chick is, and I've won a prestigious television cooking competition, been on the cover of a major food magazine, and have been named the hottest chef in the city. I've worked my way up through some of the best restaurants in the country over the last few years to make sure people know who I am. There's no way her place is going to be as big of a draw as mine.

I wouldn't even consider it competition. Not really.

But even if it were, I've never been one to back down from a little challenge. That's the one good thing Bash, Rach, and I inherited from Dad—the drive to succeed at any cost. It may have been horrible for our family life back then, but it has definitely helped all three of us thrive.

Isabella scowls again and grits her teeth. "You're going to put me out of business before I even open."

I flash her my best panty-melting grin. The one that always seems to work on the women I meet. "Again. Not my problem."

The woman growls—actually fucking growls at me. It rumbles low in her chest and slips from her lips. "You're a real jerk, you know that?"

A chuckle bubbles up my throat, and I shake my head. "I've been told that once or twice in my life."

Her steely emerald gaze holds mine. "I can see why."

Wow, this chick is full of piss and vinegar.

And the blush spreading across her cheeks with her rage only emphasizes her perfect bone structure. I almost feel bad for her. With my place opening next door, hers doesn't stand a chance. But such is the way it goes in business and life.

Sometimes, you win. Sometimes, you lose.

She glowers at me one more time before she grabs her friend's arm and drags her from the building out into the rain.

I grin and shake my head as I wander back to my spot by the window to wait for Danny.

Things just got a whole lot more interesting.

3

JAMESON

"Are you at all worried about this?" Grant's question from behind me holds the same note of tension I've been trying to ease from him since he first arrived and I told him about our new neighbor.

It's a good thing we had already made plans to meet up tonight; otherwise, I would have had to tell him about it over the phone or request a meeting specifically to fill him in, and that might have made this who conversation a lot harder.

I turn back toward the kitchen counter, where he sits nursing a glass of wine. "You think I should be? You don't know me very well, then."

Grant grins and takes a sip of his wine, then holds the glass up toward me. "You're right. I don't drink much, but this is good. We should definitely have it on the menu."

"Just wait 'til you taste it with this." I motion to the steak in the cast-iron skillet on the stove. "It's amazing with beef. And I'm already on the hunt for a great sommelier to do pairings for us."

He smiles and chuckles. "You know I love a nice meal as much as the next guy, but I promise to trust you with all menu decisions."

"As you should."

The man doesn't know the first thing about opening or running a restaurant. And while I might be fumbling around like a newborn trying to figure it out myself, at least I've *worked* in them and have done my homework on what we need to ensure everything is absolutely perfect.

"I know my role here." He points to himself. "I'm just the money guy."

Grant is more than that, and we both know it. We've become close over the last year, and if we didn't have this much trust in each other, neither of us would have agreed to become partners in this endeavor in the first place.

I flip the steak in the pan and shove it into the oven for a few minutes to ensure it's the perfect medium-rare. "You're more than that, and you know it. I could never have done this without your backing. You clearly have impeccable taste."

He laughs and sips his wine. "I won't argue there."

"I could probably use your help finalizing all the little décor and interior things. It's not really my forte, and we need it to look perfect."

"Where are we looking on the timeline?"

"Danny stopped by today and says he can have everything we discussed with the interior done in the next month as long as what he needs is in stock. And then we can start decorating and probably get opened in six to eight weeks if things go smoothly. Closer to three months if there are delays."

Grant considers me for a moment, running over something in his mind. "You're happy with that timeline?"

I rest my hands on the counter and sigh. "Obviously,

sooner is better, in my opinion. Normally, I wouldn't worry at all, considering how long it typically takes to open a restaurant, but..."

He inclines his glass toward me. "But now you have another restaurant opening right next door."

"Exactly."

While at first, I wasn't concerned, the longer the day went on and I saw people going in and out of her building just as fast as they came and went in mine, the more tense I became. For all I know, her side of the shared wall could be much closer to completion than ours. She may be able to open next week, which could be incredibly bad for us, even if she *isn't* a well-known name.

Grant takes a drink of his wine and watches the legs slide down the glass. "Do you know the girl?"

I shake my head and absently drum my fingers against the counter. "No. Never heard of her. And I only know her name at all because her friend told me when she flashed my magazine at me."

"So, she knows who *you* are."

I grin at him. "Of course, she does."

One of his dark eyebrows wings up. "And she isn't worried about opening a restaurant right next to you?"

Worried seems like a bit of an understatement after seeing her reaction this morning. She was livid—which *might* have had a bit to do with the whole parking situation —and scared at what it means to have Jameson Fury next door. "Oh, she most definitely is."

"So, it's going to be a rush to open?"

"It seems like it." I shrug because I honestly have no idea what her plans are. If we're lucky, she might decide to give up on the location and go somewhere less problematic. "But if she stays, I have no doubt she's going to try to launch before I do in order to ensure that she gets as much media attention as possible before we open and everything becomes about us."

Because that's exactly what I would do if I were in her shoes.

Worry twists Grant's lips. "Any idea what kind of restaurant she's opening?"

I shake my head and rub at my jaw. "No, but you better believe I'll be keeping an eye on her."

He chuckles and takes another sip of his wine. "Oh, I have no doubt about that. She cute?"

I turn back to the oven, pull out the pan, and transfer the steak to a plate that I slide in front of Grant. "She was drenched from head to toe when I met her and absolutely livid."

"That's not an answer to my question."

And that was completely intentional.

My new neighbor being a smokeshow is irrelevant to what's going on. "I'd be lying if I said I hadn't noticed she was hot."

It was hard not to with her nipples standing at attention in that tight, wet shirt. Even with the rain plastering her hair down around her face and the black make-up smearing under her eyes, she was still beautiful.

It's too bad we have to be enemies.

Grant narrows his gaze on me. "Why do you have that devious smile on your lips?"

Shit.

I hadn't even known I was smiling. "I'm just thinking about ways I can mess with our new friend next door. Maybe learn some more intel about what she's up to or even get her to leave."

He points a finger at me. "You be careful. The last thing you need is another enemy."

"Another enemy? What's that supposed to mean?"

He smirks. "I watched your season of *Prime Chef*, you know, and you didn't exactly make any friends."

I shrug. "I wasn't there to make friends. I was there to cook and win the money."

"It's a good thing you did; otherwise, I probably never would've met you catering the party at the Met, and we wouldn't find ourselves here on the brink of opening this restaurant together." He cuts his steak and shoves a piece into his mouth. His eyes widen slightly. "The steak is incredible, by the way. What all did you put on it?"

I wink at him. "If I told you, I'd have to kill you."

"Hey!" His brow furrows. "I'm your business partner."

"That may be true, but anything that happens in the kitchen is my business, not yours."

He holds up his hands. "Fair enough. But you want my help with the interior?"

"Now that I think about it, maybe I should have my sister come help me pick out plates and napkins and all that little shit. A woman's touch."

Grant takes another bite, chews slowly, then swallows. "That's a good idea. And I'm glad you're going to have a woman's touch with this." He glances around my tiny apartment. "No offense, dude, but your decorating taste sucks."

I chuckle at his very apt observation. "I'm not here very much. I've always been at whatever restaurant I was working at. So, it's not like I really need to decorate."

"When you first mentioned wanting my help, I was actually going to recommend you talk to Sylvie."

I jerk back from the counter. "Oh, hell no. I know better than that."

His eyebrows fly up. "What the hell is that supposed to mean?"

"Your wife has quite the reputation."

31

"Whoa, whoa, whoa!" He holds up a hand. "You better back that bus up, buddy."

"One of my uh...friends...worked with the designers who redecorated your place a while back."

He shakes his head. "Oh, hell. So, you heard all about that, huh?"

"I sure did. And let me tell you, the last thing I want when I'm trying to get it in with a hot redhead is to hear her bitching about my business partner's wife and what a bitch she is."

His jaw drops. "She called her a bitch?"

I snort and chuckle. "She called her a lot worse than that."

"Damn."

"Yeah, she was displeased, and that made for a less than enjoyable booty call for me."

Grant winces and takes a drink of his wine. "Sorry my wife cock-blocked you, dude."

"Me, too."

"That's one thing I have to say about Sylvie, though. There's no reining her in when she knows what she wants, and I wouldn't even try. It's one of the reasons I love her."

"Yeah, plus, she's hot as hell."

"Hey!" He points his steak knife at me. "You better watch what you say about my wife while I'm holding a knife."

I hold up my hands and back away playfully. "Just making an observation, man. Would you prefer I called her ugly?"

He scowls at me, takes another bite of the steak, and chews with exaggerated violence. "Hell no, but I think it's best to move on to focusing on a different woman, if you catch my drift."

"It's okay. I have a plan forming already."

He raises an eyebrow. "Oh, yeah, what's that?"

I flash him a grin and pour myself a glass of wine. "You just wait and see."

———

IZZY

Even after twenty-four hours, my blood still hasn't fully cooled from my exchange with Jameson Fury yesterday morning. I could practically feel my blood pressure skyrocketing with each step I took toward our building, and then his attitude when I got there soaking wet only made it worse.

It isn't good for me to get so worked up. What went down with him, coupled with a long day on my feet, left me so utterly exhausted, I could barely roll out of bed this morning. But I forced myself to swing my legs over the side and get up—just like I do on all those days when the realities of life threaten to become overwhelming and I want to quit.

And Jameson Fury is just one of those realities I'm going to have to figure out a way to deal with—hopefully in a way that doesn't make my blood pressure shoot to the stars.

But it's hard not to get worked up over the situation...or him.

That man is arrogant and infuriating. The way he gave me that cocky grin and all but assured me that his restaurant was going to put mine out of business before we even opened...

I'll fucking show him.

After all the obstacles I've overcome to get here—after losing Mom and Grams, I don't have any intention of giving up *at all*, let alone *easily*.

I glance at the clock on the car dash.

Six am.

I'm getting here bright and early today to get a head start before the asshole is at his place. Avoidance may be the best way to handle this problem. Avoid the man and move ahead as fast as I can because if my blood pressure rises like that every time I see him, I'm going to end up in the hospital before I can even get my place open.

It means I'm going to need to rush the timeline a little bit.

I'd hoped to have three months minimum to really have everything perfect before the grand opening, but now that I know *that man* will be right next door, I need to make sure I get ahead of the game. And ahead of him.

That starts today.

Get it done, Iz. Get. It. Done.

I turn on the street and spot the edge of our building, and it looks like there's a big open space right in the street out front.

Hell yes!

I do a fist pump. "That'll show him."

The early bird gets the worm.

When Grams told me that old saying while I was growing up, I always laughed it off since I greatly preferred to sleep in until she pulled the covers back or until the scent of her famous cinnamon rolls baking woke me, but it's proving to be an important piece of advice that rings true.

I'm getting prime parking today. It's too bad there isn't a cloud in the sky this morning and the summer sun is already shining. Part of me wishes it were pouring again so that jerk would have to park and walk the way I did yesterday. That would be the ultimate fuck you from Karma. But it appears she's going to get him back in another way.

I move down the street closer to the building, throw on

my blinker to pull into the open spot...and slam on my brakes.

"What the fuck?"

A pool lounge chair sits across the wide space that could easily hold two cars, ensuring there's no room for a vehicle on either side, and that smug bastard lies across it in nothing but a pair of swim trunks, his hands propped behind his head, shades over his eyes.

I throw the car into park, put on my flashers, and shove open my door.

This motherfucker!

My door slamming shut makes him turn his head slowly toward me, grin firmly in place.

I storm over to him with my hands on my hips and stare down at him in all his almost-naked glory. Even in the early morning sun, his abs practically glisten...and look incredible. Almost like he was carved from marble rather than crafted by God's hand.

More likely the Devil's...

Another one of Grams' classic sayings is true: never trust a skinny chef. I don't trust Jameson, and he's more than skinny—he's absolutely ripped. Any time the man doesn't spend in the kitchen, he must spend in the gym. Either that or he's been blessed with some sort of nuclear metabolism women would kill for.

It's unfair, really. I eat a piece of bread or a grain of rice and I gain five pounds. I constantly have to watch what I eat or drink and limit my diet. Just another inconvenience my doctor says is necessary to ensure I remain healthy for as long as possible.

So damn unfair.

Thinking about that only heats my blood more. I scowl at him and cross my arms over my chest.

One of his dark eyebrows rises above the top of the shades. "Good morning, Isabella."

"What the hell do you think you're doing?"

He holds up his hands innocently, the move shifting his hard pecs in a way that makes me squirm. "I'm not sure what you mean."

I point to the lounge chair. "This. This fucking chair. Why is it here?"

"I thought that would be obvious." He shrugs. "I'm sunbathing."

Sunbathing? The nerve of this guy!

I motion toward the blue sky. "It's six in the morning."

He somehow manages to keep a completely neutral expression despite the fact that I'm about to stroke out. "What's your point?"

I growl at him and clench my fists at my side. "This isn't the time to sunbathe. Nor is this the place to do it."

Jameson angles his head down to look at me over the top of his glasses, his bourbon eyes dancing with humor. "I beg to differ. I like the early morning sun when the ultraviolet rays aren't as harsh, and this is the perfect spot to do it because with all these buildings"—he motions toward the apartments that line the street around us—"this is the only spot around to get sunlight for longer than half an hour."

I stomp my foot and take another step closer. "Move the damn chair so I can park."

"Oh?" He feigns innocence and places a hand over his heart. "You wanted to park here?"

"Yes." I motion to my car blocking any traffic that might come down the street. Thankfully, this early, there isn't much. "I would."

"Well, that's a rather unfortunate coincidence that it's my sunbathing spot, isn't it?"

I groan and throw up my hands. "You're a real piece of work, Fury."

He grins at me and waggles his eyebrows. "Thank you for noticing."

"Jesus Christ, who taught you your manners? I'd like to have a little chat with them to tell them what an asshole you are."

His jaw drops, and he presses the same hand over his heart again in mock offense. "Ouch. I'm sure if my mother were alive, she'd be deeply offended by that statement."

"If my mother were alive..."

Shit. Now I feel like an asshole.

I suck in a deep breath of the cleanish early morning air and try to calm my racing heart and flaring temper. Getting so worked up isn't healthy. And hearing he lost his mom like I did allows the tiniest hint of regret to creep into my heart. "I'm sorry I said that."

He shakes his head and shifts up until he's sitting, the movement of his perfectly toned muscles making my mouth water. "No, you're not. You meant it."

Well, if he's going to give me an out...

"Of course, I meant it. You're doing this on purpose to make my life difficult."

"Why would I do that?" He motions toward our buildings and the door to his side. "My soon-to-be restaurant is right there. This is a logical place to sunbathe so I can catch my rays and get right to work." He offers me an almost kind smile—one I might actually believe if I had never interacted with him before. "I'm sorry it conflicts with your parking situation, but maybe you'll just have to get here earlier next time."

The confident smirk he gives me signifies I'm not going to get anywhere with him.

Motherfucker.

I stalk back to my car, wrench open the door, and slide in, letting the door slam behind me.

It truly isn't in my nature to battle with anyone. I have enough battles in my life without that, but he seems intent on ruining my day and my business.

And there's nothing I can do about it.

I shift the car into drive and have to circle three more blocks before finding a different parking spot. Of course, by the time I walk back to the restaurant, he's MIA from the lounge chair, but it still sits blocking the spaces.

If I threw it on the sidewalk to open the parking, someone else would just slip in and take it before I could get back since people don't give a shit about loading zones around here. And if I walk all the way back to my car and drive over here to do it, Jameson would undoubtedly be right back to interfere.

Jerk. Jerk. Handsome fucking jerk.

The door to his restaurant stands open, and his deep, smooth voice drifts out. I shouldn't eavesdrop, but if I have any chance of winning against a guy like him, I might have to play dirty.

I stop outside the door and press my back to the brick just to the side to ensure he can't see me, but I can still hear.

"Is there any way we can get that here sooner?" The frustration comes through in Jameson's question. The man is annoyed, which brings an unnatural amount of happiness to my heart.

"Unfortunately, not. Our supplier says it's on backorder. Some production issue."

I don't recognize the other voice, but it must be the contractor for his build-out or someone he ordered equipment from.

"Shit. Can we cancel the order and you get one from somewhere else?"

38

"Not that model. Everywhere is sold out."

"What about a used model from another kitchen? A restaurant that closed? I don't even mind used at this point."

"I already checked. None available."

"Shit. Shit. Shit." Jameson sounds pissed.

Good.

Any delay in his plan is only going to help me with mine. The determination to get *Grandma's Kitchen* open before his restaurant does has kicked into overdrive. I just have to be careful not to overdo it, or I'll end up with a major health setback that will only help him win.

I rush past the door to unlock mine and slip inside.

Butterflies still dance in my stomach at the realization that this place *is* mine. All mine. Growing up, I never could've imagined this when I was using my Easy-Bake Oven and stirring whatever was on the stove with Grams. But now, my dream is finally coming true.

If I can only figure out a way to stop Jameson Fury.

4

IZZY

Taking a sip of my coffee, I review Anna's resumé again, scanning her previous employers and experience even though I'm already confident she's what I'm looking for. After almost a week of dodging Jameson and getting here before the sun comes up to ensure I can park, coffee is the only thing keeping me running. That and the joy of hearing him arrive and knowing I got here first.

Thwarting his plans feels good, even if it is a small victory in the grand scheme of things.

And although it's a bit early to be hiring people, since it will likely be six weeks at the very least before I can open, I'm going to need help getting things set up. At least one or two trusty employees I can count on. People who can have my back the way Grams always did.

Days of looking through resumés have left my tired eyes itchy and sore, but finally having a great candidate sitting right in front of me feels like a massive step forward toward getting this place up and running.

I glance up and grin at Anna. "Your resumé is perfect. I can't believe you're available and want to work in a small upstart like mine."

She smiles back at me, her soft-blue eyes twinkling in the early morning light streaming in from the windows in the back of the restaurant. "I like it." She shrugs. "I've worked at a lot of super-busy high-end restaurants, and it always burns me out. My current job is stressful as hell. This should be a little bit quieter."

A laugh bubbles up my throat, and I shove a hand back through my hair which has become a disheveled mass after working on getting the tables and chairs moved in by myself this morning. "Well, I hope it's eventually busy in here, too." I hold up a hand. "But don't worry about the high-end thing. That isn't really my style."

Anna glances around and nods. "I love your style."

I look at the still mostly vacant space and can't stop smiling. "Me, too."

There isn't a whole lot in here yet, just these tables and chairs I managed to salvage from a place Ashley found that was shutting down. The mismatched wood hues and crazy-painted chairs in a rainbow of colors make my heart soar, though. Maybe because they aren't perfect, and they remind me of myself. Grams would love them, too. They're just happy. And I could use a dose of happy these days. Most people could.

I take a deep breath and try to push that thought out of my head so I don't lose it again. Going non-stop day and night to clean and help monitor the contractors to get things built-out perfectly has left me barely able to move without pain and regret.

Once I'm done and ready to open the doors, I'll let myself have a big cry imagining Grams' reaction if she were here, but for now, I need to focus on moving forward as fast as possible and ignore all the other things threatening to derail that. "So, when can I get you to start?"

Her eyes widen slightly, and she glances around. "Don't you want to interview other people?"

I nod. "I am doing other interviews. I think I have the budget to hire four part-time people."

"Oh..." The smile she was wearing falters slightly. "I kind of hoped to be full-time."

Crap.

I sigh and chew on my bottom lip. "I can't offer you full-time because of benefits and tax issues."

Because with the hourly wage she commands with her experience, I need to conserve my small budget.

"Oh." She nods slowly. "Well, I could probably make it work as long as I was getting at least thirty hours a week."

"No problem."

"Really?"

I nod and rise to my feet. "Definitely. I don't want to lose out on having you. I hope to have you here in a couple of weeks to help get the final things in order. Does that sound good?"

She stands. "Sure. I will put in my two-week notice at my current job so that works perfectly."

I shake her hand and then walk her to the door. "I can't wait to work together."

Anna grins back at me. "Neither can I. This place is going to be really cool."

"I hope so. I'll give you a call tomorrow with a time to come in and do all the final paperwork."

"Sounds great."

She slips out the door, and I return to my seat at the table we were using for the interview, lowering myself with a groan at the little zing of pain that shoots through my abdomen and lower back.

These damn tables were heavy.

Maybe I shouldn't have moved them myself, but I didn't have much choice. I need to save money any way I can, even if that meant renting a U-Haul and "delivering" them on my own.

I run my hand across the dinged wood and sigh. These old tables are definitely a little worse for wear, but it's all I could afford, and they do give the place a little bit of character. And that's exactly the way I want it.

It's not a stuffy, uptight place where people feel like they have to wear a coat and tie or a dress to come to have a meal. Jeans and T-shirts are more my style...at least, most days.

I glance down at myself and the stains all over my shirt and pants. Although, lately, my style has been grimy and dirty with working on getting everything ready.

By the time I force myself to go home at night because my body just can't keep up anymore, I look like I've been digging in a dumpster. Which I kind of have, I guess, trying to find anything I can to help with my budget issues.

And now, I have almost everything ordered and just need the perfect staff. Anna is going to be a wonderful head waitress. She has one of the most experienced resumés to come across my email since I made my posting. I can't wait to have her help in getting the final thing set up.

I flip open my folder with the rest of the resumés to get ready for the next interview when the door swings open again.

Anna sticks her head in. "Oh, good, you're still available."

"Do you have a question?" I would have thought she'd be long gone by now. It's been at least ten minutes since she left.

She worries her bottom lip between her teeth and glances around, avoiding eye contact.

A leaden ball drops into my stomach. "What's wrong?"

"Ummm..." She rubs the back of her neck. "As I was leaving, I happened to bump into the owner of the place next door..."

Oh, no. No, no, no, no, no.

I jump to my feet.

He didn't...

She sighs and finally meets my stare. "And well...he asked if I had interviewed with you and wanted to see my resumé, so I gave him a copy, and..."

NO!

"He offered me twice what you're going to pay me, plus benefits."

Jesus. That bastard. Now he's poaching my staff?

I somehow manage to find my voice. "Are you kidding?"

Anna winces and shakes her head. At least she has the decency to look sheepish and apologetic. "Look, I'm really sorry. I know we hit it off, and I do want to work here, but..."

"You said you didn't want to work at a stuffy, high-end restaurant. That's exactly what that jerk next door is going to open."

She raises one shoulder and lets it fall. "But that jerk next door also has huge street cred and a recognizable name. I don't want to sound like a greedy bitch, but I'm probably going to get bigger tips at a place that sells more expensive food and has a celebrity chef."

That motherfucker.

I fist my hands at my sides and fight the slight wave of dizziness that tries to overtake me.

Don't let yourself get worked up, Iz.

Grams' constant reminder rings in my head.

Don't push yourself too hard. You can't give one hundred and ten percent all the time.

I take a deep, cleansing breath. "There's no way for me to convince you otherwise?"

Anna shakes her head and puts her hand on the door handle. "I'm sorry."

Shit.

I sigh and drop my head back. "Well, at least I have a whole stack of applicants. Hopefully, at least a few of them will be interested."

"Ummmm..."

Oh, God. What now?

I open my eyes and lower my head back down so I can look at her. "What?"

"Well"—she glances at the door—"I saw him grab a guy off the street who seemed to be walking this way. I think it was your next interview."

"Oh, you have got to be kidding me." I clench my jaw and storm toward her.

She holds up her hands like she's expecting a blitz attack, but she isn't the subject of my wrath. "I'm sorry."

I push past her and shove out the door onto the side-walk. "It's not you I want to dice with my kitchen knife."

Poor Anna follows me out and shuffles off down the street to God knows where. It doesn't matter. My attention is elsewhere—like at the open door to Jameson's place.

I march in there and find him leaning against a newly built, beautiful, high wooden bar top with another guy standing with his back to me. Probably my next interview.

Jameson raises an eyebrow. "I'm kind of in the middle of something here, Isabella. Can we chat later?"

"Chat later?" I scoff, and the guy he's talking to ducks his head and turns slightly away from me. "No, we can't *chat later*." I march over to them, step between the two men, and jab a finger right into Jameson's chest. "How dare you?"

"How dare I what?" The smug jerk has the balls to appear confused, his strong brow furrowing.

"Try to poach my staff!" I whirl around on the cowering guy next to Jameson. "Don't you dare think about accepting a job offer from this man. I found you first."

The guy holds up his hands and backs away slightly. "I'm not sure what I'm in the middle of here. I just wanted a job."

"You're hired."

Jameson pushes an arm between us. "Whoa, whoa, whoa. I was talking with Mr. Albertson. I don't think we've finished our conversation."

"I have an interview scheduled with him."

How can he stand here pretending he hasn't just crossed a major line?

Or maybe that's the entire problem. There is no line for a man like Jameson Fury...

Jameson glances down at the large watch on his wrist that he probably paid for with his winnings from *Prime Chef*. "What time is your interview?"

Mr. Albertson chimes in innocently. "Ten thirty."

Turning his watch face toward us, Jameson raises his brows. "Ten twenty-five." He shrugs innocently. "I haven't in any way interfered with your ability to interview him in five minutes, Isabella."

I growl and stomp my foot. It might be a little childish. Okay, a lot childish. But this man seems to know how to get under my skin and get me worked up in a way that's definitely not healthy for me...or him.

I'm not a violent person by nature. Far from it. But Jameson Fucking Fury is making me *stabby,* and I have an awfully nice set of knives just on the other side of that wall that Grams gave me as a graduation gift and I keep incredibly sharp.

"Really, Fury? That's all you have to say after you just stole Anna from me?"

Jameson chuckles and offers me a slow grin that raises heat that definitely isn't anger in body parts that definitely should not be heating up for this man. "Oh, I have a lot to say to you, Iz. I'm just getting started."

———

JAMESON

Her perfectly pink bow lips open, and her jaw drops slightly, though why she's still surprised by anything I say to her is a mystery. I would have thought the chair incident would have taught her something about me—that I'm not about to let her mess up my plans. Whether that be sunbathing or opening *Fury*.

"But I'm in the middle of an interview right now." I flash her another grin. "So, let's chat later."

My words—or maybe it's the grin—make her issue another low growl and stomp her foot again, and I can't fight back my chuckle. Getting her worked up has turned into my new favorite pastime, and this is only our third run-in. The woman has managed to avoid another confrontation by beating me here every morning over the past week—a feat only made possible by the fact that I've been so sore and exhausted that I've let myself sleep in a bit longer than usual.

There's just something about how easy it is to push her buttons that really gives me the comedic lift I need after a long day's work. It's the same joy I got from messing with Rach growing up, only this time, the end result won't be big sis running to Mom or Bash, crying about it. And I won't have Dad smacking me around because I made Rachel cry.

This time, I'm hoping the end result will be Isabella giving up and leaving...

But it feels rude to be having this argument in front of our friend here. The poor guy just came for an interview and got stuck in the middle of a war he had no idea was happening.

I hold up a finger to her and turn to Mr. Albertson, offering an apologetic smile. "I'd love to have you come work for me as front of house, and the woman you saw leaving on your way in will be the head waitress."

Normally, I would spend a lot more time checking references and backgrounds of anyone I hire, but this is too good of an opportunity to pass up—both to get a great employee and also to piss Isabella the fuck off.

Mr. Albertson smiles and claps his hands together. "Awesome."

Isabella releases a little gasp.

I ignore her and plow ahead. "Can you come by tomorrow to take care of all the paperwork?"

"Absolutely." The enthusiasm with which Mr. Albertson says the word hangs in the air, and then he seems to remember that Isabella is standing right next to him and swallows thickly. He turns uncomfortably toward her. "I have to cancel our interview."

Rage reddens her pale cheeks, and she clenches her jaw so tightly I wouldn't be surprised to hear her teeth actually crack at this point. "Yeah. I got that."

It wouldn't surprise me if she lashed out and slapped me —or hell, even him—at this point, but she just takes a deep breath in her through her nose and blows it out of her mouth slowly.

Mr. Albertson shrugs and walks away, offering me a little wave on his way out. Now that he's gone, fireworks are sure to really fly. Isabella is so wound up that she looks ready to snap. This is likely to rival her reaction to the chair in her parking space.

Let's get ready for a Fourth of July-style display.

She whirls on me, her blond hair flying out in a halo around her. The sheer rage flashing deep in her green eyes sends a jolt straight between my legs, images of what it would be like to have all that passion channeled toward me in another context flashing in my mind and causing my cock to stir. "Stop it."

"Stop what?" The woman needs to be a little more specific on that. There are any number of things I'm doing that she could be referring to. Including getting an uncomfortable hard-on the longer we have this argument.

"Stop trying to sabotage me."

I shrug and close the notebook I have on the bar with all of Mr. Albertson's information written in it, using the shift in my body to surreptitiously adjust my cock behind my zipper. "I'm not trying to sabotage you. I'm just doing what I can to ensure my business succeeds. You can't take everything so personally."

Her eyes widen. "Can't take everything so personally?" She scoffs and throws up her hands. "Stealing my parking spot is not *just doing business*. Intentionally blocking me from using it is not *just doing business*. Poaching my staff is not *just doing business*."

I hold up a hand to stop her there. Not only is there no need to list my sins, but she's so wrong on so many levels here. "First, Mr. Albertson hadn't even met with you when I hired him, so I didn't poach anybody, and second, Anna was walking by as I was opening up this morning and was curious to see the inside of the place. I had no way of knowing who she was or why she was here. *She* was the one who mentioned to me that she worked in the restaurant industry. Which seemed like an open invite from her to offer

50

her a position, plus an amazing opportunity for *me* to start hiring some staff."

Isabella opens her mouth to protest, but I stop her with my hand again.

"She wasn't even on your payroll yet, so I don't know how you can consider that 'poaching' anyone."

She fumes, stepping up to me until her chest almost brushes mine. A familiar scent, something from my child-hood I can't quite place, invades every breath I take, and I glance down at the stains all over the shirt and point.

"You have a little something on your shirt."

That cute little growl she does slips out again. The sound is so unladylike but so hot at the same time.

I wonder if she does that during sex...

She shoves a finger in my chest, heat radiating through my body from that tiny pinpoint connection between us. "That's from working hard. I can't just pay people to set up my restaurant and get things organized for me. I actually have to *work* for it."

"Whoa." I throw up my hands and narrow my eyes at her. "You think I don't work hard? You think all this"—I wave my hands around—"just miraculously fell into my lap? You think I won *Prime Chef* just because of this pretty face?"

She flinches slightly. The thought had crossed her mind, apparently.

One step brings me even closer until I can feel the warm flutter of her breath against my skin and the finger she has jabbed into my chest pushes even deeper into my ribcage. "I work just as hard as you do. If not harder. Because I have a partner who is investing a hell of a lot of money into this place, which means that if it fails, he's going to lose a hell of a lot of money. It's not just my ass on the line—other people's asses are on the line, too. That's more pressure than you could possibly imagine. Everyone is expecting me to be perfect. For this *place* to be perfect. That means I have to make it perfect. And if that means 'poaching'"—I air-quote the word because I still don't agree that that's what happened—"people you want to hire for your place, then so be it. It's the cost of doing business."

She scowls at me and finally drags her finger from me. My body instantly recognizes the loss of contact between us, and I want to lean back into her. But that would be stupid and dangerous.

Very.

I wait for her to offer some sort of reply, for her to try to make some argument about business ethics or what's "right" and "good." The kind of things someone who doesn't understand the real world would argue to someone who knows what it takes to succeed.

But she just stands there, glaring at me, her chest heaving and her lips twisted into a sneer. Finally, she releases a heavy sigh. "It's not even worth arguing with you. You clearly haven't cared about anyone or anything but yourself for so long that you forgot how to."

Her words hit me one by one, like arrows directed at the deepest parts of my soul. Then, she storms away, leaving the smell of something sweet—that I've finally placed as cinnamon rolls—in the air.

The door closes behind her, and I stand dumb for a few seconds, trying to grasp what just happened.

That woman doesn't know me. Not at all.

How can she accuse me of not caring?

I care *too* much.

Apparently, explaining my relationship with Grant and how it might affect him if we fail wasn't enough for her to believe I'm anything but a selfish prick. It can't be further from the truth. Living with Mike Fury as a father taught me what a selfish prick is and how to recognize one instantly. I'm nothing like that man. I've made sure of that.

But Isabella will think whatever she wants to. That's fine. I can't let her anger or frustration with the situation derail me. Or the fact that I find her as attractive as I do frustratingly annoying.

I start to make my way across the restaurant floor toward the kitchen when the door pulls open again.

She's back for round two already?

I turn around to face her, but instead of Isabella, I find a pretty redhead with a brilliant smile.

"Hi, I have an eleven o'clock interview. I think I'm a little early."

Oh, my...luck certainly is on my side today.

I chuckle to myself and divert toward her with my hand extended. "I actually think your interview is next door with Isabella. But since you don't have to be over there for another half an hour, why don't we have a chat? I'm Jameson Fury."

She takes my hand in hers and shakes vigorously, her smile lighting up even more. "Oh, yeah. I know who you are. I loved your season of *Prime Chef.*"

Of course, you did.

I'm banking on *everyone* loving it and recognizing my face and name when it comes time to finally open this place. I grin at her and nod toward the bar. "Come on over here, and let's have a chat."

Sorry, Isabella...but all is fair in love and opening a restaurant.

5

JAMESON

"**A**re you sure you don't need me to help with anything?"

The sincerity in Bash's question drags a laugh from deep in my chest. Ever since I graduated from culinary school, he's been offering me money that I keep refusing. He seems to think I'm going to change my mind if he just asks over and over.

"What would *you* be able to help with in opening a restaurant besides giving me cash, which I've already said no to about a hundred times? You can't even boil water."

Bash gives a mock gasp of indignation over the phone. "That's not true. I absolutely *can* boil water. I can even drop pasta into it and *not* overcook it at *least* a quarter of the times I try. Though that is about the extent of my kitchen skills."

The sad thing is, he isn't even joking about that. After having Mom, Rach, and me cook for him growing up and then being provided meals in college and when he played to ensure he was on a good diet, he never needed to learn to fend for himself in the kitchen.

"Yeah, well, if you'd spent any time with Mom instead of always out on the ice, maybe you would've learned a thing or two."

Shit.

A twinge of regret hits the moment I say the words. It was meant to be a joke, but it didn't really come out that way.

Things have been tense between Bash and me for so long that sometimes I forget he isn't the enemy. The man who is now buried six feet under back home in Michigan was, but the damage he did is etched deeply into the fiber of all of us.

Some more than others.

Silence lingers through the line for a moment before Bash releases a deep sigh. "You still blame me for that? For wanting to spend time in the one place that I actually felt like I had some control over my life?"

I grit my teeth, squeeze my eyes shut, and pinch the bridge of my nose. "That's just it, Bash. You didn't."

None of us did. We were controlled by a tyrant who ruled with brutality and anger and ensured we knew our places and kept our mouths shut.

For some reason, Bash can't seem to grasp that. "You weren't in control because when you were out there on the ice, you were always worrying about what Dad was going to think. About how you were going to impress Dad with what you could do. It was always about trying to please him and wanting him to be proud of you so he wouldn't lash out and beat the shit out of one of us."

Saying the words out loud brings bile up my throat. It's a harsh truth I knew even at a young age, but this is the first time I've ever voiced it—the first time I've ever dared to mention it to either Bash or Rachel. We've always danced around outright discussing what happened to us as children, but the older we get, and the more time that passes since that man left the world, things have started to change.

Though I'm not sure if it's for the better or worse.

What I've been doing is certainly somewhere in the gray zone from that perspective. I'm so fucked up in the head because of what he did that I can't even talk to my own brother and sister about it without having to justify my actions. One of the reasons I haven't told *anyone* where I spend my Wednesday nights...

There are too many conflicting feelings about everything. About how we grew up. Mom loved the shit out of us and did what she could, but the only way any of us got any sort of positive reinforcement from Dad—typically no more than a kind word or a pat on the shoulder—was if we did something he could connect with, and the only way to connect with Dad was on the ice.

It's why the old man always hated me and the reason I never give a shit what happened to him once I left home. He knew I had no interest in playing hockey despite showing promise as soon as I was big enough to put on skates and hold a stick. Unlike Bash, I wasn't about to bend over backward to impress a father who treated me like shit and beat us whenever he felt like it.

I might've been the youngest—the baby of the family—but I know what everyone did to try to shield me from what was happening. Bash and Mom took the brunt of his rage, and Rach stepped in when she had to. But there was only so much they could do when the evidence of what took place was written all over their bodies and I could hear it happening. Their screams and his raving echo in my ears even today, almost a decade after I left that house.

Fuck. This is not how I saw this conversation going tonight.

My free hand shakes, and I press the palm flat against the bar top to try to stop it.

Bash clears his throat like he's trying to rid it of the same heavy emotion choking me right now. "You should've talked to him before he died."

I tighten my hand around the phone so hard that it almost hurts. "Why the hell would I do that? Dad never gave a shit about me when I was alive, so why would I care when he was dying? I don't think he said five words to me in the years between when Mom died and he did."

"Because he knew you didn't want to talk to him. Because he didn't want to force you into something when you already hated him so much."

Tension builds in my shoulders and up the back of my neck, tightening every muscle and threatening to bring on a migraine I can't afford right now. "Is this why you called? To harass me about choosing not to have a relationship with that man, even now that he's dead?"

He sighs again—a soul-deep sound that makes me cringe. "No. I was actually calling to let you know we got enough tickets for everyone to come to the game when the Scorpions play the Rangers. Rach and Flynn are coming, and we were hoping we could get a little preview of your place, if it's not open yet."

I turn around and scan the space, rolling through the lengthy list of everything that still needs to happen. "Still have a lot to do."

"It's been a long time since you cooked for everyone."

It has been. And despite the tension that still exists between Bash and me, it'll be good to see him and Rachel—plus, I really do need her help to finalize all the little details.

"Text me all the information about when you'll be here, and I'll see what I can do to whip up something for everyone."

"Sounds good."

"And Bash?"

"What?"

The truth of what I've been doing sits on the tip of my tongue—a confession I haven't made to anyone yet and one I don't know that I'm ready to make now. Not when it means examining things I've long buried and held so deeply that I had hoped they would never surface.

And they won't. Not right now.

Instead of confessing what will only continue to tear open old wounds, I scrub my hand over my face and lean back against the bar. "It will be good to see you."

Way to chicken out, Jamo.

I just can't tell him. Maybe when they're here. Maybe I'll finally be at the point where I can explain it to him, too. Because right now, I don't even understand it enough to know why I do it.

"It'll be good to see you, too. You think you'll be open by then?"

It's my turn to release a heavy sigh. "As much as I wish I could say yes, I don't think so. But we should be close. I'm trying to open as fast as I can because another restaurant is going in right next door."

"Really? Who would be dumb enough to open a restaurant next door to you after all the recent publicity you've gotten?"

I chuckle and rub at the back of my neck. "A totally hot chick named Isabella, actually."

"Oh..." His deep laugh rumbles through the phone. "A hot chick, huh? Sounds like that's more trouble than actually getting the restaurant up and running."

"Nah. It's not like that." I run a hand back through my hair and instinctively stare at the wall I share with Isabella's place. "I'm not stupid enough to get involved with my competition. I'm having too much fun messing with her."

"Oh, God." Bash chuckles. "What did you do?"

"Just took a page from your playbook. Playing a little dirty."

"I gave all that up."

"Only because you pussied out."

"Pussied out?" He barks a laugh. "You just wait. One day, some woman is going to blindside you. You'll never even see her coming, and then you're going to rethink that comment and apologize to me."

"Apologize to you?" I snort. "That'll be the fuckin' day."

"Ha ha."

The door opens, and Danny walks in with his clipboard full of our work list.

I glance at my watch. "Hey, look, Bash, I gotta go. My contractor just showed up. Text me the information."

"I will. And hey, Jamo? Let me leave you with this piece of advice."

"What's that?"

"Playing dirty can be fun, and yes, even sometimes necessary, but just remember it has consequences."

"I already know I'm creating another enemy."

That's never been anything I've been concerned about.

"I'm talking about more than that, Jameson. I'm talking about the kind of consequences that are internal."

He doesn't say anything else. Nor does he need to. I know exactly what he's talking about. I watched it happen to our own father. Saw it starting to happen with Bash, too, before he met Greer and got wise.

"Talk to you later." I end the call and shove my phone into my back pocket as Danny approaches.

Bash is right about one thing—playing dirty is necessary sometimes. I have no intention of changing my tactics with the beauty next door. Not until I've won.

IZZY

"Are you sure you don't need me to come over?" Ashley doesn't bother to hide the concern in her voice—nor is it unexpected coming from her.

Over the years, as Grams started to decline and I was taking care of her more than she was taking care of me, Ash seemed to naturally step into the role of "mothering" me despite my insisting it isn't needed.

While Grams tried to monitor me and help if I needed it, my staunch independence tended to get in the way of that and cause arguments more often than not. She would say I was overdoing it and pushing myself toward a hospital stay, and I would tell her I was fine—even when I definitely *wasn't*.

It's the same with Ash. She would do anything for me, and I for her. But it doesn't mean I *want* her to. I would probably need to be on the floor gasping for my final breath before I would actually *ask* for her help.

Which I honestly *don't* need right now, despite her thinking otherwise.

I turn onto my side, which sends a slight stab of pain to my lower back. Fighting the urge to groan and alert Ash to how truly uncomfortable I am tonight, I sigh instead. "Yes. I'm sure."

"Because you know I will be there in ten minutes if you need me to be."

"I know, Ash. And I appreciate it. Really." Even though I don't say it out loud often enough, she knows I love the shit out of her and appreciate having her in my life more than I can voice. I glance at the clock. "But it's already midnight. You need sleep as badly as I do."

Maybe even more so. While I've been working day and night to try to start up *Grandma's Kitchen*, she's been busting

61

her butt working as sous chef at the right hand of one of the most well-respected chefs in New York. We both developed our love of food in Grams' kitchen, and seeing her thrive in the same profession has been almost as fulfilling as doing it myself.

"I'm worried about you, Iz. You're just coming home now? That's a long day on your feet and doing manual labor. You're not taking care of yourself."

"I'm okay."

She scoffs and chuckles. "I'm pretty sure the last time you told me that, you ended up in the hospital."

"That was different. I have things under control now."

Mostly.

She's right. I have been pushing myself too hard. Staying on my feet too long and coming home later than I should. It's a recipe for a crash. But it's only temporary. I can relax and take a small step back once my place is open and I have help from the staff getting things under control.

Ashley releases a heavy sigh. "Do you? Because it doesn't sound like it."

"Well, the situation with the douchebag next door is *not* in control. But it will be. As soon as I can figure out a way to get him to back off."

"That's never going to happen."

I chuckle, then wince at the discomfort the movement brings. "Since when are you the pessimist?"

She laughs. "I'm not a pessimist. I'm a *realist*. And I saw Jameson's season of *Prime Chef*. He's not the type to back down."

"Neither am I."

Jameson has certainly proven what Ashley said to be true in the short time I've known him, though. He doesn't relent or surrender, and I can't imagine him having a change of heart.

Still, a girl can dream...

Not only would him backing off make my job easier, but it would also make it easier on my life to avoid the way that man sends my heart racing.

Why does he have to be so handsome and such a fucking jerk?

"I know you don't, hon. I know you can take on any challenge that presents itself, just like you always have. But I worry you're not looking at the big picture here. If you burn yourself out, there won't be a restaurant *to* open."

"I know." I scrunch my eyes closed. "Believe me, I know. But I'll be okay. And I'll be careful."

She releases another heavy sigh. "Why don't I believe you?"

"Because like I said...you're a pessimist."

It's the same "argument" we've been having since middle school when we became best friends sitting on the bench at the playground, watching the other kids run around and play. At the time, I was too weak to do it, and Ashley seemed to know exactly what I needed back then—and now—a good friend.

She scoffs and chuckles. "Go to bed."

"I will in a few minutes, once...you know...it's done."

"Get a good night's sleep and try not to let that man get under your skin so much."

Don't let Jameson get under my skin?

It's a little fucking late for that. The man has been there since literally the first moment we met. And I don't see that changing anytime soon.

"Easier said than done, Ash."

"Just try. And call me if you need anything. I'm serious. Anything."

With Grams gone, knowing there is someone there who will always have my back is even more essential. Tears well in my eyes, but I brush them away.

"I will. Love ya." I drop my phone onto the mattress and relax back, trying my best to do my breathing exercises to calm myself down.

It was a stressful day—one I feel through every aching joint and muscle in my entire body. And I probably should've come home hours ago and taken care of every- thing that I needed to instead of pushing it one more hour, then one more hour, then just one more. But I just couldn't leave when I had more interviews to do and I need to make sure that man didn't poach any more of my potential employees.

At least he left the lounge chair outside so I could sit and ensure he didn't snag anyone else off the street. Without his interference, I managed to hire three solid people who will hopefully be a good fit for my place. No one quite as quali- fied as Anna would have been to handle running the wait- staff, but I have to work with Jameson's leftovers, apparently, and take what I can get.

That sucks—to know his charm, name recognition, and budget mean he will probably have better *everything* than me, but there was one added bonus for the day—a slight tan on my otherwise pale arms from sitting outside for hours.

I refuse to admit it, but Jameson was right about the spot right in front of the building. It's the perfect place to catch the rays for most of the day, and the warm sun helped ease some of the tension from my body while I was out there.

And it felt incredible. I can't even remember the last time I just *sat* in the sun and tried to relax. Not that this was exactly *relaxing*.

As soon as I heard Jameson's voice float out his door or turned to find him standing near the jamb, those intelligent eyes assessing me with the smug tilt of his lips, I tensed right back up again and my blood pressure skyrocketed.

That man does things to me.

Bad things.

Things that could get me in trouble in so many ways.

Things there is absolutely no time for.

Not when I have the range being delivered tomorrow. Once that's in, the kitchen will almost be complete, and we can finally start on all the little things that really need to get done.

It means I can open in just a few weeks. Even though the to-do list is still ten miles long, at least the hard parts are almost over.

Except for figuring out a way to deal with the handsome problem next door.

My brilliant "avoidance" plan doesn't seem to have worked out as intended. Even keeping my distance, he's still managed to find ways to get to me and drive me mad.

That doesn't leave me with many other options. Not when I don't have the money or importance or stamina to go twelve rounds with him. And something tells me that will be what it takes to drop him and keep him down for the count.

What I wouldn't give to see that, though.

I guess I'll have to keep dreaming about it until a better plan presents itself. Because I refuse to roll over for Jameson Fury—even if I am rolling over and crashing tonight for as long as is humanly possible.

6

IZZY

The honk of a horn and rumble of a big diesel engine jerks me awake.

What the hell?

Blinking rapidly, I shake my head and try to clear the fog of sleep that seems to want to keep me under. This definitely isn't my plush, soft bed, though. The hard, unyielding surface under me isn't doing my aching body any favors. It feels like I've been sleeping on concrete.

Where am I?

It takes me a moment to get my bearings as my vision finally comes into focus. The old, scratched-up table under my arms. The faint smell of sawdust hanging the air from the construction.

The restaurant.

That's right.

Somehow, I managed to drag myself out of bed this morning despite feeling like complete shit because I *had* to be here. This is the only day for the next two weeks that the supplier could deliver the range, and I can't really get things started without the most important appliance, the heart of the kitchen.

So even though my body is revolting and screaming at me to go home and climb back into bed, instead, I push myself up from the table—where I apparently fell asleep— with a groan and rush out the door onto the sidewalk.

A large delivery truck partially blocks the road. I was so tired this morning that I didn't get in early enough to beat Jameson, and the jerk left his infamous chair in the loading zone, which means there is nowhere for this damn truck to go.

The driver climbs out and comes around with a clipboard in his hand and approaches me. "Isabella?"

"Yes, that's me."

He narrows his dark eyes. "Are you okay, ma'am?"

"Huh?"

Why wouldn't I be okay?

He motions toward my cheek. "Um, your face. You have a big red mark."

"Oh! Shit!" I reach up and rub my hand across it several times to work away the evidence of my little impromptu nap. *Embarrassing.* But my life seems to be full of those moments, especially lately. I motion back toward the restaurant. "I just fell asleep. It was an imprint from my little nap."

He chuckles and nods. "Man, I could use one of those, but I have a long day ahead and a delivery for you. I just need you to sign here."

I take his clipboard and sign without even reading it. That's probably bad. A real, put-together businesswoman would examine the paperwork and know what she's signing. That clearly isn't me. Not when the excitement over what he has in that truck bubbles under my skin and makes me practically bounce in place.

This is like Christmas morning!

The only thing that could make it any better would be if Grams were here. Or if Jameson weren't. So, I guess two things could really make this day perfect. Too bad I won't be getting either.

The driver tosses the clipboard back into the truck and moves toward the back. "I'll have it in there in a few minutes."

For some reason, this delivery feels like moving a massive step closer to my ultimate goal. Even though my to-do list is still huge, having the kitchen complete feels like *Grandma's Kitchen* is finally *real*. I can nail down my menu and get final inspections scheduled.

Progress.

And this delivery is more than just getting a necessary item. Securing this range was *not* easy, and it's the one piece of kitchen equipment I truly *splurged* on. There were other options. Less expensive ones. Many of them. But ever since culinary school, I *dreamed* of having this spaceship of a stove, of creating Grams' classics as well as brand new recipes on it.

It's the kind of hardware chefs fantasize about, and now, I'll have my grabby little hands on it.

The door to Jameson's place opens, instantly shattering the joy I'm feeling in this moment. That's apparently all it takes now to ruin my day—a threat of a run-in with that man.

He saunters out, looking dangerously hot with his disheveled hair like he just rolled out of bed and his muscular arms exposed in his snug T-shirt.

Christ, why does he have to be so sexy?

He motions toward the truck. "You going to block my sun all day?

I scowl and cross my arms over my chest. "Very funny,

since you're the one blocking us from using this spot for its actual purpose right now."

He snorts and grins at me in a way that goes straight between my legs. Jameson is a man who knows what he does to women. It's written in every smirk, smile, grin, wink, or waggle of an eyebrow. Men like him use it to their advantage, too, to charm the "weaker sex" and get what they want.

Well, he won't get it from me.

He wants me to cave and give up. He wants to crush the competition before I even open. But I've been fighting too many things for too long to let an arrogant, shameless man like Jameson Fury get in my way.

The driver raises the back door of the delivery truck, and I move behind it to watch him unload—and to put a little more distance between myself and the ridiculously hot chef who makes my blood boil.

Of course, Jameson steps up right next to me, watching intently while the driver maneuvers the range onto the lift that will bring it down to the ground.

One of the pieces of cardboard pressed to the side falls away, and Jameson freezes and takes a step toward the truck. "Is that..." He glances back at me and points to the massive piece of equipment. "Is that the seventy-two inch Vulcan with dual convection and steam?"

I smirk at him, not even trying to hide my glee. "Sure is."

His jaw drops almost to the street we're standing on. "How in the hell did you manage that? I've been trying to get one for weeks."

Aha. Finally. A victory.

The score may still be Jameson five, me only one, but at least I'm on the board now. Having something *he* wants shouldn't give me such joy, but the weight resting on my shoulders placed there by what's been happening with him and the impending fight over our openings suddenly feels lighter somehow.

"It wasn't easy to get." A miracle, really. But I'm not going to let him know how much work I had to put into it and how I almost cried, thinking I wasn't going to succeed. "I called Vulcan and around to every supplier and had them put me on the top of a waitlist if anyone canceled an order or one randomly came in used or on return. I told them to call me with literally *any* leads on one."

"Shit." He clenches his jaw, and the heat of anger reddens his neck. "I should've done that."

I don't bother fighting the smug grin pulling at my lips, and I turn and offer him a shrug. "Yep. Guess you should've. Sorry."

Not sorry.

It's about time Jameson feels what it's like to be on the losing side. It can't be good for his already inflated ego to keep having things go his way all the time. Not good at all. A man like this needs to be knocked down a peg or two regularly to be reminded he's human and not some god.

Jameson eyes my prize with a lust I'm sure most women would kill to have directed at them. The driver starts to move it toward my door, but Jameson holds out a hand, stopping him, and turns back to me. "I'll buy it from you."

"What the hell?"

The man has clearly lost his mind.

His jaw hardens. "I'll buy it from you."

I snort and shake my head. "Uh, no. You *won't*."

"You paid what? Twenty grand? I'll give you double what you paid."

Until this moment, I wasn't aware it was possible to choke on one's own saliva just trying to swallow, but somehow, I do and sputter out a cough. "What? That's *insane*."

A muscle tics in his jaw as he glances between the range

and me. "Let's not beat around the bush here, Isabella. I want that shiny new range. You have it. But one thing I have that you don't is deep pockets." His typically hard bourbon eyes soften slightly. "Can you honestly tell me that having an extra forty thousand dollars wouldn't be potentially a game-changer for you right now?"

Well, shit. He has me there.

I glance at the stove and sigh. That kind of money would make a huge difference in what I'm able to accomplish in the grand scheme of things. Game-changer doesn't even begin to describe what it would mean.

But this is my *one* win. I don't want to lose it just because it might stretch my budget a bit—or a lot. A whole *hell* of a lot.

He steps closer to me, lowering his voice so the delivery man waiting impatiently can't hear him. "Isabella, don't dismiss my offer outright just because you hate me."

"Hate you?" I shake my head and run my hands through my hair, pushing the strays back into my bun. "I don't know that I *hate* you."

It's a strong word and not one I use lightly. It breeds the kind of poison in your system I already have enough of. While I definitely find him pompous and annoying, I don't know that I *hate* the man standing next to me.

Jameson chuckles and leans in a little closer—too close for what I would consider proper etiquette. Even outside with the smells of Brooklyn surrounding us, a rich, spicy scent invades my next inhaled breath with him only inches from me. "I'm happy to hear that. Though, I don't know that I believe you."

Neither do I.

I don't know *what* I believe when it comes to Jameson. He's as infuriating and arrogant as he is handsome and talented. It makes it really hard to say no to him...

About this. Definitely *just* about this.

———

JAMESON

Standing this close to Isabella, it's easy to momentarily forget what I'm trying to accomplish here. The woman twists me up in ways that make me very uncomfortable, especially when that sweet cinnamon scent floats off her and toward me, coming into my lungs with every breath even though we're outside in the warm summer air.

And while she says she doesn't hate me, the animosity with which she's greeting my offer suggests otherwise. This is a no-brainer. A way for her to pocket forty grand by doing *nothing*. Yet, she seems unwilling to budge.

No matter what she says, she *definitely* hates me.

The beauty next door takes a deep breath and releases it in a huff. "Even though I *don't* hate you, Jameson—despite what I'm sure you think and the fact that you've given me *every* reason to—I can't accept your offer. As much as I may need that money, I need the range more."

Bullshit.

That doesn't make any sense. There are dozens of other commercial ranges she could buy for what I'm offering her, even cheaper ones that would put even *more* cash in her pockets that she can use elsewhere.

This isn't a rational decision. She's saying no just to spite me, to rub in my face that she finally has something I want. The only reason she won't give it up is that it's *me* asking for it.

It's stupid to reject such a generous offer just because of pride. While I've been known to let my own pride get in the way a time or two, I hate to see it happen to her when she clearly needs the money, if only to hire more help to get her place up and running. Really, I'm offering her another way to beat me—to use the funds I'm giving her on a silver platter to beat me to opening. It's the ultimate win for her. I just need to convince her of that if I want this Vulcan in my kitchen.

"Think about it, Iz. I told you I'd pay you double, which would allow you to hire more help and open sooner. *And...*" I can't even believe I'm going to say this, but it will sweeten the deal so much that even hatred won't be able to stop her from accepting it. "I'll even throw in *my* range, which I can assure you, is top of the line."

Just not the Vulcan *she* has.

Her pretty pink lips part on a scoff. "Jesus, you just don't know when to quit, do you?" She motions toward my place. "What do you have in there? A Vulcan?"

I nod. "Actually, the sixty-inch Vulcan with a fabulous broiler, convection, and steam, which is even *more* expensive than this." I tap the top of the beauty in front of us. "And you can have it."

"You're just going to *give* that to me along with *double* what I paid for this? It doesn't seem like a very wise business decision on your part." One of her blond eyebrows rises. "What would your partner think?"

Fuck.

She's probably right about that. If Grant knew I was offering her this much for a damn range, he'd probably have a coronary and back out of our deal immediately...if he survived the shock.

But he doesn't get it. He doesn't live in the kitchen the way I do. There's no way he can comprehend that equipment like this can make such a huge impact when running a kitchen for a packed restaurant. But I think, just maybe, if I laid it all out for him in easy-to-understand laymen's terms, he would understand. Otherwise, I'll just have to figure out a way to cut the budget elsewhere—as painful as that may be.

"Let me worry about my partner and what's good for my business. You think about what's good for yours."

A car horn blares and inches around the truck, partially blocking the street.

The driver taps his foot impatiently and clears his throat. "Where am I taking this thing?"

"My place." We both say it at the same time and point to different doors.

The poor man throws up his hands. "I'm giving you sixty seconds to sort this shit out. I have other deliveries to make today."

Isabella plasters on a smile and points to her place. "Take it to my place. If anything changes, we'll take care of getting it moved." She returns her hard gaze to me, the softness in it before apparently reserved only for the driver. "But I doubt that."

She has zero intention of budging on this. But if I don't try *everything* to convince her, I'll regret it. I need to appeal to reason.

"Go in my place and take a look at what I have, Isabella. See if it's something you want to work with. Don't dismiss my offer without at least looking and thinking about what all that money can do for you."

She scowls at me again and appears ready to argue, but then her eyes dart over to my place.

Yes. She's actually considering it. I might have a chance here.

I motion toward my door. "Go ahead. I'll keep an eye on things out here and make sure it gets into your space."

The dirty glare she gives me makes me steel myself for some sort of verbal attack, but instead of arguing, she heads toward my door, swaying her perfect hips almost violently in her frustration. She reaches for the handle and glances back like she's expecting me to pull something.

This driver seems like he's on the up and up, so even if I wanted to try to do something under the table, this man doesn't seem like the type to let me interfere with her contract.

"So, are we good?" His question turns me back to the street.

Reluctantly, I incline my head toward her place. If she changes her mind, it's easy enough to have Danny come over and get it from her and move it to my side.

The driver rolls his eyes and throws up his hands. "Thank God!"

He pushes the stove across the sidewalk, and I open the door to Isabella's place and hold it for him to load in.

With her over at my place, this is a good time to scope out the competition. No doubt she's doing the same in addition to examining my stove. That's fine. I want her to see what she's up against. It might help her to fully appreciate the position she's in.

I follow the driver inside and immediately scan the space.

She's been busy.

Even if this side were partially started like mine was when she moved in, she's been doing a lot more work than I realized. And on her own, too. Unlike on my side, where Danny and his crew are constantly going in and out and it seems work is happening twenty-four-seven, over here, things have been relatively quiet. A few deliveries. Some construction workers here and there. Isabella must be taking on most of this herself.

It's both impressive and a bit concerning. Opening a restaurant from scratch isn't a small undertaking. I'm feeling overwhelmed even with a partner who offers me a basically open budget and endless support from essentially anyone I ask for it. I also have my Wednesday evening activities to help me destress from it all. Isabella is alone, and while it shouldn't bother me so much, a strange ache forms in the center of my chest.

That only gets more intense as I take in what she's already accomplished.

Tables and chairs...

Though they're mismatched and appear like they were pulled out of dumpsters—not exactly the fine dining I'm going for—they actually don't look too bad in the space considering its industrial roots. They're easy and welcoming, like something you'd find at a small café in the South. The style definitely fits Isabella's more casual and laidback vibe. And while she doesn't have any décor on the walls yet, I can already tell what she's going for.

It's smart, really. A relaxing space that will probably serve super approachable food to people who may not be one hundred percent on board with fine dining the way I plan to present it.

She may be more competition than I gave her credit for in the beginning. It makes my insistence to Grant that we didn't have anything to worry about from her seem a little less true.

I wander after the delivery driver toward her kitchen, but an open notebook on one of the tables makes me pause.

Her to-do list. I shouldn't read it. That's intrusive and completely inappropriate, considering I'm her competitor.

But I do it anyway...

1. Get sign hung.
2. Hire at least two more servers.
3. Finish interior décor.

4. Schedule with the inspector.
5. Choose an opening date.
6. Line up vendors and place first orders.
7. Set employee schedules.

A grin spreads across my face at the final one, and I reach out and brush my finger over her delicate script and the knives with dripping blood she drew around it.

8. Kick Jameson Fury's ass!!!

Three exclamation points. She must really mean it.
I'd like to see her try.

JAMESON

"And now we would like to welcome celebrity chef, Jameson Fury, who's here to talk about his new restaurant that will be opening soon over in Bushwick."

I plaster on my best panty-melting smile and offer it to Becky and Tim, the hosts of the Channel 7 news morning show. "Thanks so much for having me. I'm excited to be here to talk about my venture."

Becky's bright-blue eyes dance at me the same way they did when I banged her in the back of the studio after I appeared on the show following my win on *Prime Chef* a year ago. It's too bad the woman is vapid as hell because she was a decent lay. But I just can't imagine spending time that isn't horizontal with somebody whose only talents are talking, reading off a teleprompter, and sucking cock.

It's why I never pursued anything more with her after our fun the last time I visited with the show, and it seems she holds no ill will toward me over it. Something tells me she'd be willing to go for another round in the back when we're done if I asked. But it's another blonde who seems to occupy my thoughts lately...

One I certainly can't be thinking about right now when I'm on live television. This is my time to talk up *FURY* and start the hype leading to opening.

Becky turns slightly toward me. "Jameson, I am so thrilled that you finally have your own restaurant opening up. I got to taste some of your amazing dishes when you were here last time, and I can only imagine the kind of menu you're putting together for your own space. Want to tell us about it?"

"Of course." I smile and glance toward the camera like I was instructed. "It's going to be called *FURY*."

The co-anchors burst out laughing, and Tim points at me.

"Clever naming."

I grin at him and shrug. "It seemed fitting. We are going to be mostly modern upscale American and European fare, but, of course, everyone knows I always love to throw a little twist into something to make it my own."

Becky and Tim both nod vigorously. Tim glances down at the menu I brought with me, examining the dishes.

I only had a second to glance at it when I picked it up from the printer on my way over here this morning, but the menu looked good. The print is fancy enough to look upscale but easy to read in dim lighting. I really wanted to be able to show it on camera, and I'm glad the printer was able to do the rush job so I could have it with me today, but it meant there wasn't time to really prepare Tim and Becky on what the menu contains.

Tim freezes for a second, glances over at me, then back down at the menu before smiling at the camera. "Well, Jameson, I have to say...you have some pretty *interesting* dishes on your menu."

"Oh, definitely. I think the octopus salad is really going to blow people's minds."

Tim chuckles and hands the menu to Becky. "You mean the 'octo*pussy* salad?'"

"What?" I jerk my head to the side and find both of them fighting full-on laughter while looking at the printed paper.

What the fuck is he talking about?

I clear my throat and peek at the camera while trying to keep a smile on my face. "I'm not sure what you mean, Tim."

That's kind of an inappropriate comment for him to be making on live television. A little lowbrow—even for a man who has a reputation as quite the ladies' man around NYC. I still wouldn't expect that to come out of his mouth. Seems like a big risk to his job.

Tim points to the menu, and Becky holds it out to me with a smirk.

She taps a long, manicured nail on it. "I think you have a couple typos on here, Jameson. You might want to get these corrected before the restaurant opens."

Typos? What the fuck?

There's no way. I went over this menu a dozen times before I brought it to the printer. It was perfect. I made sure to hand write each item clearly so there wouldn't be *any* problem reading it.

I snatch it out of her hand, and the fact that the cameras are running live on me suddenly pushes to the back of my mind. Scanning the menu, my hands tighten on the paper. Each word flashes through my head, and my vision goes red.

Octopussy salad...
Boner-in ribeye...
Spanked pork butt...
Roasted cock with a creamy white sauce...
Roast beef curtains with ass jus...

Motherfucker!

It goes on and on. Almost the entire menu.

These are not *typos*. This was a deliberate attack. Someone intentionally changed every single menu item.

And there's only one person who could have done it.

Izzy...

I left the handwritten version on the counter in the kitchen when I was over looking at her range. She was alone in there...with the damn menu. And I never bothered to review it when I dropped it off at the printer because I had finalized it already.

That sneaky little woman.

It seems I underestimated the feisty blonde next door. Izzy has more guts than I gave her credit for. Apparently, my offer to buy her range was a shot across the bow I didn't know I fired. She was ready with a response attack and found the perfect opportunity with the menu.

Well played.

Only now, I'm on one of the most-watched morning news shows in New York, looking like a fucking idiot.

I finally force a smile and glance back up at Becky and Tim. "Looks like somebody decided to play a little joke on me, that's all. I can assure you—the menu is going to dazzle everyone."

God, that sounded lame.

Becky's fake tinkle of laughter floats over to me, and she places her hand on my arm. "Do you have an opening date set yet?"

At least she steered the topic of conversation *away* from the menu disaster. I shake the paper in my hand. "Once I get these corrected, we'll be almost ready. A couple of final inspections and I anticipate opening in a few weeks."

She claps like an excited child. "Excellent. And why did you choose Bushwick for a location? I imagine with your name recognition, you could have opened up anywhere in Manhattan and been successful."

"I'm very excited to be opening a restaurant in the Bushwick neighborhood. It's a very up-and-coming area, and the people there have been very underserved in the past in terms of options for more upscale dining. I'm happy to be the only restaurateur looking to expand in this area of Brooklyn right now."

Tim nods and points at me. "And I heard you partnered with Grant Mason. That's impressive. Everything that man touches is like gold."

Let's fucking hope.

I smirk and look directly at the camera. Izzy thinks embarrassing me like that with the menu stunt was slick, but I now have a massive stage to knock her down another peg. "I can assure you, Tim, we're going to be the best restaurant in all of Brooklyn and certainly in Bushwick."

Becky turns back to the table in front of us and spreads her hands wide. "And I hear we're going to have a little taste of something after the commercial break. What you going to be making for us?"

Not the Octopussy salad.

"Oh, I have something interesting in mind."

Something that will show them what I have in store for the patrons who come to *FURY*.

And that will show Izzy what she's up against.

———

83

IZZY

The look on Jameson's face as he reads the menu and sees all the changes I made almost makes suffering through all the shit he's done to me worth it.

It was too good of an opportunity to pass up. After walking through his restaurant and seeing how much he's accomplished and then standing there in his kitchen, looking at his set-up, the menu sitting there was like an open invitation.

All I could think was: *If he wants war, I'll give him war.*

And this was just the first shot on my part. When he figures out what else I did, he's really going to melt down. As it is now, Jameson Fury is at a complete loss. I never thought I'd see it, but this even tops his knowing that I got the Vulcan he wanted.

He's pissed. Good.

It's about time he knows how I felt with all the under-handed stuff he's been pulling on me. And the fact that Becky and Tim are giving him shit only adds to my glee.

Payback's a bitch. And so is what he will undoubtedly try to do to me after this. But it's worth it. Well worth it, just for that one moment, that one look of embarrassment on the most-watched morning news channel in New York City.

But he finally seems to come to his senses again and shakes his head. "Looks like somebody decided to play a little joke on me, that's all...."

Damn, he handled that well.

He's far too polished to let what I did throw him off too much, and as I sit and watch, he casually rejoins the conversation and levels blow after blow at me. "I can assure you that we're going to be the best restaurant in all of Brooklyn, and certainly in Bushwick."

That bastard!

I knew he would insist on payback; I just didn't think it would be this fast. He is making it clear and sending me a message. He intends to take me down.

Well, he can give it his best try, but I'm ready for him.

As long as I can keep dragging myself out of bed.

Today was rough, and it seems to be getting harder and harder every day. If I hadn't had a meeting with Barry to finalize a few interior construction issues, I probably would have stayed curled up and just slept to regain some of my energy.

But as it stands now, I don't have time to relax. Not with Fury breathing down my neck.

I close the app on my phone I've been using to watch the morning show and glance around the place. It's time to dig into some work. Maybe trying to perfect my own menu will distract me from waiting for Jameson to return and the inevitable confrontation that will happen when he does.

Because there's no way he's going to let what he said on air be the last word about this.

It's like bracing myself for an oncoming hurricane— batten down the hatches and all that jazz. I may have unleashed a monster, but I'm ready for him.

Despite feeling exhausted and physically weakened right now, I'm mentally tough as nails. Or steel. Or are nails steel? Whatever is the hardest, that's what I am.

I make my way back into the kitchen and grin at my prized possession. Saying no to Jameson's offer to buy the range stung—especially when I went home and looked at my finances. But the victory somehow seems sweeter after what just went down on the morning show.

I've secured two major "wins" in the last few days— three, if you count the *other* little prank I pulled in his kitchen while I also messed with his menu. He can't have discovered that one yet, because I'm sure I will hear about it immediately—likely from cursing and screaming coming through the shared wall.

So, for now, I cook and wait for him to return from his few moments in the spotlight...with a smug smile on my face for as long as I can wear it before he comes in and wipes it clean off.

The prick.

I drag out all the ingredients I need for Grams' chili, throw my hair into a messy bun, crank up the music from the radio on the far end of the counter, and set to work making one of my absolute favorite dishes.

It doesn't really need any *work* for the menu, but I know some people don't like too much spice in their food. I want to please as many customers as possible, so the plan is to make two versions—Grams' classic and a slightly "watered-down" version that removes a lot of the spice and makes it more palatable for people who can't handle it.

I hope you understand, Grams.

Altering her recipes feels sacrilegious somehow, but if I want to compete with *FURY* right next door, I need to offer something he doesn't—approachable food that doesn't scare off customers with fancy names and ingredients...or by burning off their tongues.

I'm feeling spicy today, though. Maybe because of my tiny wins. So, this batch will have a little something extra. The workers will probably appreciate a free lunch later, so it won't go to waste even though I can't possibly eat it all myself.

Time flies, chopping, stirring, and swaying my hips to the music, and I almost miss the sound of the front door closing.

Almost.

It makes me freeze with the spoon held over the pot. If it's Jameson, he's going to come swirling in like a tornado.

And I'm not expecting anyone else 'til later this morning when Barry is supposed to return with his guys and what he needs to build the benches for people to use while waiting in the hostess area.

I shift my shoulders back and brace myself.

Only instead of a furious Jameson Fury, he appears in the doorway to the kitchen with a smug smirk tilting his perfect lips and leans against the jamb, crossing his arms over his muscled chest. Intentional or not—and with *this* man, I'm almost certain it's *always* intentional—his biceps bulge against his pale-blue T-shirt.

He clears his throat, and I jerk my gaze away from the taut muscles there and to his eyes that dance with humor.

Dammit. The jerk caught me staring...again.

It was bad enough when he was out on that damn chair sunbathing practically naked, but he's clothed now. My attention should be focused on how to take him down, not on the ways I want to *take* him. And there are *so many* ways dancing through my head right now.

Why does he have to be so infuriatingly hot?

He raises his dark eyebrows at me, the corner of his mouth curling up even more. "You don't have anything to say to me?"

I stand up even straighter, a move that shifts my breasts out and causes Jameson's focus to drift south of my face.

Ha! At least I'm not the only one.

If nothing else, at least I got that little ego boost today.

"What would I have to say to you?"

For some reason, playing dumb seems like the right response here; though, he *has* to know it was me. None of his construction crew would have any reason to mess with his menu, and I was the only other person back there while he was working on it. Plus, his jab at me on live TV was in clear retaliation.

But the way his amber eyes bore into me, I don't want to admit what I did. Even though only hours ago, I was so proud I could have burst. Now, that pride has been replaced with a tiny quiver in my belly of something I don't even *want* to consider.

Almost like an anticipation, a desire for him to move closer, to be angrier, to demand some form of penance from me.

Christ, I'm a mess.

It's been so damn long since a man has touched me in that way that I'll apparently fantasize about it with the one who has become my mortal enemy in the span of only a few weeks.

Get a grip, Iz.

He pushes off the jamb and takes a step toward me. "Oh, I don't know." He holds out his hands. "Maybe an apology for embarrassing me on live television?"

Another couple of slow steps bring him even closer, close enough that the rich, spicy scent he always carries with him overpowers the seasonings from the chili on the stove to assault every one of my breaths.

Still, I don't answer.

We've stood like this before, but somehow, the energy between us today is different. A crackle. A spark. Something building and threatening to light the whole kitchen ablaze.

His heated gaze narrows on me. "Not going to say it, huh? Well, I have a few things to say to you."

Oh shit. Here we go.

8

IZZY

This is what I've been waiting for. The storm I knew would come with his anger. This playful sexy act when he first got here was simply to get me to let down my guard. It's time for him to strike. But I'm ready for whatever he throws at me.

I think.

He examines me, waiting for some kind of response, his eyes raking over me like he can see straight through to the intimate thoughts I'm trying to push to the back of my mind.

I stand my ground, refusing to quiver under his assessment.

He takes another step closer until our chests are practically touching while I still hold the spoon over the pot. The side of his mouth tics up slightly. "Well, I have to say, Iz, I underestimated you. Fucking with my menu was genius. Well played."

Wait...what?

I shake my head to try to clear it because I can't have just heard him right. "Well played?"

He nods slowly, his eyes locked with mine. "I'm actually impressed. I'm not so sure I would have been quick enough to come up with that if I had been in your position, standing there in your kitchen with the menu just sitting out unprotected."

Impressed. He's IMPRESSED with me?

Those words shouldn't feel so good. They shouldn't make warmth swell in my chest and flood my cheeks. They shouldn't make me all swoony and light-headed, yet I wobble slightly on my feet and drop the spoon into the pot of chili.

A strong arm wraps around my waist, holding me steady. He narrows a concerned gaze at me. "Are you okay?"

Shit.

I squeeze my eyes shut for a moment and inhale deeply, but that only brings that incredible scent that's all Jameson into my lungs. My heart flutters again, the rush of blood filling my ears, and I force my eyes open. "I'm fine."

His brow furrows. "You don't look fine. You got really flush then really pale."

"I'm fine. Really." I smile at him, trying to ignore how incredible his palm feels pressed to my back. And how his firm chest brushing against mine only makes my heart beat faster. "Really."

I'm not sure who I'm trying to convince—him or me.

But just as quickly as the little "event" happens, I start to feel the energy rush back, and with it, the reality of how close Jameson really is. And how much I like it.

Nope.

Shaking my head, I push at his chest. "I'm fine. Thank you."

If he doesn't stop touching me and back away, I may wrap my arms around his neck, sag straight into him, and let the rivalry between us go to the wayside for a few minutes.

That can't happen. Not now. Not ever.

Jameson looks like he's going to fight me or question me again, but instead, he sucks in a deep breath and blows it out slowly before inching back. "Good, then let's get back to you apologizing to me."

A laugh bursts from my lips, echoing off all the stainless-steel equipment in the kitchen. "I will apologize to you when Hell freezes over."

He scowls and leans his hip against the range he wants so badly. "You embarrassed me on live TV."

I wave my hand back toward the restaurant. "You stole my parking space, intentionally blocked it, and then snatched employees right out from under my nose! What I did was nothing compared to that."

He snorts out a laugh and shakes his head. "I didn't do in front of millions of people."

I scoff and prop my hands on my hips. "First, it doesn't matter if you did it in front of people or not. You've been screwing me over at every turn. Second, I had *no way* of knowing you were going to bring the menu onto the show today."

"Maybe not, but you were willing to let me get them printed and potentially hand them to customers like that."

I wave him off. "Bullshit. You're way too big of a perfectionist not to check them over a thousand times before you open. They never would have reached the hands of your customers, and you know it."

He smirks at me and crosses his arms over his chest again.

"What?" I glower at him. "Why are you smiling? That wasn't a compliment."

A deep chuckle rumbles from his lips, and he leans

toward me slightly and winks. "Doesn't mean I won't take it as one."

Grrr. This man is too fucking much.

I need him out of my restaurant and personal space soon, or I'm liable to say or do something I absolutely shouldn't. Like start to actually *like* him. "Was there anything else you needed besides an apology you're never going to get?"

He glances into the pot on the stove, grabs the spoon sticking up, and stirs it while inhaling deeply. "What's this? It smells incredible."

Another compliment from Jameson Fury. I better watch out —maybe Hell is freezing over.

I snatch the spoon out of his hand and stir even though it doesn't need it. "Nothing you need to concern yourself with."

There's no way I'm revealing any of my menu plans or recipes to this man. He'd steal them and somehow manage to nail a distribution deal with some massive food conglomerate that would make him millions.

Maybe I'm being a bit paranoid about it, but with someone as sneaky as Chef Fury, one can never be too careful. And Grams would roll over in her grave if she ever saw any of her recipes being sold with someone else's name on them.

He holds up his hands in surrender with a dropped jaw. "Wow! I just wanted a taste of whatever smells so good. God forbid I try some of your food."

Well, maybe not God...

But *something* prevents me from handing the spoon back. Maybe it's pride or lingering anger over everything he's done. Or, even scarier, maybe it's because he's already paid me two compliments when I was expecting him to be volatile when he showed up, and that worries me far more than if he had come in here guns blazing.

This isn't the time in my life to get involved with anyone —emotionally *or* physically—and even if I were to, Jameson would be the last one on the list of potential suitors.

He takes a step back from the stove and shakes his head. "I didn't realize you were doing top-secret shit over here."

I scowl at him and stir the chili. "It's not top secret. Far from it."

Suck it up, Iz. Let him have a taste and tell him to move on back to his place.

One taste won't hurt anything.

And it might be enough to get him to hightail it out of here in search of a beer or something to tame his palate with as hot as I made this.

Wait...

I fight the sinister smile threatening to spread across my lips. I've been thinking about this all wrong. Most people can't handle this kind of heat. Grams' original recipe is hot enough, but when I add my "extras" to it, it becomes almost like napalm. Maybe Jameson will be one of those pussies who can't deal. If I'm lucky and he's not, it could throw off his whole palate for days.

It may be tempting fate to try for a third "win" today, but something makes me fill the spoon and bring it up for him. Something that wants to top the "prime chef" just *one* more time.

———

JAMESON

Something mischievous twinkles in Isabella's emerald eyes. Something completely foreign. Typically, the only thing I see there is anger and annoyance. But this look...this one excites me as much as it worries me she might be up to something.

What are you doing, clever girl?

I wouldn't put it past her to try to pull one over on me again after what she already did. Truth is, I had hoped to catch her off guard and perhaps secure a little payback myself.

When I came in here today, I thought our confrontation was going to go a lot differently. Because I was *pissed*. The entire drive, all I could think about was what a huge moron I must have looked like when I was sitting there staring at that menu on camera—bright lights shining on me, Tim and Becky chuckling at my expense.

I imagined all the potential customers laughing at me and wondering what a shit-show I must be running if I can't even handle a menu. All the people who will forever be giggling about "octopussy salad" every time my name is mentioned for the rest of my fucking life.

Yet, the moment I laid eyes on her standing at the range —the one I want so badly, the one she refuses to sell me— her hips swinging to the beat of the music blasting from the radio, something a lot different than anger took hold.

It was *pride*.

I was fucking *proud* of her for finding a way to get back at me.

Not that I think anything I did was that bad or under-handed—just the cost of business—but she's standing on her own two feet, refusing my money I know she needs, and not just *not* budging but actively *fighting* back.

It wasn't what I expected from the perky, tiny blonde. Though, perhaps I underestimated her. The soaked woman who stormed into my empty restaurant space weeks ago to let her disdain for me known is far different from the one standing before me now, holding out a spoon. This one has something devious in her eyes and a lot more spunk in her after what she did to me.

She flashes me a grin and nods to what looks like chili. "Try some. My grandmother's chili recipe."

Her lips twitch like she's fighting a grin, and I hold her gaze while I lean forward and wrap my mouth around the spoon.

Fuck.

Almost instantly, the fruity heat of what can only be habanero peppers hits my tongue...and burns violently across my palate.

I fight the urge to cough against the heat, and instead, swallow again and take a second to try to savor the other flavors present beneath the searing fire of the pepper.

And boy, are they there.

The chili is *hot*—there's no denying that—but it's also layered with depth of flavor I haven't ever experienced in a dish like this before. It's truly incredible. Her grandmother was an excellent cook.

Izzy watches me expectantly, spoon clutched tightly in her fist.

She thought she was going to get me with this shit.

I grin at her and reach out to tug the spoon out of her hand. Her mouth drops open slightly, and she watches me expectantly. I meet her gaze and hold it while I lick the remnants off each side slowly, making sure to swirl my tongue over every little bit of the surface before darting it out across my lips.

Isabella swallows thickly, and her tongue darts out across her lips, mimicking my own action. My eyes can't help but follow the motion, and my cock twitches, imagining what it would feel like being the focus of that attention.

Fuck.

That is a dangerous road to go down, but something about Izzy and her fiery responses to everything I've thrown at her has left me more frazzled than I was even looking down at that menu this morning. She's stood her ground since the moment I showed up and punched right back at me—refusing to apologize, tossing things back in my face that prove her points.

She's pretty fucking incredible.

And watching her react to me flirting with her is only spurring on something that is a very bad idea for both of us. Because I'm going to have to crush her—or her restaurant, at least.

But that doesn't mean we can't have a little fun until that time comes.

Or a lot of fun.

I take a step closer to her until I can feel each breath floating from her slightly open mouth.

Her eyes lock with mine, and her bottom lip trembles slightly. "Wh-what are you doing?"

Asking myself the same question here, Iz.

I place the spoon on the edge of the stove and reach out to brush a stray strand of blond hair from her face. "Just putting the spoon back."

She sucks in a sharp breath. "Uh-huh."

Her eyes drop to my lips, and almost of its own volition, my hand moves to cup her cheek. Smooth, buttery-soft skin touches my palm, and a tiny little gasp slips from her lips.

I lean in slightly until I can smell the spice coming from her, proof that she's been testing her own food. She freezes, and I wet my lips to try to numb the tingling still there from the chili.

"That was very good chili, Ms. Baldwin. Spicy. But I like things that way." I gently drag my thumb across her cheek, making her quiver under my touch, then drop my head down until my lips brush her ear. "I know what you were trying to do by giving that to me. But you failed, Iz. Because you see, I love *all* things hot and live for a challenge. Besides, you know what they say, 'if you can't take the heat, get out of the kitchen.'"

I take a step back from her, and she almost falls forward following me. She stands in front of me dazed, her eyes glassy, her body practically vibrating.

Maybe fucking with her isn't nice. But I'm paying for it, too.

This hard-on isn't going to take care of itself, and I have a lot of work still to get done today. That won't happen if I stay in her domain any longer.

I turn and make my way out of her kitchen without looking back. If I do, I'll be too tempted to stalk back over to her, kiss her, and fuck her on the damn counter.

Jerking off in the bathroom of my place like some perv is going to have to do.

At least...for now.

9

IZZY

"Wow! This is not how I pictured it at all."

I jerk up my head from where I had it buried in a stack of paperwork spread out across one of the tables. Considering how jumpy I've been ever since my little incident with Jameson the other day, I can't believe I didn't hear the door open.

I've been working the last week with my heart in my throat, waiting for another run-in with Jameson. But the man has remained elusive—whether intentional or not—leaving me a bundle of frazzled nerves.

At least I knew I was safe last night since he always seems to disappear on Wednesdays. I've noticed him sneaking off several times in the early evening and not returning when other nights he's here burning the midnight oil. He's definitely up to something, though what it is—on those nights or with me the other night in my kitchen—remains a mystery.

And it's all left me out of sorts, especially when unexpected visitors arrive. Only it isn't my enigmatic neighbor standing just inside the door. A stunning woman with bright-red hair who looks vaguely familiar stands just to the left of the door, shrewd gaze assessing every inch of my restaurant.

Unease creeps over my skin. "Can I help you?"

She turns her head in my direction and smiles. "Oh, hi. I didn't see you there." One of her manicured hands flits out. "I was just commenting that this is not what I expected."

I raise an eyebrow at her. "Um, what do you mean?"

Why would she expect anything?

She waves a hand around again. "Oh, just that this isn't really the style I had pictured."

Who is this woman, and why she picturing anything for my restaurant?

"And you are?"

"Oh." She extends her hand to me and walks over to the table. "Sylvie Mason. I'm Grant's wife."

"That explains it." I roll my eyes, sigh deeply, and motion to the wall I share with Jameson. "You're in the wrong space."

Her eyebrows fly up, and she glances around. "Am I?"

I point at the wall. "Jameson and your husband have the space next door."

Her mouth drops open slightly. "Well, that certainly explains *this*."

She motions around her absently.

What the hell is that supposed to mean?

My initial unease shifts to anger. Like I need Grant Mason's wife here reminding me what a piece of shit my restaurant is compared to what they're doing. "Well, if there's nothing else I can do for you..."

Her eyes fly wide. "Oh." She presses a hand to her chest. "No, no, no! I didn't mean it like that. I *love* all of this." She gestures around her again. "It's so eclectic and welcoming and homey and not at all what I imagine would come out of my husband or Jameson's heads."

I snort and roll my eyes, unable to hold it back. "You can say that again."

She chuckles and offers me a sympathetic look. "I take it you've had some run-ins with Grant?"

"Your husband isn't the one who has been a pain in my ass."

This time, she drops her head back and laughs, and instead of moving toward the door and her inevitable date with my enemies next door, she points to the chair across from me. "Sounds like there's a story I need to hear."

This woman is a total stranger, the spouse of the man who, for all intents and purposes, is going to try to ruin my business before it even gets off the ground, yet something inside me wants to open up to her for some strange reason. That's very odd for me—letting anyone into my very private world. Yet, Sylvie seems genuine, and at this point, maybe a non-neutral party holds the insight I need.

I incline my head to the chair and lean back in mine.

She slips into the seat across from me. "So, you're having a problem with Jameson? That doesn't surprise me. There's a reason he and my husband get along so swimmingly."

My hands fist involuntarily on the table in front of me. "He's just so..."

A low growl comes from my lips that surprises even me while Sylvie's eyes widen.

She laughs again. "I get it; I really do. I can imagine trying to open a restaurant right next to them isn't going to make any of you friends."

I don't know...

Jameson certainly acted like he wanted to be a lot more than friends the other night. The way he looked at me. The lingering touches. The almost kiss.

"Nor will what you did to him with the whole menu thing."

"Shit. You know about that?"

Her tinkling laughter fills the room, and she shakes her head. "Well, I knew someone had done it, and Grant told me it was another restaurateur. I just put two and two together."

I scowl and rock back in my chair, the old wood creaking ominously under me. "It was just payback for everything he's done to me."

"Again, I feel like I'm missing something here. Care to fill me in?"

I sigh and give her the quick rundown of all the shit Jameson has put me through since my first day here. She listens intently, nodding along and laughing a few times. "And then, the day of his TV appearance, he showed up in my kitchen afterward. And while I was expecting anger, what I got was a lot more like..."

She shifts forward, clenching her hands on the table, her bright eyes dancing with curiosity. "Like what?"

"Like...flirting."

Rapping her knuckles on the old wood, she laughs. "Jameson is a hopeless flirt."

For some reason, that makes bile churn in my stomach and threaten to work its way up. Understatement of the century. And what happened with Jameson the other night was far more than a simple, flirty run-in. That man had me practically melting with one look. And that near kiss left me breathless and dizzy again.

I swear opening a restaurant next to him is not good for my health. "You know him well?"

She shakes her head, sending her red locks flying around her face, and sits back. "I wouldn't say *well*. But I met him after his appearance on *Prime Chef*. He was catering an event we were at as the celebrity chef, and he and Grant really hit it off. I know enough to understand that he's a shameless flirt and is probably just as likely to try to fuck you as to stab you in the back."

I snort and shake my head. "That's reassuring."

This woman's analysis is spot-on the vibe I've gotten from him since the day I set eyes on him in the pouring rain. He's a man who knows how hot he is and uses it to get what he wants. He never fails, and he enjoys a challenge much more than having something handed to him.

Am I that challenge? Or is the restaurant?

Sylvie grins at me. "I wasn't trying to be reassuring. I was trying to be realistic."

I scrub my hands over my face and let the chair drop down onto all fours. "Christ, I can't believe I'm telling all this to a perfect stranger."

She chuckles again. "Don't worry. I'm like the Fort Knox of secret information, especially when it comes to matters of the heart."

Something tells me I don't have to worry about her revealing any of this to anyone. Though these circumstances do seem a bit unique.

"Even though your husband is his partner and my business rival? Seems like a bit of a conflict of interest, if you know what I mean."

She shrugs nonchalantly and leans back in her chair. "I like to support the underdogs. The people who may not get such an easy lot in life and have to fight their way up every rung on the ladder of success. Something tells me that might be you."

Damn, she's good.

Almost too good. It's a little unnerving how easily she can see me.

Am I that transparent?

I shift uneasily in my seat, suddenly self-conscious about

everything—the second-hand tables and chairs, the hand-made items decorating the space that I sourced from local donations since I can't afford pricey décor, my own outfit of a stained T-shirt and ripped jeans.

Sylvie offers me a soft smile. "I think there's room in this area for more than one incredible restaurant. And I will gladly do everything I can to help you make yours successful."

"Really?"

She nods. "Of course."

"But...you don't even know me."

Pushing to her feet, she rests her palms flat on the table and winks at me. "I know enough. Now, let me go scope out the competition for you."

She throws her purse that probably costs more than the damn range Jameson wanted so badly over her shoulder.

I groan, close my eyes, and pinch the bridge of my nose. "You're going to be impressed."

"Why do you say that?"

Opening my eyes reluctantly, I meet her gaze. "Because *I* am."

That man may drive me bonkers and make me want to stab him with my kitchen knife...but he knows how to create an incredible restaurant space. As much as I complain about fine dining, he's done it right. It's elegant yet rustic. Stunning and comfortable without being stuffy.

She offers me a sympathetic smile. "Sorry."

I offer a laugh I don't feel and wave her off as I climb to my feet to walk her to the door. "You don't have anything to be sorry for."

"I know. It just felt like the right thing to say. I mean...I don't want my husband's business to fail. But I don't want yours to, either. There has to be some middle ground."

For a brief moment the other night, I thought perhaps

that was true. When Jameson's hand brushed over my cheek so tenderly. When he stared into my eyes and sent my heart fluttering. But then, just as quickly, his mask of assholeness slipped back into place and he walked out of here without a glance back like he owned me.

Well, no man has ever owned me or ever will.

I have no intention of letting Jameson Fury win this restaurant battle or me. "I appreciate any help you can offer, Sylvie."

She pats me on the shoulder and steps out into the warm summer air and sunshine. "I'll do my best. Now, the boys are waiting for me. Let me see what I can find out."

With another wink at me, she makes her way next door. The thought of following her in is very tempting. And honestly, I doubt they would kick me out if I tried to get a peek of what they've done since the last time I was in there.

It's not like I could copy them even if I wanted to steal any of their ideas. I don't have the kind of money or resources to do anything even remotely like what they have going on.

But my feet remain planted as she disappears inside. Sylvie offered to be my eyes and ears over there. I'm going to let her.

It's best that I keep my distance from Jameson.

For his sake and my own.

JAMESON

The door to the restaurant opens and closes, the sound echoing through the vaulted ceilings and off the empty tables back to me in the kitchen.

I stick my head out and see a familiar red shock of hair. "Hey, Sylvie. We're back here."

She waves and makes her way across the hardwood floors, her heels clicking on the surface as she takes in everything in a way that makes me hold my breath in anticipation.

Shit. I didn't think I'd be this nervous for her to see the place.

I wasn't kidding about what my "friend" said about Sylvie. The woman is shrewd, and she knows exactly what she likes when it comes to interior decorating, food, and men and certainly isn't afraid to speak her mind about her feelings. She doesn't make things easy on Grant, and there's no way she is going to here, either.

If she doesn't like something, she's going to let us know quickly and without mincing words.

She reaches me and leans in to plant a kiss on my cheek. "Hey, where's my husband?"

I tilt my head toward the kitchen. "Stuffing his face with various menu items."

With a laugh, she follows me back to where Grant sits on a stool pulled up to the counter, several dishes spread out in front of him.

He glances up at her and waves his fork. "Hey, babe."

Sylvie leans in and gives him a kiss that would definitely not be appropriate if children were around, and I offer an exaggerated gagging noise as I return to the pot on the stove.

"Oh, stop it!" Sylvie chuckles. "We're all adults here. And we get so little time alone without the kids that we need to take advantage." She scans all the items on the counter. "I thought the menu was already set?"

Grant gives a bemused grin. "That's what I said when I got here."

I just scowl at them. "It is. It *was*." This is difficult to explain to anyone who doesn't share my obsession. It has to be *perfect*. And now, I'm second-guessing everything. "But after my little moment on the morning show, I'm starting to reconsider."

Sylvie raises an eyebrow. "Why? You're not happy with what you selected?"

"It's not that."

I shove my hand back through my hair and sigh, wincing slightly at the pain in my side left from last night's activities. Even my usual stress relief did nothing to erase what went down with Isabella the other day.

Nor can I forget that damn chili.

It won't leave the back of my mind. The flavor still assaults my tongue every time I think about it. And so does Isabella's scent. Can't get it out of my fucking head. But those are two completely different issues.

The one at hand is the delicious item she's going to have on her menu and how it compares to the things I had planned before she tore mine apart with her wicked pen.

"I'm starting to wonder if my menu might be a little too ambitious for this area."

Grant climbs from his seat to offer it to his wife. "I told him he's being crazy."

She nods and motions to the couple of dishes I have laid out—some from the old menu and some potential new items. "I don't understand." Her eyes drift over to the side with the more elegant plates, and she points. "I thought that this was the kind of food you cook."

I clear my throat and glance toward the joint wall. "It is. But it's not the type of food the people in this area are used to. It might be a little too conceptual for them."

Sylvie chuckles and shakes her head. "I can see you're just as much of a worrier and perfectionist as my husband. No wonder you two get along so well."

I scowl at her. Even though she's one hundred percent

right, it doesn't mean I have to like it. "Why do you say that like it's a bad thing? Being a perfectionist is what got me to where I am today."

Grant nods and raises his hand. "Same."

His wife smacks him on the arm. "I'm not saying it's a bad thing. But I do think you need to consider whether you want your restaurant to be all concept or to have a little heart." She inclines her head back toward the shared wall like I just did. "Isabella?"

I narrow my eyes on Sylvie. "What about her?"

She shrugs slightly. "I may have stopped over there on my way here. And accidentally slipped in and talked to her for a while."

Grant glances at her. "Accidentally? I told you the girl next door was the one who messed with the menu."

Sylvie offers a faux innocent shrug. "I can play dumb."

I laugh and smack my hands together. "All right. A spy. Just what we need."

She holds up her hands and shakes her head. "Oh, no. I am no spy. I'm just letting you guys know that I really dig the vibe of her place. It's casual and inviting and very homey."

I cringe at the word. "That is definitely not what we're going for."

She shrugs. "I get that." She reaches out and grabs a bite of the new roasted chicken dish I came up with from the plate in front of her, unceremoniously popping it into her mouth. Her eyes roll to the back of her head, and she groans. "Damn. That's good."

Grant leans in. "Don't make those noises and say things like that in public. You know how I get."

Sylvie laughs and smacks him again. "Behave." She turns back to me and offers a sympathetic smile. "Look, I think you need to do whatever you want to do and not worry about what the beautiful blonde next door is doing. If you do, you'll end up second-guessing everything until the day you open and probably long after that. That won't be good for your business. But that doesn't mean you shouldn't also put your heart and soul into each thing you make."

My partner points at me. "Exactly what I told him."

One of her slim shoulders rises and falls. "Yeah, but he probably doesn't listen to you."

Grant points at her and laughs. "No, he certainly doesn't."

I scowl at him. "That's because I know what I want. This is *all* I've wanted since I was about five."

He chuckles and shakes his head. "I still don't understand how the son of hockey royalty, whose brother was also one of the best players in NHL history, ends up as a chef instead of out on the ice."

His words freeze my blood faster than being out on the morning ice ever did, and I school my features and try not to react to his comment. Grant and I may have become fast friends, but there are a lot of things I'll never discuss with him, no matter how much I like the guy.

The Fury family dynamics are one of them. Mike Fury was a beloved player, a hall of famer champ who could do no wrong on the ice. It was at home where he had trouble. But there's always been an unspoken agreement between Bash, Rach, and me not to taint his image. Not because we're trying to protect him, but because we're trying to protect ourselves from having to relive those moments through invasive questioning from reporters.

So, I have no intention of answering Grant's question. Instead, I shrug and turn back to the stove.

Almost as if she can sense the tension, Sylvie springs to her feet and claps her hands together. "Whatever the reason, I'm so glad you ended up in the kitchen. Otherwise, we wouldn't be here in this lovely place. Really good job, boys." She glances between us. "Really, you guys did a great job. I have every confidence this place is going to take off."

Grant snorts and reaches out to pop a piece of the artichoke salad into his mouth. "I sure as hell hope so; otherwise, we'll be in the poor house."

That brings a laugh from everyone, but I can't help thinking about Isabella and her financial situation. If her restaurant fails, that's likely exactly what's going to happen to her.

Yet, having her compete with me isn't good for my business, either.

I can't let my concern for her get in the way of having my own successful restaurant. Nor can I let the fact that she is beautiful and talented and sexy as hell disrupt my focus.

That woman is a liability in a lot of ways.

And a liability is the last thing I need right now—no matter how much fun it may be to mess around with her.

I need to keep things professional—as much as anyone can in this situation.

Yep, professional. I can do that.

Grant sweeps his hand over the dishes. "So, what's your final verdict on the menu? We don't have a lot of time left to make this decision."

"No, we don't." I press my palms down on the counter and stare at the mix of food laid out before me. "Something just isn't right. I'm going to stay and play around some more. Hopefully come up with something that really sings."

The way Isabella's chili did the other night.

Otherwise, she's going to be the one putting *me* out of business.

10

IZZY

The smells coming from Jameson's kitchen are so mouth-watering; they're not just tempting... they're downright torturous.

I would never give that man the satisfaction of knowing that, though.

His ego already occupies so much of his perfect body that I'd be worried it might start taking up residence in the parts of the brain he needs to function daily if it gets stroked and grows any bigger.

But my stomach seems to disagree, growling at me like a starved lion on the savannah. It's been a long day—*another* long day. I've stayed far later than I had planned—again—this time trying to clean the kitchen spotless after the construction crew traipsed through here to install a few other smaller items I've been waiting on.

I deeply appreciate their help in getting things set up, but I could do without the mud and dirt on their damn boots. Seeing it on my pristine white tile floors was giving me hives all evening.

So, instead of heading home, eating, taking my meds, and doing what I need to stay healthy, I find myself here on my knees with a metal bowl of hot, soapy water and a damn sponge. Because, *of course,* I don't have a mop and proper bucket here yet.

Add that to the to-do list, Iz.

Along with the ten thousand other things that seem to just pile up higher and higher each day. The mountain is starting to feel overwhelming, more like Everest than the moderate hill I thought it would be when I got my keys.

It's not that I didn't understand how much work this would be. It's just I was so determined. *Am* so determined. The idea of failure never even crossed my mind. Until I met the shameless chef next door.

Now, all I can think about is how easily one mistake on my part could fuck up any chances I might have to actually compete with *FURY*. Hell, even if I do everything absolutely *perfectly*, there's still a chance that I don't *stand* a chance.

If I think about it any more tonight, I might become overwhelmed with the possibilities again and only make things worse. So, I try to push away the growling in my stomach and the stab of pain in my lower back as I scrub away like Cinderella.

"This is a very dangerous position."

Shit!

I jerk up and whirl toward the door, knocking over the bowl with a loud clang. Jameson leans against the jamb again, shirtless, with a dark-blue apron stretched across his chest, exposing his hard, rippled biceps and impressive pecs.

My heart thunders against my ribs, and I press my hand against it and try to take a deep breath to calm myself. "What the hell are you doing here?"

He raises a plate I hadn't even noticed was in his hand. "I went out to grab something from my car and noticed you were still here. Thought you might be hungry. I also wanted to warn you that it's probably not safe for you to be here alone this late at night with your door unlocked. Quite dangerous, really, especially if you're going to be waving your ass in the air like that. Some perv might come in and try to take advantage of the situation."

"A perv, huh? That would explain you being half-naked already. Did your shirt spontaneously jump off?"

A panty-melting grin spreads across his face, and he shrugs nonchalantly before taking a step forward. "It was hot as hell in my kitchen. This is far more comfortable." He waves the plate in front of me. "You hungry?"

My stomach growls in response, and I press my hand against it.

God, that's embarrassing.

"I do work in a kitchen." I wave a hand around. "I'm perfectly capable of cooking something for myself if I'm hungry."

Which I am. I just haven't had the time to do it yet.

"Oh, I have no doubt you're perfectly capable. I just already had all this delicious food made. But if you don't want it..."

I eye the plate in his hand, examining each item as carefully as I can from a few feet away.

He shifts closer. "Why are you looking at it like a venomous snake is going to uncurl from the center and lash out at you?"

Venomous snake. Quite the apt comparison.

I raise my focus up to meet his humored gaze. "Maybe because I don't fully trust you."

His dark eyebrows fly up. "You? Don't trust me?" He barks out a laugh and shakes his head. "That's fucking rich coming from the woman who altered my menu *and* put *salt* in my sugar jar."

Oh shit.

I was wondering how long it was going to take for him to discover that one.

He takes another step closer. "I had to throw away what would have been a pretty delicious, sweet and sticky Korean barbeque ribs this evening once I tried it and promptly spit it out." His eyes dance with amusement. "Again...well played. I thought I was impressed with the menu thing, but that was really above and beyond. Makes me wish I had thought to do it when I had a few minutes alone in here. You got me twice."

An unbridled sense of glee warms me from the inside out. I fight a grin and push some of the sweaty hair matted to my forehead and temples back from my face. "Don't forget the chili."

Crap. Where did that come from?

I've just admitted exactly what he accused me of—trying to mess with him yet again the other night with Grams' altered, special recipe. And something tells me that won't go unnoticed by him.

He narrows his eyes on me and holds up the plate. "Despite the fact that you embarrassed me, tricked me, and tried to burn my mouth off, I promise you, this plate is completely safe. I'll take a bite of everything myself if it will ease your mind."

Christ no...

The thought of watching him wrap his mouth around a fork or a spoon, or God forbid, lick it...brings up far too many fantasies I've been trying so hard to forget. If he were to do it right in front of me again, I'm not so sure I'd be in any position to deny him anything he asks of me.

I shake my head and grasp the plate. "That won't be necessary."

A grin pulls at his lips, and he grabs the fork resting

across the various delectable looking items and stabs the tines into what looks like whipped potatoes with fresh herbs mixed in. I try to pull the plate from his hand, but he maintains a firm grip and lowers the fork until the bite is right in front of my mouth.

He doesn't utter a word, just moves it forward to brush against my lips. I dart out my tongue and lick carefully, savoring the flavors of butter, garlic, parsley, and something deeply rich and funky that can only be black truffle.

The man probably put four hundred dollars of truffles on a dish he was only testing. But I can't complain, especially not when he pushes the bite between my lips and into my mouth.

I swallow, watching his gaze drop down my neck before returning to meet mine.

"Well?"

Christ, that was good.

His lips tip up into a knowing grin without me saying a word, and he leans toward me. "You can tell me it was amazing, Iz. I already know. These might be the best potatoes I've ever made."

Dammit.

His arrogance should be a massive turn-off. It should make me want to simultaneously smack him across his handsome face and run far away from his reach. But he has reason to be arrogant about this.

"Shit. Yes. Incredible."

He chuckles and stabs a piece of steak. "Was that really so horrible to admit?"

I open my mouth to protest, but he pushes the meat between my lips before I can get a word out. Chewing, something familiar yet exciting and new mixes with the deeply beefy flavor of the filet. "Mmm. What's on this? It's a béarnaise, but something is different...."

Instead of answering, he swipes the fork through the sauce drizzled over the steak and gently wipes it across my lower lip. The move is so sensual that a shiver rolls through my body and a jolt of pleasure flutters between my legs.

Oh, hell.

"Tell me what you taste."

I flick my tongue across my lip. "Butter. Lemon. Vinegar. White wine. Tarragon, of course. Pepper. Shallots. Cayenne."

He draws the fork over my lip again. "You got something wrong. Two things, actually."

"Hmm." Those are the classic ingredients in a béarnaise sauce, one of the basics we learn in culinary school. Yet, something *is* different. I just can't put my finger on what it is. Though, it shouldn't surprise me that he would mess with one of the most classic sauces. That's kind of Jameson's MO.

His warm bourbon eyes watch me intently, waiting for me to come up with the answer, but all I can do is stare into them, swim in their warm depths—all ability to think gone in an instant.

He sets the plate onto the counter to our side and runs the fork through the sauce again. His tongue darts out to lap it off, then he leans in, brushing his lips to mine until I open my mouth enough to let him slip his tongue in.

That same incredible flavor mingles with a taste that is all Jameson, coating my tongue and eliciting a moan from somewhere deep inside me. He drags me up against him, wrapping his arms around my waist and crushing my chest to his. I shift his grip down to my hips and groan into his mouth, looping my arms around his neck, clinging to him like he's an anchor in a storm rather than the man creating the raging tempest in my life.

What the hell am I doing?

Something stupid. Something reckless. Something

highly inadvisable. Yet, I can't bring myself to care in this moment. Not with him pressed against me, with his tongue tangling with mine and his hard cock brushing the spot between my legs that hasn't had any action in literally years.

I am in so much trouble.

JAMESON

I swipe my tongue against Izzy's again, relishing the feel of her in my arms as much as I enjoy seeing her struggle with my little test. It was never my intention to kiss her. To touch her. To do *this*. I honestly just wanted to feed her and make sure she was safe here alone at night.

But walking in to find her perfect ass in the air like that, wiggling side to side seductively kind of threw my plans out the proverbial window.

She stills in my arms and jerks back her head, eyebrows raised. Her pink cheeks redden even more with her proud smile. "I got it. Spring onion. You used spring onion instead of shallots."

I grin and brush my thumb across her kiss-swollen lower lip. "Yep. What else?"

"It's spicier than normal, though not super-hot. The burn is gone as quickly as it's there. Something familiar."

"Very..."

Her eyes light up. "Habanero instead of cayenne!"

"Inspired by your little trick with the chili the other day."

"It shouldn't surprise me that you can't just use the classic recipe. Your culinary school professors would probably shit themselves."

I issue a low, deep chuckle and lean in to kiss her slowly.

"I don't give a fuck what someone who taught me years ago thinks."

"You don't care what *anyone* thinks."

For some reason, her words bother me more than they should, tightening my skin and making my stomach squeeze.

It's definitely what I want the world to think—that I do whatever I feel like and don't care about judgment from anyone. But the lie coming from *her*, knowing that *she* believes it, twists something deep in my gut. Especially knowing what I've been doing secretly and the likely reason why.

"That is absolutely not true, Izzy. In fact, I probably care what people think too much."

Her green eyes analyze me before she brushes her fingertips across my temple. "There's a lot more to you than meets the eye, isn't there, Jameson Fury?"

The fact that I'm letting her see that part of me, even if it's only a tiny glimmer, feels both freeing and terrifying at the same moment. This can't be anything more than a release of the tension between us. I can't let myself believe it ever can be, and opening up in any way will only confuse things more.

I push my hard cock against her and attempt to redirect the conversation away from things I have absolutely no desire to tell her. She rolls her hips into mine, almost like they're seeking the very thing I'm looking to give her.

And I'm more than willing to oblige.

It will be good for us—to get rid of the pent-up energy simmering since we first met. It will make doing what I have to do to ensure success later so much easier once she's out of my system.

At least, that's what I'm telling myself.

I reach down and grab her ass to lift her and set her on

the counter. If she wants to stop this, if either of us wants to apply the brakes to this runaway train, now would be the time. This should be when we come to our senses and realize what a horrible idea it is. But the look in her eyes and the way her hands roam over my exposed chest and biceps tell me she is just as lost in the moment as I am—what's good or right or smart for either of us be damned.

The tangled complications this could create get pushed to the back of my mind as I reach for the waistband of her yoga pants and slip my hands along her smooth, soft, pale skin.

She jerks slightly and shifts her hips up, giving me even better access, and I drop my head and capture her mouth with mine, kissing her with clear intent, giving her one last chance to tell me to fuck off. But despite all the bickering and the battles we've had, it seems it's been building to something wholly unexpected between us.

Well...maybe not wholly unexpected.

Grant hinted it would be coming and could potentially be a problem before I even acknowledged it. Bash, too. Yet even knowing it's a huge problem, that it creates a massive conflict—both personally and professionally—I don't stop it, either.

I tug the waistband of her pants, and she lifts her hips fully to allow me to drag them and her underwear down her legs. She kicks off her shoes, and I take a step back, pulling her clothes from her feet and letting them fall to the tile floor.

Her pink pussy glistens with arousal under the bright lights in the kitchen, and I've never felt so starved in my entire life. My cock strains against the zipper of my jeans.

"Fuck, Izzy."

I slowly run my hands up her inner thighs, and she shudders under me, reaching around my neck to drag me to her for another mind-bending kiss. Every swipe of her tongue only winds me tighter. Gives me more resolve.

My hands find the hem of the tank-top barely containing her breasts, but she pushes them away and reaches for my waistband.

She wants to do this with her shirt on? Okay.

This woman has absolutely nothing to be self-conscious about, but as much as I want to suck and lick and touch her breasts, crave to see *all* of her, I'll do whatever it takes to make her happy in this moment.

Izzy manages to undo the button on my jeans and lower the zipper, finally giving my cock room to breathe. I groan into her mouth and graze my hands up to find her center. Her hips buck against my palm, and I brush my thumb up over her clit, swallowing her resulting moan. Her rolling hips seek more contact, but I have something else in mind.

I drop onto my knees on the hard tile floor, and before she can utter a word, I lower my head and drag my tongue between her legs and to the apex of her thighs.

Sweet fuck!

"Oh, God..." Izzy drops her head back and closes her eyes.

Every lap of my tongue makes her twitch and my cock ache. But as badly as I want to get her ready and be buried inside her, playing games with Izzy is far too much fun.

I want her to suffer the same way I did, staring down at the menu while the cameras were focused on me. I want her writhing and desperate. Begging. I want her to know I'm the one in control even though she somehow managed to pull off a major victory.

And the perfect plan forms in my mind almost instantly.

Kissing my way up her inner thigh, I reach to the plate on the counter beside her and drag the fork through the béarnaise sauce. Until I tasted Izzy's cunt, I thought this was the single greatest thing I ever had on my tongue. The opportunity to have them both is too good to pass up. An added bonus—it's going to drive her mad.

I dribble the delectable sauce over her thighs, as close to her pussy as I dare get.

She jerks, and her eyes fly open and find mine. "Wh-what are you doing?"

My gaze locked on hers, I slowly lower my head and draw my tongue across the deliciousness on her seductively soft skin.

"Oh, God." She drops her head back again and rolls her hips up against me.

Having my tongue so close to where she wants it must be pretty uncomfortable.

Good.

Because right now, I don't even care how much my dick is throbbing or how badly I want to drive into her. Torturing her is so much more fun. Knowing I'm bringing her to the brink of madness by not giving her what she wants.

I lick my way up and down her thigh, then move over to the other one to repeat the process, allowing my hand to glide over the wet flesh my tongue just occupied. Her fingers tangle in my hair, and she pushes at my head, urging me, begging me for something that I'm unwilling to give her at this moment. The release she wants so badly.

The same thing I want. Only I plan to be buried inside her when that happens. I want to feel her cunt tightening around my cock. Want to relish the feeling of her body letting go as I empty myself inside her.

And by the time I remove the last of the sauce and move up to her center, I'm more than ready. I glide my tongue, still dancing with the glorious flavors I created over her wet lips again, and probe inside her. The combination almost makes me come before I even get started.

If the tiny bit of heat from the habanero in the sauce that lingers on my tongue hurts her, she certainly doesn't show it. She digs her nails into the back of my head and shifts her hips, trying to bring me to her clit to gain her release. I chuckle against her and finally relent, licking and nipping my way up until I suck it between my lips.

"Oh, fuck!"

Swirling my tongue over her most sensitive place, I press two fingers inside her welcoming heat. She clenches around them almost instantly, and I curl them to find her G-spot. Each pump of my fingers and flick of my tongue coils her tighter. Her rolling hips get almost wild.

She's going to come soon, and when she does, something tells me it will be life-altering for both of us.

Her body stills, and she sucks in an awkward breath. If I were a gentleman, this is where I would let her come. I would let her release fill my mouth and coat my tongue the same way the béarnaise did. And God knows, with as good as she tastes, I want that, too.

But I want inside her more. And bringing her this close to orgasm, leaving her dangling over the edge, is going to teach her a lesson—that I always win.

11

JAMESON

When I drag my head away from between her legs, Izzy gasps, her eyes flying open to meet mine. "What are you—"

I shove my pants down my thighs, letting my dick spring free between us and taking it in my hand. "I want to fuck you, Izzy." Stroking myself slowly, I drag the thumb of my free hand up the sensitive flesh between her thighs, making her entire body shudder. "I want my cock buried deep inside you when you come. So deep I get lost inside you."

Because that's what this feels like. Being lost and being found at the same time. Losing all the bullshit. Letting it float away on a cloud of lust. Finding a release and moment in time to share one thing we both need.

She shudders, raising her hips in offering.

I lean in to brush my lips across hers. "I want to feel your entire body contract and your pussy clamp down on me like a fucking vise when you come." I dart my tongue out across my lips, the taste of her cunt still there. "As incredible as you taste, I want *that* more tonight. I have every intention to make you come harder than you ever have in your life."

It can't be any clearer. I've made my intentions known.

I drag the head of my cock through her soaked pussy, and she groans and clings her arms around my neck.

"But one thing I don't have is a condom."

Izzy stills and meets my concerned gaze. "I've had the shot. And it's been..." She glances away, almost like she's embarrassed, before returning her eyes to meet mine. "A long time since I've been with anyone, and I've been tested for everything under the sun. I'm good."

How the hell has it been a long time since she's been with anyone?

Men must be climbing over themselves to be with a woman like Izzy. She's beautiful, talented, and clearly driven to succeed. There's nothing sexier than that combination.

Cradling her face in my palm, I pull my head back. "Despite what you may think, it's been a while for me, too. I've been tested."

She wraps her legs around my waist and urges me closer with her feet. One of her heels digs into the spot where I'm sporting a giant bruise, and I clench my teeth and bite back the grunt of pain threatening to come out. This isn't the time to be a pussy—not if I want some.

Izzy tugs my mouth back down to hers and slips her tongue between my lips. "Then fuck me, Jameson."

Holy fuck!

It's the ultimate statement of trust from someone who probably has every reason not to trust me after everything that's happened since we first met. We've gone out of our way to trip up each other at every move, and now, we're both trusting each other in the deepest way possible.

Hearing those words from her mouth does something to me. It unleashes something from deep inside—a need to possess her, to take her in every way imaginable, to stake my claim, especially here in *her* fucking kitchen. Right next to the range she refused to sell me. To let her know I own her and this place even if she doesn't want to concede it.

It's so wrong. But as I push inside her, it feels so fucking right.

Her body stretches to accommodate me. She moans into my mouth and clamps down around my cock, making herself even tighter.

I drop my forehead against hers and groan, my muscles tense and burning while I hold back what I desperately want to do. "Fucking eh, Izzy. I can't do this slow."

"I don't want you to." She squeezes my dick again. "I'm a big girl. I can handle it."

Fuck yes, she can.

She's so fucking here in this moment with me. Whatever else might exist between us forgotten—even if only for a few minutes. I truly believe she can take anything I can give her.

And I will. I'll give it all to her.

I drag my hips back and drive into her hard, pulling a gasp from her throat and rocking her backward slightly. Her damn nails dig into the back of my neck, and I plunge into her again and again. But a little pain mixed with my pleasure has never stopped me.

It only spurs me on. Gives me more focus. I want her so crazed that she makes me bleed, that she leaves marks on my body—actual physical reminders of having her in my arms and my cock inside her.

It's some sort of animal desire, something I don't understand and maybe never will. But it's there all the same.

I drop my hands to her ass and shift her closer to the edge of the counter, altering the angle and ensuring the head of my dick drags against her G-spot with every thrust. That part of me catching in that perfect little spot deep inside her, combined with the way she keeps clamping down around me, sends pleasure rippling through my body in a way I've never experienced before.

I've fucked hard and hot in the past—pretty much all the time. There isn't any reason this should be any different, yet somehow, it is.

And that's fucking terrifying.

For someone who has spent his entire life pushing people away and seeking solace anywhere but in another human being, wanting to be closer to her, feeling more, striving to lay my claim isn't just scary; it's downright dangerous.

I draw my cock out of her and smack the outside of her thigh. "Turn over."

Something about fucking her from behind feels so primal, so right for what's happening tonight, and my body craves it.

Izzy doesn't question me, just complies and lowers her feet to the tile, then turns around and spreads out across the counter, gripping the far edge and offering that sweet ass up to me just like it was when I came in tonight.

Fuck yes.

I smack my palm against her ass cheek again—hard this time. She bucks forward and yelps, my red handprint almost instantly appearing on her creamy skin.

"Fuck, Iz. You have a beautiful ass."

She glances over her shoulder at me, her eyes hooded with lust. "Fuck me, Jameson. Don't toy with me."

I lean over her, pressing myself to her back, and brush my lips against her ear while one hand slips around her hip and down to find her clit. A gentle pinch sends her jerking forward again. "But toying with you is so much fun."

———

IZZY

Jameson is an absolute monster. A beast who gets off on torturing me and leaving me hanging. After driving me mad with his mouth, now he's intent on doing the same thing with his cock.

He pushes into me hard then retreats slowly, letting me feel every fucking inch of him each time but never giving me quite what I need to reach that release.

It shouldn't surprise me, given what I know about him. Nothing should, really. Yet his reaction to my question earlier did. It shook him. And he opened up just enough to leave me wanting to know more. More about what makes him tick. What makes him shift from foe to *this* so easily.

What about him makes me let him do this to me...

He gets me so twisted, I'm not even sure where I am anymore. And now I've found myself surprised by him again, this time by how goddamn good he feels. How much my body responds to him. By how instinctive this feels despite us being natural enemies.

None of it makes sense.

This.

Us.

It's all wrong.

It's a recipe for disaster.

Throwing gasoline on an already raging inferno.

Yet every time he drives into me, it feels like some tiny broken part of me getting put back together again.

That's a dangerous thought, and not just because this is Jameson Fury. Because I can't have that. I can't have someone like this for any length of time, for anything more than a quick release. Because it gives me false hope for things that will never happen and can never be. It makes me want a future that's just out of reach and always will be, no matter how hard I fight for it and try.

This is just one time.

One. Time.

Even though we never said it, we both know it. All the hostility and tension worked out on the counter of my new kitchen.

I'll never be able to work in here again without thinking about how he feels inside me, of his hands digging into my hips, holding me steady. The burn in my fingers as I struggle to cling to the counter while he drills me from behind. The sound of skin on skin and his hot pants in my ear. The gentle brush of his kiss against my shoulder blade, so soft and different from the pace he set.

The man is more complicated than I can imagine. Capable of such brilliance and such brutality at the same time.

And he's hiding so much more.

I'm convinced of that. Something he conceals under his façade of arrogance and apathy. When you've spent as long as I have hiding something, it's easy to recognize it in others. Easy to see someone else struggling to contain whatever is eating away at them—physically, mentally, emotionally.

It's precisely what he does. Buries himself in his work and conceals his wounds with his attitude in order to prevent anyone from getting close to him, someone who might rip open those old scars and make him bleed again.

But this isn't the time to explore that. Not when his cock is banging into my G-spot at just the perfect angle. Not when I've been so close to orgasm for so long that my entire body is vibrating and sweating. Not when I'm going to scream if I don't come soon.

His fingers dig into my sides, and a brief flash of them slipping across my abdomen almost makes me stop the bliss and end this on the spot. But instead of pondering the many complicated facets of the man behind me and my own hang-ups, I concentrate on the feeling.

The feeling of *everything*.

Cool stainless steel...

Slapping flesh...

The push and pull...

A battle for something we both want. A race we're both intent on winning.

His hand snakes around my hip and finds my clit, rolling it in time with his hard thrusts. And it's exactly what I need to cross the finish line.

I gasp as lights explode against my eyelids, and my body vibrates, jerking back against him. He continues his punishing pace, dragging out my release until he finally finds his, pushing into me one final time with a mumbled curse before he sags along my back.

My legs threaten to give out, but he wraps a strong arm around my waist and drags me back up against him. Instinct tells me to move his arm, to get it away from where I absolutely don't want it. But being held this way feels so good.

I reach back and grip his side, and he winces with a grunt.

The post-orgasmic haze starts to clear, and I twist my head to look back at whatever caused his response. A massive bruise on his side has me sucking in a breath. "Oh, my God, are you okay? What happened?"

His eyes darken, and he drops his head and presses a kiss to my neck, which I instinctively tilt to the side to give him greater access. "Nothing. Don't worry about me. Are you okay?"

Almost involuntarily, my pussy clenches around his dick still buried inside me.

He offers me a groan in response. "Is that a yes?"

"Most definitely."

For now.

We both know this moment won't last. He's going to need to let go of me, pull his cock from inside me, and walk away, leaving a hell of a lot of things unsaid and making the situation between us as neighbors and rivals even more complicated.

Because we aren't going to talk about it. We aren't going to acknowledge what we just did.

Shit. We may have really fucked this up.

Maybe it would have been better if we continued to dance around each other and pretend there was no attraction there. Better if we had concentrated on what we hated about each other rather than giving in to our base needs.

It would have been better...because the awkward silence between us now, only broken by our heavy breathing and the music playing in the background, starts to weigh down on the amazing feeling that just enveloped me.

Anything good never remains. It's the way of the world I learned at a very young age.

The moment was too good to last.

12

JAMESON

"Jamo, I am *seriously* impressed."

I glanced back at Bash, where he stands just inside the door of *FURY*, to try to discern whether I should take his comment as a compliment or insult. He scans around the restaurant in awe, Greer by his side, looking equally impressed.

"Thanks...I think."

Flynn and Rachel wander around behind the bar, whispering to each other. She giggles and says something to him that makes him freeze on the spot. Rach tosses him a look and grins, and he narrows his eyes on her.

Ick.

I know that look she gave him, and I don't even want to think about my sister giving that look to a guy, even if he is the love of her life.

Bash takes another step inside, and his eyes connect with mine. "Mom would be incredibly impressed and so happy for you."

He might as well drive a knife straight into my heart

with that comment. Though, I know it wasn't his intention. It just makes me miss her more than I already do and wish she were here with us to have this family dinner.

I was always the closest to her, the one constantly under-foot in the kitchen, helping mix and stir, measure and bake. As a child, the kitchen was my safe place. Freedom from Dad's anger and violence and the constant wondering what any of us might do that could set him off when he actually *was* home.

That's what I had hoped to build here. My own place, where I can find solace and freedom to do whatever my heart desires without fear of repercussions, but instead, everything I've done since coming here has had a ripple effect.

And doing what my body desires has left me out of sorts.

Instead of relieving the tension simmering between us, what we did in Isabella's kitchen has only wound me even tighter, made me more aware of her and that she's just right next door. Or at least, she should be.

In the almost week since I left her there with the evidence of what we had done still inside her, I haven't seen her, heard anything, or even smelled anything coming from her place.

Not that I've been watching for her like a stalker.

Nope. Definitely not.

Even if I had seen her, I don't know what I would have done. Definitely not ignore her—I'm not *that* big of an asshole. But I've never been in a situation like this before—I actually *care* about someone I fucked. And I have to see the person day in and day out for who knows how long.

I'm completely unprepared for the depths of what that means, and it makes her absence even more troublesome, not to mention makes me even more uneasy that something might be wrong.

She's a workhorse, like me, here early in the morning and late at night. Always doing *something*. It's not like her to duck out and not be around.

If I had her number, I would be tempted to call and check in on her, but that might also give her the wrong impression. Or maybe the *right* impression I want to be wrong about. Because I can't actually have *feelings* for this woman. That wouldn't do at all.

Fuck. I royally fucked this up.

"Jameson?" Rachel's voice draws me back to the present matters at hand. "Can we open one of these?" She holds up a bottle of wine she must have pulled from one of the wine fridges along the back wall of the bar. "Or two?"

I've already chosen wine pairings to go with the food tonight, but Rach is always telling me I need to break free of my stringent plans and "live a little." Maybe a random bottle of wine can be her "win" in that regard.

"Of course."

Flynn claps his hands and rubs them together. "Excellent, man. I'm fucking starving, too. It was a long flight."

Greer steps up next to me and pushes up to kiss my cheek. She lays a gentle hand on my shoulder. "You really did an amazing job. I'll make sure to tell everyone I know in the league to come here when they're in town."

That would be huge. Me on the NHL upper echelon's radar. Media covering players and management eating here. *FURY* splashed across social media by the stars of various teams.

I offer her a genuine smile. Greer is so nice and good-natured; it's hard not to like her. I can see why Bash didn't stand a chance once he met her. He was doomed from day one...almost like it seems I was with the blonde next door.

Bash joins us in the center of the restaurant next to the

long table I had custom-made to seat large parties. "When do we eat?"

I sigh, glance at my watch, and then toward the kitchen. "Maybe an hour? I have a few more things to finish up. I wasn't expecting you guys so early."

It would have been nice to have my full kitchen staff here to help me prepare everything for tonight, but that seemed a bit like overkill for a family meal—even if I am cooking almost the entire menu for them to try. I've already had my new employees come in a few times to test some recipes with me, and I'm confident in who I've hired, but this felt more like a family thing. Not something I want to be interrupted by work.

Flynn and Rachel join us with their bottle of wine and five glasses and set them on the table. It's disgusting how happy they are together, but we all saw it coming years ago. The surprise was really how long it took them to figure it the fuck out.

Rach grins at me and waves the bottle back and forth. "Well, before you head back to your domain, I propose a toast."

She pours some of the Pinot Noir and hands it out. Everyone raises their glass, except me, because it seems awfully weird to be toasting myself.

Tears shimmer in Rach's eyes, and she swallows slowly, like she's trying to force down some emotion clogging her throat. "To Jameson, who finally got his shit together."

I groan as we all clink glasses. "Jesus, thanks."

She grins at me, the true depth of how proud she is of me shining back. "Anytime."

Movement at the propped-open front door catches my attention, but by the time I shift my focus, there's nothing but an empty sidewalk visible. On a gorgeous summer night like this, it wouldn't surprise me if there are people out walking the neighborhood and trying to catch an early peek at what's happening in here since we have the door ajar.

Rachel squeezes my arm and motions to the table. "We can set the table while you're finishing up. Where are all the place settings and cutlery?"

I groan and pinch the bridge of my nose. "I meant to talk to you about that. I have some temporary stuff in the kitchen we can use tonight, but it's one of the last things I've been dragging my ass on—choosing place settings, cutlery, wine glasses, and all the other little shit. Grant says I need a woman's touch."

She chuckles and nudges me with her hip with an eyebrow raised playfully. "Are you asking for my help?"

Everyone, including her, knows exactly how much I hate to admit that. The glee growing on her face while she waits for my response makes me twist my lips into a frown. But if I want her help, I'm going to have to concede.

"Yes. Would you be willing to go shopping with me tomorrow during the day? I have something going on tomorrow night, and I don't think we'll have time before the game Thursday."

"Was that really so hard?"

I scowl at her. "Yes."

She tickles my side just like she used to when we were little and she was trying to get me to laugh. "Of course, I'll help you."

Greer pouts. "Dammit. I want to go shopping, too. But I'm going to be tied up with pregame stuff all day tomorrow."

Bash presses a kiss to her temple. "You could always step down as coach and let me do it. It would free you up."

She elbows him in the ribs, and he feigns injury. Greer rolls her eyes. "That's never going to happen, buddy."

It's still hard to believe that Bash is here now. And so

happy. Same with Rach. These two have managed to get their shit together in a way I never will, to get past what we all experienced as children to let someone in and let someone love them.

How do they do that?

I almost broke into hives just offering that tiny insight to Izzy the other night, yet these two have given themselves completely to someone else.

It's insanity. I want no part of it.

Another flash of movement at the door has several of us turning toward it. Bash's gaze meets mine, and he raises an eyebrow. I shrug. It could be anything, but he can't just let it go and heads in that direction to check it out.

He always was the protective one. When he was around, that is. When he wasn't out on the ice with Dad, getting trained to become one of the greatest hockey players of all time by one of the greatest hockey players of all time.

Bash can check it out. I'm confident he can handle anything he finds out there. Instead of worrying about some nosy neighbors, I turn to head back into the kitchen to grab plates and silverware for Rachel, but multiple sets of footsteps behind me stop me in my tracks.

Shit.

I sense her before I see her. Even with my back to them, Isabella's presence fills the room and makes my skin heat and cock stir.

"Jamo! Look who I found outside."

The last person I want to see right now because she's the *only* person I do want to see. I can't let the family witness that. That would raise too many questions I don't have answers to. Open up discussions I am not prepared to have.

I plaster on my most neutral expression and turn to face them. Izzy looks naturally beautiful as always, in a flowing black tank-top, black and white yoga pants, Chuck Taylor's, and her blond hair piled high on her head in a messy bun more like a crown fit for a queen.

She smiles nervously, twisting her hands in front of her. "I'm sorry. I didn't mean to intrude. I was just walking by, and..."

Just walking by...

A tiny grin pulls at my lips despite my best efforts to remain unaffected by her. "Everyone...this is Izzy. She's opening the restaurant directly next door."

Everyone's eyes widen. Even Flynn and Greer. Clearly, Bash and Rach have informed them of our recent conversations about the chef next door and our antics. Though *no one* has any idea what that all led to the other night.

Bash flashes her a grin. "It's wonderful to meet you. I've heard a lot about you already."

Izzy's head whips toward him. "What? Where would you have heard..."

Her eyes dart over to me, and I chug my wine and swallow what suddenly feels like cement.

"Guys, I need to get to work if we want to eat anytime soon."

Rachel scoots over to Isabella and extends a hand. "I'm Rachel. These two assholes are my brothers. Want to join us for dinner?"

Thank God I had already swallowed my wine; otherwise, I would have just choked on it.

What the hell is Rachel doing? Trying to torture me?

Izzy throws up her hands. "Oh, no." She shakes her head with wide eyes. "I couldn't intrude on a family dinner."

Greer waves a hand dismissively and approaches them to slip her arm through Izzy's. "Nonsense. I'm Greer—this one's wife." She motions to Bash with the hand holding her wine glass. "The more, the merrier. Right, Jameson?"

Shit. I'm going to need something stronger than wine tonight.
A lot stronger.

———

IZZY

I wasn't trying to spy on them.

Yeah, right, Iz. Go ahead and tell yourself that...

The laughter and voices from inside drew me to the door, even though I had only intended to run into my place to grab a few things and then go right back home tonight.

So maybe it was spying...a little. Or a lot. But I couldn't *not* check it out. Not after the way Jameson and I left things. Not after that awkward few moments of finding pants and underwear and pulling them back on in silence while he tugged up his jeans and stood there rubbing at the back of his neck like he'd never been in a more uncomfortable position in his life. Not after he finally motioned to the remainder of the food on the plate and said, "Well, enjoy it," and then hustled out like his damn ass was on fire.

It has to be the single worst post-sex moment of my life. Not that I've had a lot of those to speak of, but it was, *by far,* the one that left me reeling the most. Because the sex was incredible. *He* was incredible. Even with the way he toyed with me and made me want to simultaneously punch him and ride him, he was just...magnificent.

And I let him walk out of there with no sort of resolution or discussion about what anything that had just happened meant.

Maybe it meant nothing. That would certainly make things easier for both of us if we mutually felt that way. And I, honest to God, don't know *how* I feel about Jameson. All I *do* know is that whatever he did to me that night wore me out so much that I've barely been able to get out of bed since. Even days later, I can still feel him between my legs every time I take a step.

So yeah, after *all* that...curiosity has gotten the better of me.

And...*maybe* a little hint of jealousy came into play when I heard a woman's voice filled with affection say his name. The name of the man who gave me the best night of my life. The man who, until only minutes before that, I thought I would always be at odds against even though I denied not wanting to be.

How fucking insane is that? Me. Jealous over Jameson Fury.

It's not like I have some sort of claim on him just because we banged it out once in my kitchen. That wasn't anything special—just two people who had a bit of tension figuring a way to work it out so we can continue to be neighbors and rivals without so much animosity.

At least, that's what I keep telling myself.

But now, my spying got me caught, and Jameson's family has invited me to what will surely be a very awkward dinner. If Jameson agrees, that is.

He stands, staring at me, his darkening eyes never wavering from mine. Completely unreadable. He lifts his wine glass and drains it in one gulp, then swallows hard. "Of course. The more, the merrier."

He doesn't mean that.

It's written in the tic of his jaw and the way his knuckles whiten where they clench around his wine glass.

Jameson doesn't want me here.

That realization makes acid crawl up my throat. I fight to swallow it back down. It never occurred to me that he might *regret* what we did; that he might be sitting over here wishing he had never brought over that plate of food, that he had never kissed me, that he had never touched me...

It made things a bit awkward, yeah, but *regret?* That hadn't crossed my mind until seeing the way he's looking at me now.

"I-I really shouldn't. I need to get over to my place and check—"

"Nonsense!" Greer guides me forward with her arm looped through mine until we're mere feet in front of Jameson. "Why don't you go help Jameson in the kitchen? That might get things moving a little quicker. We're all starved!"

She doesn't even bother to try to hide the wink she tosses at Jameson, nor does he make any attempt to hide his scowl back at her. But when his focus finally lands on me again, his lips shift slightly into a weak smile.

He inclines his head toward Greer and motions toward the kitchen. "Come on, Izzy. We have a few things to finish up."

I almost say *no.* The word sits on the tip of my tongue, threatening to spill out. It would be so much easier to walk away now. To turn and race from his beautiful restaurant and back over to my totally lame one where I can drown myself in mac and cheese and wallow in self-pity.

But I've never been someone who runs away from anything. I'm not going to start now. So, I pull my arm from Greer's and prepare myself to follow Jameson into the kitchen.

He glances over my shoulder at the group gathered around the table and sets his empty glass on it. "Rach, come grab the plates and stuff."

Thank God we won't be alone back there.

The thought of being in *his* kitchen. His domain. Within his physical reach. Without anyone to act as a barrier against the weirdness between us...

I don't even want to consider it. It makes my body

shudder with anticipation for something I'm not even sure I *want* again.

Who are you kidding, Izzy? You want *it again. And again. And again.*

I blow out a deep breath as we step into the kitchen, and Rachel turns toward me with a concerned raised brow. "Are you okay?"

"Oh..." I wave her off and watch Jameson move to the range to check something on one of the burners. "Yes, perfectly fine."

She considers my answer for a moment like she's trying to read me and determine if I'm lying through my teeth or not, but then she shrugs and grabs the dishes and silverware off the corner of the counter before she scurries out of the kitchen with a wink at me and a, "Have fun!" called over her shoulder.

Leaving me exactly where I *didn't* want to be. Where I am not anywhere *near* ready to be. Alone. With Jameson. In his hot kitchen. With a dozen delicious scents enveloping us.

My mouth waters—and not just remembering the incredible taste of what he fed me that night. More the taste of him—his kiss, his lips, his tongue.

I wonder what he really *tastes like?*

That question has my gaze drifting down to his ass since I can't see the object of my inquiry when he's facing the stove. But just my luck, he turns to face me at exactly the right time to catch me staring inappropriately.

Because of course he does.

"My eyes are up here, Iz."

I jerk my head up and scowl at him, hands on my hips. This man will *not* embarrass me. I refuse to give him that satisfaction.

Pretend everything is normal and totally fine. That's the

only logical way to proceed here. The alternative is unthinkable—actually *talking* about the fact that we fucked like rabbits?

I'd rather not.

He smirks at me and leans back against the counter next to the range. "I need your help. Come over here and stir the risotto while I get the lamb out of the oven to let it rest."

Stir. I can do that.

Quite competently, actually. Even if my brain is half fried from being in the same vicinity as this man when only days ago, he had me bent over a similar counter while he plowed into me.

Still, I approach the stove with trepidation. It brings me dangerously close to being *too close* to Jameson. He turns and pulls the lamb out of the oven, then tents it and sets it aside on the counter.

I stir meticulously, sure to scrape the sides of the pot and bottom. Concentrating on doing just that so I won't think about the fact that he's only a foot away from me.

Stir. Stir. Stir.

A warm hand slides slowly down my upper arm, and Jameson presses the front of his body against my back. I swallow a tiny moan at the contact, and while one hand closes around mine on the spoon, the other wraps around my waist and pulls me back even tighter against him.

Don't think about where his hand is, Iz.

I can't. Not right now. If I do, I'll let all those fears I try so hard to keep locked in the deep recesses of my mind free to wreak havoc on my psyche. And I need my wits about me now.

Jameson presses his lips against the exposed skin at the back of my neck. It's all it takes for me to practically melt against him. His strong arm wrapped around me keeps me steady, the wobble in my legs both embarrassing and incredibly hot.

This man can literally make me weak-kneed with a single kiss to an oh-so-sensitive place. He uses his hand wrapped around mine to continue stirring.

Thank God he's thinking to do it because God knows I have suddenly lost my innate ability to stir.

His warm breath flutters against my ear, and with each inhalation he takes, my body shifts back with his moving chest, desperate not to lose that connection.

Pathetic, Iz.

But he doesn't give me any time to consider just how much. He nips playfully at my ear, sending a little zing straight between my legs. "I wasn't expecting to see you tonight. I thought you were avoiding me."

Avoiding him?

Definitely not. Though I may have extended my stay in bed a little longer than needed because I just wasn't sure what to say to him when I did see him.

"Uh, nope. Not avoiding you. I wasn't feeling well."

Shit.

That just slipped out. More than I wanted him to know, for sure. If this man smells weakness, he'll pounce on it like a lion who finds an injured gazelle in the Sahara.

He stills behind me, then his hand leaves mine on the spoon, and he uses it to turn my head to the side to meet his gaze. "Are you okay? I didn't hurt you, did I?"

Gosh, that almost sounded sweet.

"Oh, God no. Nothing like that. Just tired. Needed to recharge a bit."

A tiny grin pulls at the corner of his mouth. "Good." He glances over his shoulder toward the door out into the restaurant. "And you'll probably need to do it again after spending the night with my family. I'm apologizing ahead of time for anything they say or do that's going to be wildly inappropriate. I wasn't really prepared to have you thrown into this mix."

I chuckle and stir. "I doubt they can do or say anything *that* bad."

He laughs into my ear, his chest vibrating against my back before he steps away from me. "You don't know Bash."

The loss of his body heat radiating through me is like getting doused with a bucket of ice water.

Jameson pressed against me shouldn't feel so good. I shouldn't let it. This whole thing is a recipe for disaster. And just because he kissed my neck doesn't mean he wants a repeat of the other night. Or that *I* should want one.

Dammit. This was so much easier when I tried to hate the guy.

13

IZZY

"I'm sorry. I don't really follow sports." I shrug in apology and take a sip of my water. "I never would have known if you hadn't mentioned it."

Greer laughs and smacks Bash in the chest. "Oh, stop it. Don't apologize. I wouldn't expect anyone to know who I am." She hitches her thumb toward Jameson's brother. "But this guy, he's the one with the ego. You may have mortally wounded him."

I chuckle, relieving a bit of the tension that had formed in my shoulders when everyone was discussing "the game" they're in town for and I had absolutely no *clue* what they were talking about.

Now knowing Bash played in the NHL and Greer coaches, I vaguely remember hearing at least *his* name at one point in time. Probably Ashley ogling him on the cover of some sports magazine or something.

But I never would have put two and two together on my own, let alone recognized either Bash or Greer without Flynn jumping in to rescue me with some basic knowledge about the Fury legacy and how Bash and Greer ended up together—somewhat scandalously apparently.

Hockey royalty.

I never would have guessed it. Jameson seems about the least likely person I've ever met to go play a violent sport like hockey, yet apparently, his father was one of the best in the game and his brother was at the top of his when he retired. "Jameson, how come you didn't end up in the NHL?"

Rachel and Bash exchange a look and laugh, but Jameson's face almost immediately hardens, and he goes stiff in his chair beside me. I hadn't missed the tension radiating off him when the conversation turned this direction, but my question seems to have struck some sort of nerve I didn't intend.

He swallows whatever was in his mouth and takes a long drink of his wine. "I was never very interested in it. That was Dad and Bash's thing."

His tone makes it unmistakable that's the end of that conversation.

I clear my throat. "Is that how you ended up cooking?"

He glances at me out of the corner of his eye and nods. "Yeah, spent a lot of time with our mom."

Who I insulted pretty badly when we first met...

Cringing internally, I take another bite of my mouthwatering lamb, waiting for someone else to take the lead on another topic of conversation—*any* topic at this point to break up the thick air of discomfort hanging over the table.

Rachel leans forward and rests her elbows on the wood, swirling the wine in her glass. "Too bad that didn't help you develop any sense of style or taste."

Jameson fakes indignation and then grins at her. "Seriously, sis. Ouch with the jabs tonight."

She waves a dismissive hand at him, then turns her

focus on me. "Jamo and I are going shopping tomorrow for a bunch of stuff for this place. Do you want to join us?"

Crap.

Jameson peeks over at me. "I'm sure Isabella has plenty to do at her restaurant without tagging along to help with mine."

It isn't meant to be an insult or brush off. I'm almost positive about that. But still, his comment makes me shift uncomfortably in my chair.

This dinner has been full of moments like this—his siblings and their significant others poking and prodding and trying to get one of us to say something that would reveal that we're something more than neighbors who happen to have the same profession. But we've both remained tight-lipped. Me mostly because I have no fucking *clue* what we are.

I smile at Rachel. "I appreciate the offer, really. But I have a lot scheduled tomorrow with my contractor. Little things here and there that need to be addressed before we can have the inspector come for approval of things."

Flynn sips his wine and motions toward my unused wine glass. "Are you sure I can't get you a glass of this? It's pretty incredible stuff."

The heat of a flush spreads up my neck, and I press my hand against it in an effort to conceal it from the table. "No, thank you. I don't drink."

Bash raises an eyebrow and looks down the length of the table at the three empty bottles they've already killed off since I arrived. "Well, shit, you must think we're all total lushes."

I shift upright and shake my head. "Oh, God, no. Nothing like that. It's not a judgment thing. I just can't—"

SHIT!

Everyone around the table waits for me to finish my

147

sentence, but instead, I feign a cough and take a tiny sip of my water, trying to play it off that I didn't almost reveal a lot more than I intended.

Jameson's narrowed eyes watch me with concern. After a moment, he seems appeased I'm okay and motions down the table at the spread of dishes off his coming menu. "Well, what did everyone think?"

Greer raises her glass. "Fabulous!"

Bash nods his agreement. "Amazing!"

Rachel beams at Jameson. "Everything was incredible!"

Flynn rubs his stomach. "I loved the octopus."

Shit. Shit. Shit.

Jameson slowly turns his head toward me. "I bet you did. It's one of my favorite dishes on the menu. Or it was...."

Oh, God. Please don't go there.

I've gone from feeling really fucking proud of myself for what I did to Jameson's menu to thinking about it non-stop and wondering if I went too far. It happened on the most widely watched morning news show. I didn't *know* he was going on there when I messed with the menu.

Though, if I had known, I'm not confident it would have stopped me from doing it. It felt too good to have a win. But not as good as being with Jameson the other night. That makes this incredibly dangerous territory.

I thought he had gotten over the whole menu thing, but his current reaction suggests he may still be harboring a bruised ego from the whole thing.

Bash's jaw drops open. "Oh, my God! Was that *you* who changed the menu?"

I drop my face in my hands and groan. "Um...yes."

Uproarious laughter fills the room, and I peek between my fingers to find everyone in hysterics.

Everyone except Jameson, who looks anything but

148

amused. "Fine. Laugh at my being humiliated. I see how much you all care."

Bash smacks his palm against the table. "Oh, stop it. You were not humiliated. That was *hilarious*, Izzy. Be proud of yourself. He would have done the same damn thing to you. Don't let him tell you otherwise."

"And on that note, I think it's time to start cleaning up." Jameson pushes away from the table and stalks back toward the kitchen with his plate in hand.

"Shit." I watch him disappear into the kitchen then turn back to his family. "I really pissed him off with that."

Rachel shifts over to take the chair Jameson vacated and pats me on the arm. "Don't worry about it. He always was the moodiest of the three of us. And from what I hear, he was giving you just as much shit before you pulled that stunt, so he deserved it."

I chuckle and smile at her. "Thanks, I appreciate that."

"So..." She grins at me and sips her wine, eyes wide and expectant.

"So...what?"

She shifts closer again and glances toward the kitchen. "What's up with you and my brother?"

I scan the table to find all eyes locked on us intently. Nothing like having an audience for a super-awkward conversation with the sister of the guy you boinked. "Um, nothing? We're neighbors, and soon, we'll be running competing restaurants. It's just a little friendly competition."

Bash nudges Greer and smirks. "Kinda like us, Coach."

"Uh, no." She crosses her arms over her chest. "That wasn't friendly competition. That was you trying to put me in my place and knock me down a peg."

Flynn laughs. "And see how that worked out for you."

Rach finishes her wine and pushes the glass away. "Friendly competition can lead to a lot more."

I shake my head before she opens her mouth to continue. "No. Not this time." I plaster on my best smile, the one I use when I'm trying to convince the people who know matter that I'm okay when I'm really crumbling inside and in agony. "Jameson and I are all we're ever going to be. Business acquaintances and neighbors."

JAMESON

"Jameson and I are all we're ever going to be. Business acquaintances and neighbors."

I guess that settles that.

The words are innocuous enough. They shouldn't hurt me. They're a statement of fact. Of how things apparently *really* are. Of what she feels about the situation.

One I apparently misread.

I overstepped in the kitchen the other night and again preparing dinner tonight. But both times, something drew me to her, made my hands itch to touch her, to feel her pressed up against me, to smell that sweet cinnamon clinging to her skin. Seeing her in *my* kitchen this time, helping me, standing in front of my stove...it was such a fucking turn on. I almost bent her over and took her right then and there despite the fact that I initially wasn't ready to broach the subject of what happened between us.

But I'm glad I didn't take it any further than that kiss to her perfect, smooth neck. If I had, it sounds like I would have been making a fool of myself...more than I already have.

I suck in a deep breath and make my way toward the table. "Yep. What she said..." My eyes lock with Isabella's, and a hint of something indiscernible shimmers beneath their surface. "Just business acquaintances and neighbors." I try to keep the venom out of my words, to hide how much they hurt to say, but I'm not so sure I do a good job of it given the pained expressions of everyone around the table. "But we're done fucking with each other, right?"

Those words were chosen very carefully, specifically for their double meaning only Isabella will know.

It's a definitive statement that whatever we did was a one-time thing. That I won't pursue it again. That anything that happens between us going forward will remain strictly professional—both in how we run our businesses and how we conduct ourselves when it comes to our *personal* interactions.

Getting it out in the open and cleared up should feel like a massive relief. Instead, it feels more like a rock has settled into my stomach.

I lower myself into the seat Rachel vacated next to Flynn and grab his half-full wine glass to down it. Everyone watches me intently, like they're expecting some sort of bomb to go off. I pour myself another glass and shrug. "What?"

Greer shifts nervously in her seat. "Uh, nothing. Was the menu you served tonight the final one?"

I wish I knew...

It's been a constant battle since I left the television studio. My head can't seem to land on the right answer for some of the dishes. Continuously tweaking things. Over and over and over.

I thought I had finally found exactly what I wanted for a few dishes when I brought that plate over to Isabella. But now...the thought of having to make that damn béarnaise sauce again, of having to taste it each night and know I won't be able to without also tasting her cunt on my lips is too much to handle.

Changes are in order.

"I'm still fiddling with a few things. But I don't have much time left. I need to nail everything down soon for the opening."

Flynn slaps him on the shoulder. "I hope we're invited and will get the VIP treatment."

I snort a laugh and shake my head. "Of course, you're all invited. But you have to sit at the shittiest table in the place. I need to save the great tables for the critics and celebrities."

Bash jerks upright in his chair. "Hey! I'm a celebrity. So is Greer."

Laughing, I point to Isabella, who has remained quiet and subdued since I reentered the room. "I think she just proved your celebrity is in your head...or, at the very least, only exists in very small circles of people who enjoy hockey."

Greer cringes. "Ouch, Jameson. Way to destroy your brother's fragile ego."

Bash's mouth drops open again. "Fragile ego? Me?"

Rachel's tinkle of laughter overpowers Bash's objections. "God, I've really missed this." Her eyes sweep over everyone at the table. "I've missed you guys. It's been way too long since we all got together."

A heavy silence settles over the table, all of us remembering the last time we were all in the same place—Mom's funeral. Bash and Rachel saw each other when Dad died last year, but I wasn't about to insert myself back into that shit situation when I spent my entire life trying to get away from it.

Isabella stands abruptly, rattling the glassware on the table and bringing everyone's attention to her. Her normally pale skin carries a slight tinge of pink. "I need to get going. Thank you so much for inviting me to dinner."

Rachel stands next to her and places a hand on her arm.

"You don't need to rush off. We're just going to sit around talking for a while. And I think Jameson has dessert."

She glances at me, though whether it's for confirmation about dessert or to get my assistance in trying to make Isabella stay, I can't exactly tell.

"I do have dessert. Three options, actually."

That doesn't seem to be enough to sway Isabella, though I hadn't anticipated it would be. She looks uncomfortable, like she's finally realizing she doesn't belong here in the middle of the Fury family table. After what she said, it seems she made that choice, so she shouldn't look so upset.

Isabella steps back from the table and offers a small wave to everyone. "It was nice meeting all of you." Her gaze connects with mine for a moment longer than is warranted for two people who are just business acquaintances and neighbors. "Thanks again, Jameson. For everything. I'll see you around."

I'll see you around.

That's a brush-off if I've ever heard one. I guess we'll go back to being rivals and rushing to get our places opened first and pretend what happened was all some strange dream and the attraction that still exists between us is just some hallucination brought on by the long work hours and little sleep we've both been experiencing lately.

I swallow through the lump in my throat and watch her make her way toward the door. "Yeah, see you around."

Each step she takes feels so finite. Like she's going to disappear out that door and I'll never see her again even though she's right next door.

Fuck, am I fucked up.

I take a long drink of wine and watch her finally leave. Almost immediately, everyone at the table turns their focus on me expectantly.

"What? What are those looks for?"

Someone's phone rings, and Greer scrambles in her purse and pulls it to her ear, buying me at least a momentary reprieve. "Hello? What? When? Well, shit." She glances at Bash and uses her hand to cover the phone. "Mac just called Doc and said he's been puking all night. He's likely out for the game unless he feels better tomorrow."

Bash rubs a hand across his jaw. "Shit."

Greer nods at something the person on the phone is saying. "Uh, huh. Sure. We'll be there shortly."

One of Bash's eyebrows rises. "We're leaving?"

She offers him an apologetic look as she slips the phone back into her purse. "Doc said he's concerned it may be a stomach virus that could spread to the whole team. We need to get back and make sure everyone's okay and maybe move rooms around if people are feeling sick."

Bash pushes to his feet with a heaved sigh. "Shit." He glances at me. "And this was just getting fun." A grin pulls at his lips, and he reaches out to bump fists with me. "Excellent meal, bro. Truly. We'll see you at the game?"

I rise from my chair and nod. "Yep, absolutely. I have plans tomorrow, so I can't hang out, but I'll be at the game Thursday. Wouldn't miss it."

Though I've spent the better part of my life trying to avoid doing anything that would remind me of Dad, I would never miss the opportunity to see Greer coach or to spend time with Rach, Flynn, and Bash while they're in town. Not even if it means facing the ugly lie I keep telling them and myself.

The urge to tell them what I've been doing makes me open my mouth, but I can't manage to get the words to come out. I watch Bash and Greer hug Flynn and Rachel and say goodnight, then accept the same from them.

They hustle out to find a cab while I lower myself back

into my seat and stare at the pile of dishes strewn across the table.

Rachel pours herself another glass of wine and motions to the cluttered tabletop. "We should get this cleaned up before we're too drunk."

Flynn chuckles and pours another glass into the one I took from him, then takes a sip. "Too late for me. We're on vacation, babe. Live a little."

I sigh, grab my glass from my spot at the head of the table, and pour myself another one, too. "Leave it. I'll clean it up later."

It will give me something to do to try to keep my mind off both what just happened with Isabella and also what might bubble to the surface stepping foot into the stands at my first NHL game in almost twenty years. I thought I could handle it, thought I had desensitized myself to the idea, but my hand shakes as I bring my glass to my mouth, and the fruity, slightly bitter liquid does nothing to help ease the sourness in my stomach.

But game night isn't about me. It's about Greer and her team being so damn close to the playoffs again. It could be their year, and I don't need to put a damper on anything by spouting off about my own bullshit.

I'll figure it out. I always do.

Except with Isabella.

14

JAMESON

"**A**re we really not going to talk about it?"

I glance up from the pile of tablecloths at Rachel. "Talk about what?"

She props her hand on her hip and raises an eyebrow at me. "Um...the stunningly beautiful woman who had dinner with us last night and the massive amount of sexual tension between the two of you."

Shit.

Here I thought I had managed to save myself from the guillotine of a Rachel inquisition when she and Flynn left the restaurant pleasantly sloshed last night without bringing up the Isabella situation.

Apparently, she was just biding her time until we were alone. Or she was sobering up. Maybe both. But now that she's brought it up, the chances of me walking away from this conversation unscathed are slim to none. Especially since we've only just begun our shopping trip at the restaurant supply store. This may end up being an all-day interrogation.

I sigh and pull out a red tablecloth with an intricately stitched pattern around the outside edge. "What do you think of this one?"

She snatches it out of my hand. "Actually, I love it. But don't deflect."

"I wasn't deflecting." I move around her and over to the side of the store where the glassware towers on high shelves.

Her quick steps follow me.

Literally no escaping.

Rach may look all sweet and innocent, but she's like a shark who smells blood in the water. Now that she knows about Isabella and has seen us interact, she isn't going to let this go until she gets the answer she's looking for.

Too bad I don't even know what the answer is.

I grab a wine glass from one of the shelves and lift it up to the light. "These are pretty."

Rachel snatches it from my hand and sets it back down. "No, these look like medieval goblets. And not in a good way." She reaches up and grabs a different glass. "You need something like this for Pinot."

While simple, the red wine glass beautifully reflects the light in the store. "Yeah, these are cool."

"I say you get these and some for white wine, then when you hire a sommelier, you can let him or her pick out other ones."

"That was kind of my plan."

"Good." She shifts her attention from the glasses back on me. "Now that that's settled, let's talk about Isabella."

I sigh and walk away from her as fast as the crowds in the store will allow, but Rach is quicker than she looks and weaves her way around people to get in front of me, blocking my path. I grab her upper arms and move her to the side easily. "There's nothing to say."

"If that were true, you wouldn't be running away

from me."

Shit. That kind of backfired on me.

Relenting, I stop and turn back to her. "We messed with each other a little bit, played a few pranks. Hooked up once, and that's all there is to it. Please, just let it *go.*"

She props her hand on her hip again and raises her eyebrows at me. "All there is to it, huh?"

"Yep." I snag the wine glass from her hand and make my way over to the counter to ask the checkout person if they can box up a whole hell of a lot of these.

"It didn't feel like that was *it* last night."

The truth of Rach's words eats away at me as we stand in line.

It didn't feel like that for me, either.

Not when we were together in her kitchen. Not when she was in my arms in mine. Not when I tasted her on my lips or when she sagged gently back against me.

But what she said was pretty clear—her words still ringing in my ears even now.

"Didn't you hear her? She said we were just *business acquaintances* and *neighbors.*"

"Wow."

I peek down at Rach and find her wide-eyed.

Well, fuck.

I may have put a bit too much emphasis on those words. My anger and frustration might be showing a little more than I would like. It makes it really hard to convince people you don't give a shit when you act like you do.

Rachel laughs as we shift forward in the line. "You're an idiot, Jameson."

Despite the frustration I'm feeling—not to mention the annoyance at her sisterly persistence—I chuckle and glance at her. "You're not the first woman to tell me that."

"I'm sure I won't be the last, either. That girl is most definitely not done with you. I don't care what she said. Or why." She taps her finger to her chin. "Maybe it was because she was overwhelmed with all of us at the table. Or maybe she didn't want to assume something more was happening between the two of you that she wasn't sure about." She tosses up a hand. "Either way...I definitely got a vibe."

"A *vibe*? What the hell does that even mean?"

She scoffs and crosses her arms over her chest. "You don't believe in the vibe?"

I narrow my eyes on her. "Is this the same *vibe* you managed to miss between you and Flynn for five years?"

Her mouth drops open slightly, and she snaps it shut in a huff. "Totally different situation."

Yeah, right...

I bark out a laugh, and the people in line in front of us turn to glare at me. Ignoring them, I lean over to Rachel to try to make our conversation a little more private. "Really? Because we all saw it."

"Well, I see it here. You need to talk to that girl, Jameson. Figure it out."

"There's nothing to figure out. I'm about to open a restaurant. Not only is my reputation on the line but also a hell of a lot of my own money, plus Grant's money."

"Grant has plenty of that."

She isn't wrong, but that's irrelevant. Just because he agreed to partner with me and has money to spare doesn't mean I can flush it down the drain by not concentrating on what's important right now—that's getting my place open, not my sexual attraction to the girl next door.

Rachel wants to believe in happily ever afters and true love, and maybe she and Bash both found that. But it doesn't mean it's for everyone. My restaurant is my focus, not my heart.

We finally make it to the front of the line, and a pretty

blonde employee smiles, her eyes scanning me with appreciation. "Good morning. Wait...are you Jameson Fury?"

I grin at her and nudge Rachel in the side with my elbow. "Sure am."

She claps her hands together like a giddy teenager, even though I would guess she's at least in her early twenties. "Awesome. So exciting to have you in the store. How can I help you?"

I hold up the glass. "I'm going to need fifty of these and another fifty of one of the white wine glasses I can show you back there. Do you have enough in stock to accommodate this quickly, or am I going to have to do a special order?"

"Oooh. Let me see." Her gaze drifts over to Rachel, and she frowns slightly. "Is this your girlfriend?"

First, what a wildly inappropriate question for a store employee to ask the customer. Second, eww.

"This is my sister."

Rachel snickers and covers her mouth with her hand. She leans in while the girl types away at her computer screen, checking inventory. "You certainly do have a way with women, baby brother. I'm sure you can get things figured out with Isabella."

I bite back the growl of annoyance threatening to rip from my throat. "Let me concentrate on one thing at a time."

Rach steps back with a sigh and raises her hands. "Fair enough. We have the glasses, the linens, and the silverware. What's next?"

I lean against the counter and picture the inside of my place exactly how I want it. "Table decorations. Some sort of centerpiece or something. I don't just want lame little votive candles."

"Oooh!" Rach jumps up and down and claps. "I have an idea."

I snort and shake my head. "Why do I have a feeling I'm

going to regret asking for your help with this?"

More than I already do...

She smacks my shoulder. "Oh, stop it. You love me, and you know it."

I grin at her. "I do, but it doesn't mean I can't also find you annoying."

Blondie looks up from her computer and smiles. "We can get those for you by tomorrow, Mr. Fury. Give me a minute to find someone to cover the register, and I'll assist you with anything else you need to order."

"Thank you."

Her interruption gave me a little break from Rachel's persistent pushing, and it will be nice to have relief tonight and tomorrow before I have to sit with the entire family for the game. My usual Wednesday night melee will be a great stress relief and reprieve from the constant questioning and ball-busting.

I dish it out to them just as much as they do to me, but I fucking hate being the focus of it. Especially when they keep bringing everything back to the blonde with the green eyes who haunts my dreams.

"Is that why you're ditching us tonight, because I'm *annoying*?"

She's fishing, trying to determine if I plan on spending my night away from them in a certain woman's bed. As nice as that would be, she made it clear that isn't what she wants. And I have other plans. Ones I don't intend to share with Rach or anyone else, for that matter.

"I'm not ditching you. I had plans well before anyone gave me the date for the game. But I'll meet you guys for dinner before, and we'll have three hours to enjoy each other's company and watch Greer's guys beat the shit out of the Rangers."

"Ugg. Fine." She points a finger at me. "But I know you're

hiding something. I'll figure it out. I always do."

I sure as shit hope not because I am so not ready to explore that rabbit hole.

IZZY

"Are you sure you don't want me to help?"

I tighten my hand around the spoon and glance at her. "For the last time, Ashley, no. I got this."

Everything else may be a total shit-show, but I can definitely stir mac and cheese.

She leans against the counter in my kitchen, arms crossed over her chest. "Fine, but you know you didn't have to cook. We could've just ordered something. We both cook all day, every day. Sometimes it's nice to let someone else do the work."

I stir the noodles and cheese in the pot and pour in more shredded cheddar. Never enough cheese. I've been craving my comfort food all day. After that meal with the Furys, I needed something that would remind me of easier times with Grams. "I know, believe me. But I really haven't been cooking all that much, and I can't just sit around."

I've been restless. Antsy. Unable to sit still despite being utterly exhausted.

"You clearly haven't just been 'sitting around,' Izzy. You look like shit."

"Gee, thanks."

She shakes her head. "I don't mean it like an insult. Just an observation. I don't think I've ever seen you look this exhausted, not even when we were in school or busting our asses as prep cooks." A sigh slips from her lips, and genuine concern hardens her gaze. "I'm worried about you—"

"And I feel like a broken record telling you I'm fine."

Even I wince at the tone of my response. It's not like me to be so snippy with anyone, let alone Ashley. Everything just feels off lately. Like I can't keep anything in order or on track. It's made me feel like crap—mentally and physically.

But I shouldn't take it out on her.

Ash presses her lips together and scowls in a way that tells me she isn't buying it for a second. Maybe I'm not as good of an actress as I thought.

Somehow, I've managed to hide what's really been happening in my life from everyone—employers, other friends...Jameson. But Ashley has always known and can apparently see straight through my best efforts to appear unaffected by the long hours and lack of care I've been giving myself.

Because the truth is, I am weary to the bone. There's no other way to describe it—the kind of tired that makes it impossible to get out of bed in the morning without *physically* dragging yourself out and that makes you crash the moment your head hits the pillow, even if you've left important things undone.

And something tells me it's only going to get worse the closer I get to the opening.

"You're going to burn out, Iz. Have you even spoken to Thaddeus since all of this started?"

My hand stirring the pasta freezes, and I glare at her. "No. And you better not call him, either. I'll talk to him *if* and *when* I need to."

Which will hopefully not be for a very long time.

"Fine." She pushes off the counter and wanders over to the papers spread out all across my small kitchen table—my final checklists. Everything I still need to do before we can actually open. Ashley sits down and laughs. "Why is this one crossed off?"

"Which one?"

She waves the paper back and forth. "*Kick Jameson Fury's ass.*" One of her brunette eyebrows rises. "It seems to me that rather than kicking it, you've been kissing it."

I let my jaw drop and turn to face her. "I have *not*."

"Really?" She drops the list, forms a circle with one hand, and sticks a finger from her other hand through it. "You don't think letting him bang you in your kitchen counts as a loss on that front?"

Smartass.

One thing I've always appreciated about Ashley's friendship is her willingness to call me out on my crap. It keeps me honest, and I know I can always rely on her to tell it like it is when I need to hear some hard truths. But I don't think I'm ready to face the *hard truth* about my feelings for Jameson Fury just yet.

Ignorance is bliss.

I scowl at her and give her my back again. "That was a moment of weakness."

She snorts. "I'd say. But I guess I can't blame you. He is one magnificent specimen, isn't he?"

"You have no idea." Though I tried to say it under my breath, she obviously hears me since she bursts out laughing again. "Look, I really don't want to talk about Jameson anymore."

"I'm sure you don't. You also don't want to talk about what you're doing to yourself physically or how worried Grams would be if she were here. Or how you should probably be calling Thaddeus or what I might be able to do to help you to take some of this stress off your shoulders." She offers a shrug. "I'm not sure what that leaves as viable topics of conversation here."

While I want to object to the accusatory tone of her statement, she isn't exactly wrong. I'm avoiding all those things. At the moment, I just don't have the energy to discuss anything that isn't a little *lighter*.

"Why don't you tell me how things have been going for you at work."

She raises an eyebrow. "Really?"

"Yes, really."

Her sigh of resignation fills the room, and she leans back in her chair. "Fine. We can pretend all of these other things aren't happening because ignoring things always makes them better."

A tiny twinge of guilt hits me at her words. It's not about ignoring them. It's about being physically incapable of dealing with everything at one time. But I can't admit that to her. I can't admit how overwhelmed I've become or how many times I've been tempted just to give up before I collapse. She already worries about me too much. If I told her how I really felt lately, she undoubtedly *would* call Thaddeus for me.

I just need to make it to the opening. Once I do, the staff will be able to help me pick up some of the slack, and things will calm down a bit.

Unless they get ten times worse.

Like the situation with Jameson has.

With my luck—or should I say lack thereof—chances of that happening are pretty good. Though Grams, who was ever the optimist, would tell me to stop thinking that way.

I spoon two helpings of mac and cheese into bowls and carry them to the table.

Ashley digs into hers the moment I place it in front of her and moans. "God, it's so good. Even after eating this in this kitchen for twenty years, it only seems to get better."

Another recipe Grams handed down to me that we both grew up cooking with her.

"It's going on the menu. I know it's simple, but sometimes simple done perfectly is what people want."

At least, I hope so.

Ashley rests her hand on mine on the table. "People are going to love it, Iz. Really. Your grandmother was the best cook I ever met, until *you*. You take her recipes and make magic with them. The people of Bushwick are lucky to have you."

I aimlessly stir the food in my bowl, my appetite suddenly vanishing. "That's what I keep telling myself. But you should have *seen* this spread Jameson did last night. It was incredible. I always knew I had talent, but he's *truly* gifted."

She scoffs and takes another big bite. "Stop it. Stop comparing yourself to him. Stop fantasizing about his monster cock. Just stop. You're going to drive yourself nuts."

I chuckle and force myself to take a bite of the dinner intended to warm and settle me like a soothing balm. Instead, the familiar taste only makes me wish Grams were here more so I could get her perspective on things.

"I think I already *am* nuts, Ash."

"Then get un-nuts and get your ass back on track. Don't let a man distract you from your endgame."

My endgame.

I thought I knew what that was, but Jameson has blurred the lines and various paths so much that I can't keep them straight anymore.

It's embarrassing since I never thought I would be *that* girl, yet here I am, pining away and wondering where things went awry with a guy I never intended to even *like*, let alone get under my skin so badly.

If Grams saw me now, she'd probably literally kick me in the ass and tell me to buck up. So, I guess I need to do it for myself now. Too bad I'm not anywhere near that flexible.

15

JAMESON

The simple act of climbing out of my SUV is painful enough that it makes me groan like an old man. It feels like I was hit by a Mack truck, and I guess I kind of was.

It wasn't even this bad last night, sitting at the game with everyone. That's because the pain always seems to be worse the second day. If it had been like this last night with Bash, Rach, and Flynn next to me all three periods, someone would have noticed and called me out.

It was hard enough explaining away the shiner. They seemed to buy my story about a board falling when I was helping Danny get the partition wall up for the server station, but I think they secretly thought Isabella had given it to me after some clandestine meeting I didn't tell them about.

If I had revealed the truth, that would have led to questions I'm not ready to answer.

Today is going to be long, feeling like this. I lock the car door and make my way toward the open restaurant door.

But something makes me stop and direct my attention at a different door. Okay, not something...someone.

Is she there?

A brand new Mercedes sits parked just a few cars up from mine. It's possible it has nothing to do with her. Still, the idea that it could be a guy—someone she's romantically involved with and that's why she said what she did the other night—circles around my head violently.

Knock it off. None of your business.

I force myself to enter *FURY* and find Danny and his crew are busy putting the finishing touches on the art installation along the back wall. We waited until anything that might kick up dust into the air was completed before hanging it because it will be a *bitch* to clean once it's up on the wall.

Danny waves to me and approaches. "Hey, man. Great game last night, huh? The Scorpions are pretty much unstoppable."

I run a hand through my hair and bite back a groan at the pain that slices through my ribs. "Yeah. It was fun to be there with Bash, Rachel, and Flynn to see them clinch a playoff spot. How are things coming?" I motion toward the giant metal sculpture leaning against the back wall. "That thing looks even bigger in here than it did at the art gallery."

He glances that way. "We've got most of the anchors set and should be moving it into place soon."

"Awesome."

He turns back to me and runs a hand over his chin, shifting his weight awkwardly. "Grant stopped by earlier."

"Shit. Was I supposed to meet him here?"

Danny shakes his head. "I don't think so. He was with his wife, and it seemed like they just wanted to pop in."

Pop in?

"And check up on me and the place."

The fact they didn't just call or arrange a time brings unease creeping up my spine. Grant knows I would meet him here anytime he asks, which means he did it intentionally to either catch me off-guard or when he thought I wouldn't be here.

"He kept asking me about an opening date. He seems pretty anxious to get the ball rolling."

I wander over to one of the tables and slowly lower myself down, biting back a grunt. "So am I, but everything has to be perfect first. And we need the final inspections."

"I think we're about ready to get those scheduled."

That should bring a wave of relief through me—to finally be to this all-important point with the finish line in sight—but instead, a sense of dread settles on my shoulders. "Already?"

He nods slowly and scans the place even though he knows it better than the back of his own hand, just like I do. "Pretty much."

This is it. Everything I've worked for, basically my whole life, is just on the horizon. Only now, all the ways it could go horribly wrong won't stop racing through my head.

The critics could hate my food.

The people could hate my food.

I could give someone food poisoning.

I could be overpriced and no one will come.

My food might suck and no one will come.

I rub my temples and squeeze my eyes closed against the growing headache. "How much more time do you need?"

He shrugs. "A day or two tops. I can call and schedule the inspections right now."

"I'm sure Grant will be thrilled about that."

Danny rushes off to make his calls while I pull out my phone to make the one I need to. As if today isn't already painful enough, now I have to deal with a call to my partner, who apparently doesn't trust me.

Grant answers on the second ring. "Jameson."

I clear my throat and try to keep the tiny bit of anger I have at him for checking up on me out of my voice. "I hear you had a bright and early inspection today."

He chuckles. "We just happened to be in the neighborhood."

"Bullshit. Nobody just happens to be in Bushwick."

"Okay, fine. I wanted to check in on the progress and make sure there weren't going to be any delays. I want an opening date, Jameson. I hate paying for a building and everything else without any idea when we'll start having some money coming in."

"Danny is scheduling the inspections."

"That's good to hear, but I hope there won't be any more surprises from next door."

He means any more pranks like the menu thing, but the way he says it—like an accusation that she did something criminal and is some sort of shitty person—tightens my skin.

"Nope. We've come to a truce of sorts."

"Good. Any idea of her opening date? We need to make sure that girl doesn't try to steal any of our thunder or ride our coattails."

As if Izzy would intentionally do that.

I may have thought so at the beginning. I might have harshly judged her because she was the competition and maybe done a few underhanded things in the name of business that were morally questionable.

But despite what she did with the menu and the whole swapping the salt for the sugar thing, I don't really think she has a malicious bone in her body. I can't believe she would ever even consider doing anything to sabotage our opening or try to "ride our coattails" the way Grant is suggesting. It wouldn't work, anyway. Her style and food are so different from ours that I can't imagine much of an overlap in our clients, even if she *tried* to steal them.

"I don't know when she's opening."

I have to bite back the desire to defend her. If I do that, Grant will latch right onto it and know something happened. And there's no reason to let him know. Not when whatever that was is over anyway.

"Find out and let me know. So how long will you need after the inspection? Two weeks?"

"Yeah."

"That gives you enough time for food orders and for me to get everyone who is important invited."

I lean forward, rest my elbow on the table, and pinch the bridge of my nose. "We'll do a press release. I assume your people can handle that."

He chuckles, his humor apparently returned now that we've figured out an opening date. "Of course. Press release, print, radio, and television ad campaign."

"And I'll get some sort of formal invitations designed and sent out to anyone who is anyone in town."

"Don't worry about that. I'll have Sylvie take care of it."

"No offense, Grant, but I don't exactly trust your wife."

"Why the hell would you say that?"

"Because I'm pretty sure I saw her car parked outside, and she isn't in here, which means she's probably next door with Isabella again."

"Goddammit." He releases a heavy sigh. "We brought separate cars this morning. She said she had an appointment she had to go to when we left. I didn't know she stayed. Don't worry about it. I'll take care of it."

I just hope he doesn't do anything rash. He doesn't understand Isabella, and while I'm not sure I do, either, at the very least, I know she isn't malicious. She's not going to do anything to try to tank our opening. If we fail, it's going to be totally on us. Or more accurately...me.

It's *my* name on that sign. My recipes. My hands cooking everything that comes out of the kitchen.

I'm the one going on the news and touting how incredible it's going to be. Any failure, any slight misstep, is one hundred percent on me.

It's the kind of pressure I imagine Dad and Bash were under every time they skated onto the ice. *Prime Chef* was hard. Knowing the cameras were on me twenty-four-seven and some of the world's best chefs were judging everything I created was almost unbearable. But there was an end in sight. Either I was going to win, or I was going to lose.

With a restaurant, I have to be *on* every single meal every single day for the indefinite future. Even *one* mistake could be enough to crush this place and my reputation.

I swallow the lump in my throat and rub a hand over the stubble forming on my chin because I didn't bother to shave. Mostly because the act of raising my arm hurts too much. "Look, Grant, I'm just as worried, if not more so than you are, about getting this place up and running as soon as possible and properly. Please have some faith in me."

He snorts. "I do. You think I would've gone into business with you in the first place if I didn't?"

"I know you put your neck on the line to back me on this and a whole lot of your money. But just because you own fifty-one percent of this place doesn't mean I'm not putting in one hundred percent effort. My blood, sweat, and tears are literally the only thing keeping me going right now."

I bite back the rest of what I'm about to say—that I'm both emotionally and physically spent at this point.

Having Bash and Rachel here was both incredible and tiring in a way I hadn't expected. The more they're around, the more certain memories work their way from the back of my mind, where I push them to rear their ugly truths. And the fact that I couldn't just tell them what I've been doing, talk to them about it, and maybe try to rationalize it, makes me feel even more like shit. Like I'm some sort of criminal, hiding something from my own siblings.

I fucking hate this feeling, and I refuse to live like this forever. One of these days, I will have to come clean with the family. But today is not that day. Nor do I feel like opening a can of worms with Grant about my feelings for Isabella when they're irrelevant to how we're moving forward.

The opening is imminent. There's nothing that can stop it now.

Grant sighs again. "I do trust you, Jameson, and if I didn't have faith in you, I would never have agreed to go into business with you. We're a great team, and we're going to do great things with this restaurant. But I'm a businessman, first and foremost, and I need to ensure that we've dotted every *I* and crossed every *T* so there won't be any surprises."

"There won't be. I promise."

He grunts. "Don't make promises you can't keep, Jameson. Let's get this place opened. You think we'll be ready by two weeks from Saturday?"

"Yep. Two weeks from Saturday."

The first day of my future.

IZZY

"You really think I'm ready?"

Sylvie wanders around the restaurant for what feels like the hundredth time, examining every nook and cranny with the kind of scrutiny that makes my stomach churn and my skin feel tight. "I really do. You've done a fabulous job, and people are going to love it."

"You think?"

For some reason, validation from this woman I barely know is suddenly so damn important to me. Maybe because Grams isn't here to see it and I don't fully trust myself or the choices I've made in here, knowing what's happening next door.

She leans back against the counter near the door and releases a heavy sigh. "I really do. But I feel like you don't."

"It's not that exactly."

She inclines her head backward toward Jameson's place. "Does it have anything to do with a certain someone next door?"

It would be stupid to lie to her. After the conversation we had the last time she was here, she already knows there is tension between Jameson and me. But she doesn't know that tension boiled over in the kitchen she was just standing in.

Should I tell her? Give her all the dirty details about what Jameson did with his tongue, hands, and damn cock?

It could potentially get Jameson in a lot of hot water with Grant if he found out. But the fact that she actually knows him makes me want her insight despite my reservations. Because dinner the other night only confused things more, and I need some clarity on that situation before I can move on and focus on getting this place opened.

"We slept together."

Her eyebrows fly up, and she pushes off the counter. "What? When did that happen? How?"

I sigh and run a hand back through my hair that fell out of the messy bun I had it in at some point during the day. "A week ago. And...it happened like how all sex happens. He... you know..."

Does she really want me to give her the nitty-gritty?

"And?"

"And what?"

"Well, what the hell *happened*?"

The ultimate question I haven't found an answer to yet.

"We, you know, did the deed, and then, he left."

"Left where?"

Shit. Now I'm going to sound like a total hussy.

"Left here."

"You had sex *here*?" She glances around the restaurant, almost like she's looking for evidence of our shenanigans.

"The kitchen."

My domain. My safe space. The place I always feel closest to Grams and not so alone on those days when missing her becomes overwhelming. Only now that's tainted by the memory of what that man did...of what *we* did.

Sylvie bursts out laughing, then slaps her hand over her mouth. "Shit. I'm sorry. I was just thinking about the health code violations."

My laugh tumbles to join hers before I release a frustrated groan. "God, Sylvie, it was good. Really, really, *really* good. But then it got weird, and he left, and then I didn't see him for a while because I—"

I barely manage to catch myself. I'm so used to only having these conversations with Ashley that I almost let my weakness slip to Grant's wife.

"And then his family showed up, and I got roped into dinner with them."

"How was that?"

"Awkward as fuck, if I'm being honest."

She chuckles and crosses her arms over her chest. "I can see that. If his siblings are anything like Jameson."

"It was like being thrown into some massive inside joke. I felt like I was missing out on a lot of information I needed to understand what was going on. Lots of good-natured ribbing but also some tense moments. Some things they were keeping close to the chest."

All families have secrets, things they don't want to discuss, especially with an outsider there. I shouldn't be surprised by it, not when I'm keeping my own from everyone around me, but the fact is, I *wanted* to belong at that table more than I care to admit.

I wanted to laugh at their inside jokes and actually understand them. I wanted to be able to jump in with a witty jab and bring laughs to everyone around the table. I wanted sisters like Greer and Rachel who so clearly love with their entire hearts.

It never seemed like I was missing much growing up with Grams, but when I see a family together like that—even without their parents there—it definitely showed me what could have been had the world not been such a cruel place.

"Did you and Jameson resolve anything? Are you two together?"

"God no. No, we are very much *not* together. He made that definitively clear at dinner."

"So, you guys had sex, then you had some awkwardness, now you're not going to have sex again, but you're still opening a restaurant right next to his, and you feel what? Guilty about that?"

"No. Not guilty. More like overwhelmed? I'm not sure I can compete with what Jameson and your husband are offering."

Plus, that man just...gets under my skin. It feels like he's exposing me with every look. Like he can see my weaknesses and plans to exploit them.

And I hate being vulnerable and *refuse* to be weak. It's a promise I made to Grams—to always *fight*. I don't want to fail her, but as the weeks pass and I move closer to opening, it feels like a battle I may not be able to win.

She motions back toward *FURY*. "There's no way you can compete with that, honey."

"Jesus...thanks for just ripping the Band-Aid off, I guess."

"No." She steps forward and rubs my arm. "That's not what I meant. You shouldn't *want* to compete with that. Jameson has a totally different style—one that can't be matched by anyone else on this planet. You have your own that you shouldn't bend from. You do your thing and let Jameson do his. I don't even see you guys as rivals, to be honest with you."

"You don't?"

She shakes her head. "No. Your food and concepts and styles are so different, you're either going to attract completely different customers or the same customer when they're looking for different things. Think about Manhattan. How many restaurants are there on a single block?"

"Dozens."

"Exactly. And yet, many of them thrive."

"There are a lot more people in Manhattan than Bushwick."

"That's true. But other than Jameson, you don't have much competition, do you?"

"Not in this immediate area of town. It's why I picked it, besides the beautiful building. There aren't any sit-down restaurants within at least ten blocks."

"Exactly. Stop second-guessing yourself or letting Jameson Fury get under your skin." She holds up a hand to stop my protest even though it's true. "Believe me, I know that's hard. The man seems to have it nailed down as a science. But all you can do is concentrate on you. Make this the best restaurant you can. Stop worrying about *him*. Move on. I don't care how good the dick was. It's not worth getting hung up on him."

"That's easy for you to say."

She shakes her head and laughs. "No, it isn't. I have been in your shoes with Grant. That man can frustrate me quicker and more than anyone else on this planet."

"Yeah but...you married him."

"I did...because all the frustration he brings out in me is nothing compared to how much he loves me. But if Jameson isn't ready to give you that—and it sure as hell sounds like he isn't—then move on, leave him in the rearview. Put all your energy and effort into this place." She waves her hand around. "Think of it like some one-time stress relief you got out of your system."

Out of my system.

It would be so much easier if that were true.

As it stands, I know I'm going to spend the rest of the day wondering what's going on next door and maybe even fantasizing about our little escapade every time I set foot in the kitchen.

So. Damn. Frustrating.

I walk Sylvie to the door and offer her a hug before she makes her way out.

Don't look over there. Don't look over there.

Forcing my eyes to watch Sylvie's car drive away instead of looking at Jameson's open door is agonizing. I hate tension, and it seems like there's more between us now than there was when we hated each other.

But I make myself step back inside and take a long, slow, deep breath. Being alone in here feels odd, especially knowing that very soon, the staff will be here every day, helping me set up things and preparing for the opening.

I can almost picture everyone bustling around and serving

all the happy customers, assuming Jameson doesn't poach them. And I wouldn't put it past the man. Not only is it his MO, but there was something in his eyes the other night at dinner. I still can't wrap my head around how he touched me and kissed my neck in the kitchen only to make it clear shortly thereafter that what I feared was true—it was just a fuck to him.

No more.

Maybe that's all he wanted in his kitchen, too. A quickie while his family waited out in the restaurant. The rush of knowing we could get caught.

Regardless of his motives, he has now made his intent clear, and Sylvie is right. I need to concentrate on *me* and *my* space, not Jameson and *his*.

I wander back to the kitchen and get to work on finalizing the menu.

This is it. Final inspection is scheduled. Staff is hired. Décor is complete. I release a heavy breath as tears well in my eyes.

Grams, I wish you were here with me right now.

She would be so proud of me. Of course, she would also tell me that I'm working myself into the grave, but I have to do it. I have to push myself—even if my body is on the brink of breaking down. Because if I don't do it now, it may never happen. This might be my only chance to have my dream, and I can't let that go for anything or anyone.

I lean over the counter almost exactly where Jameson had me bent over it and work on handwriting the menu to bring to the printer tomorrow.

Something is missing.

Tapping the end of my pen against the metal counter, I run through the whole list again—all Grams' recipes, with a few slight modifications to make them my own.

Corn bread! How could I have forgotten that?

Grams' jalapeno cornbread is to die for, especially with her chili recipe or the mac and cheese.

Crap.

Without anything cooking in the kitchen, I smell him before I hear him or see him—that spicy, rich scent hitting me almost instantly.

I need to put bells on that front door. Because it sure as hell isn't safe to have Jameson Fury sneaking in here unannounced.

It would be so much easier if I had time to prepare myself, to steel myself against his bourbon eyes that I just want to drink down. To tell my body no when it yearns for him to reach out and touch me.

Be strong, Iz.

I look up to find him approaching me slowly. Almost like he doesn't want to startle me despite the fact he's intentionally made no noise coming in.

For the first time since I first met him, Jameson looks uncertain. Disheveled. Like something is weighing on him. And he's sporting a pretty good black eye that looks painful. "Hey."

"Hey, what the hell happened? Are you okay?

My first thought is an angry ex got to him, but he said he hadn't been with anyone in a while. So, unless he lied to me, it's something else.

"I'm fine." His lips press together into a hard line, and he shoves a hand back through his hair almost violently, glancing away from me to try to hide the wince and grinding of his teeth. "Shit."

While the word was mumbled, barely audible, the frustration and evident pain he's in pulls at my heartstrings more than it should.

"What's wrong?"

He shakes his head and sighs, returning his gaze to

mine. "I'm not sure, just feeling very..." He waves his hand in front of him like he's searching for the right word.

Only one comes to mind to describe his demeanor. "Anxious?"

"Yes."

It takes a lot for a man like Jameson to admit that. He doesn't like to admit any kind of weakness. He always wants to be the one in control and to convince everyone that his control is unwavering.

He shifts on his feet and scans the kitchen, avoiding making eye contact with me again. "I just had a very frustrating phone call with Grant earlier this morning, and I tried to forget about it and get on with my day, get shit done, but some things he said are just driving me a little crazy."

"Things like what?"

Jameson finally levels his gaze on me. "Things he said about you."

I fully stand and turn to face him. "What about me?"

"He wanted to know if you were going to be a problem for us...for me."

"What did you say?"

He watches me for a moment, then closes the distance between us until all he has to do is reach out an inch to touch me, but he holds back. "I told him you wouldn't be."

The words hurt more than anything I've been through in my life, and that's saying a lot. They slam into me like wrecking balls—one by one. He's definitely a problem for me, but apparently, he can blow me off without a second thought.

Why come here to tell me that? To reiterate how little I mean to him?

I clear my throat and try to tamp down the tears. "That's good? I guess?"

"But that was a lie..."

183

Wait. What?

I drop my pen onto the counter. "What does that even mean—"

His lips descending on mine steal my words before I can voice them. I groan and sag against him, everything else forgotten for a tiny moment in time. Even though I have no fucking idea what's going on, I let him lead me down the same road that got us into this position in the first place.

Soft and demanding at the same time, the kiss asks a question and demands an answer, though I'm not sure what either is.

He drags his head away and captures my face between his palms. His warm amber eyes ripple with need and another emotion I haven't seen there before, one I can't quite identify. "You are most definitely going to be a problem for me." He brushes his thumb over my cheek. "Come to my place tonight."

It isn't really a question. More of a statement. Almost a command.

I never wanted Jameson to have control over me, but with his body pressed against mine, my lips tingling from his kiss, his scent enveloping every breath I take, I'm helpless to resist him.

"Yes."

16

JAMESON

The *yes* that fell from Isabella's kiss-swollen lips had to have been the single sweetest word I've ever heard in my entire life. I hadn't even realized how badly I needed to hear it, to have that confirmation that what I've been feeling isn't all one-sided. That I'm not *completely* insane like I've been thinking was a true possibility.

After spending the day stewing about what Grant said about her, I found myself drawn to her place despite all the reasons to stay away. Maybe to prove to myself that I was right about her and he was wrong. Maybe to convince myself I could look at her and not care. Or maybe just because I can't get her out of my head.

I never thought I had an addictive personality. I've never done drugs or drank heavily. I've never been the type to get obsessed with things or people—other than putting everything I have into cooking and being the best of the best—especially things that could be very bad for me.

But Isabella is quickly becoming a major weakness. An

unexpected fork on what I thought was a pretty straight road to achieving what I've worked my entire life for.

She'll walk in my door in mere seconds, and the drive back to my place alone gave me plenty of time to think. Plenty of time to reconsider what we're about to do and end it. Go back to how things were before we ever touched each other with anything other than disdain.

It would make things a lot easier—professionally and personally, especially with Grant. If he finds out, it could be the end of this partnership and my chance at success, but I can't bring myself to care when the tentative knock on the door makes my heart leap into my throat.

She came.

If she is second-guessing this in any way, it didn't stop her. She could have changed course at any point on the way here, driven home, and given me the ultimate *fuck you* by leaving me here hard and waiting. But nothing stopped her, just like my reservations about whether this is a good idea or not don't stop me from yanking open the door and dragging her inside to devour her soft lips.

So fucking sweet...

She moans into my mouth, looping her arms around my neck and pushing her hips forward to rub against my hardening cock.

Hell, who am I kidding?

The truth is, I've been rock hard since the moment I walked into her kitchen, and it made for a very uncomfortable drive. Maybe I should've jerked off before she got here. Given myself a little bit of relief and ensured that I could go all night with her. But it seems that when it comes to Isabella, I want all my pleasure from her body. From her soft hands and this mouth that I can't bear to pull away from. From the tongue tangling with mine...

Fuck.

186

My dick aches to be inside her, to be cocooned in her hot cunt, feeling her come apart in my arms and screaming my name. Almost as if in answer to my silent prayer, she reaches down with one hand and rubs against me. I grunt into her mouth and thrust my hips into her hand, backing her against the door she just came through.

I drag my mouth from hers, and her tongue darts out across her lips like the taste there is something she can't get enough of.

God, that's hot.

Placing one hand against the door to the side of her head, I capture her face in my other palm; the pain that's been plaguing me all day suddenly eases with the rush of hormones and determination flooding my body. "I wanted you here so I could have you all night. So I could do every depraved thing I have fantasized about over and over again without any threat of interruption. But Christ, Izzy, the bedroom seems so far away right now."

She squeezes my cock harder and nods. "It sure does." Her words come out breathless and full of the same need I feel building inside me. "I feel like I've been waiting a long time to see what you taste like, Jameson. And I don't want to wait any longer."

"Oh, fuck..."

Isabella slides down the door to her knees on the hardwood floor and deftly unbuttons and unzips to free me from the confines of my jeans. The brief moment of relief quickly becomes another form of sweet agony when she takes me in her hand and squeezes. I release a groan, burying my fingers into her hair as she leans forward and lets out a hot breath across my most sensitive flesh.

She peers up at me from under long, dark lashes. "Everything I've ever tasted from you has been incredible, Mr. Fury."

I stare down at her glittering green eyes, sparkling with humor. "I sure hope I can live up to your expectations."

A tiny laugh falls from her lips, and she swirls her tongue around the head of my cock. I jerk and tighten my hold on her hair.

"I'm sure you will." She sucks me into her mouth slowly, like she wants to either torture me or experience every bit of it.

My bet is on the torture.

The way she slides her tongue along the bottom of my shaft, then up across that place right under the head of my cock is clearly designed to torment me. To make my hips rock forward in an attempt to drive deeper. To push me to the brink of self-control.

She moans around me and changes the angle of her assault so that she can take me even farther down.

Oh, fuck. I won't last. No fucking way.

If I want any chance of coming inside her, I need to end this before she does it for me. I tug on her hair and drag my hips back to free my cock from her mouth's vise-like grip.

She gazes up at me, her lips wet and swollen, her hand still wrapped around the base of my shaft. "What?"

I tug her up and against me, pressing a brutal kiss to her lips before making my way to her ear. "As much as I would love to see you swallow my cum, I want to be inside you more right now."

The hand wrapped around me strokes, and she gives a tiny nod. It's the only confirmation I need that's she's fully on board with this plan.

That control I'm barely clinging to finally snaps, and I push her back against the door and fumble to find the waistband of her pants. She releases her grip on me long enough to shove them down along with her thong and kicks them off to the side along with the flip-flops she was wearing.

The urge to drop to my knees to worship her again and get the warm taste of her release on my tongue wars against the need to feel her clamping around me, but she brushes her thumb over the head of my dick and urges me back toward her, making the decision for me.

Thank fuck, I don't have to make that choice.

I grasp her hips and lift her to wrap her legs around my waist, then pin her to the door. The bruises on my side issue a little scream of objection, but there isn't any time to worry about how sore this might make me. Aligning my cock with her wet heat, I lock eyes with Izzy and drive into absolute bliss.

It isn't what I had in mind when I invited her over tonight. I pictured something a little more romantic, or at least a soft mattress beneath us. Romance isn't a word I've ever really associated with how I am with women, and most would consider this a little barbaric. But this feels right with her, right here in the damn living room against the front door barely inside my apartment. Everything else between us has been fast.

Immediate hatred.

Immediate frustration.

Immediate tension.

Immediate attraction—at least from my end.

Why should this be any different?

Izzy deserves to be worshipped. To be shown how beautiful and irresistible she is to me. She needs to know just how she drives me fucking crazy in a way no other woman in my life ever has.

And I'll do all those things...once I get some fucking relief.

My hips mimic the push and pull of the relationship we've always had. Every retreat feels like losing a little something, while every drive in is like coming home to a place I hadn't known I needed.

She groans and drops her head against the wood, digging her heels into my lower back to push me even deeper.

I still for a moment and put my forehead against hers. A huge part of me wants to stay like this forever, buried inside Izzy, but the need to move makes me drag my hips back and slam into her again.

Her nails score my nape, and I lean forward to suck the breath right from her lips.

And good God... she seems more than willing to let me.

————

IZZY

I wasn't hallucinating. It wasn't just a fantasy I had built up in my head, some exaggerated remembrance of a moment in time made to be something that it wasn't. No...I wasn't wrong about what happened in my kitchen the other night. Jameson really is *that good*.

The first time, I thought it was just the tension build-up that made it so perfect. The typical hate-fuck everyone talks about being so incredibly hot. But I don't hate Jameson anymore—if I ever *truly* did. And given what he said earlier, I don't think he hates me, either.

You are most definitely going to be a problem for me.

The statement could have been taken a lot of ways, but it only said one thing to me—he wants me. Truly wants me, even with all the bullshit between us.

While I would love to convince myself that it's just the fact that it's been so long, that I'm lonely and need this connection and affection from someone, I can't deny the reality of what's happening with Jameson.

And apparently, neither can he.

Because even now, as he slams into me, I see the struggle deep in his bourbon eyes. He knows all the reasons why this is wrong. All the complications it brings. Yet, we're doing it anyway.

What does that say about us? That we're both weak? Or is it just that our connection is that strong? Something undeniable that no one could ever fight?

Either way, it doesn't matter right now. Because it feels *good*. And I haven't felt *truly* good in such a long time that it feels like I deserve this. One more night of reckless abandon, of throwing caution to the wind and letting natural need take over before I have to face reality and decide how to handle telling him what he needs to know.

I should be at home right now doing all the things I need to in order to keep myself healthy and sane, but instead, I'm in the arms of the one man I shouldn't be. I'm losing myself in the competition who can ruin everything I've ever dreamed about and worked for if I really let him. And in this moment, I just might.

Just might give him everything...

Especially if he keeps doing that thing with his hips that makes the head of his cock drag against my G-spot.

"God, yes!" The words tumble from my lips, and I roll my hips to meet his, harder and faster, reaching for that one moment of sheer bliss I know is just on the horizon.

It's raw and rough and all Jameson.

He isn't the type of man who ever makes love. I doubt he even understands the meaning of the word, but with the pleasure coursing through my veins like heroin right now, I can't care about that missing fantasy.

I can momentarily brush aside the fact that he looked

like he'd been in a fight when he arrived—banged up and battered the way I feel, even though it might not be as visible. He's hiding something from me just like I am him, something that can wait for another day. Until his hand shifts from my thigh to the hem of my shirt, and I quickly reach down and plaster my hand over his to still his progress.

Oh, God. Not now...

I am *so* not having this conversation with him right now, not in the middle of feeling like this. I'm not ready to expose any more weaknesses to Jameson when he already has me torn open and practically naked in front of him. When he's already worked his way under my skin and into my heart.

He stalls the movement of his hips and drags his head back to look at me. "What's wrong? Why won't you let me touch you?"

I answer him with a kiss and by squeezing my pussy around him.

Distraction always works.

His eyes snap shut, and he groans, his chest rumbling against mine in a strange mixture of need and frustration. He pulls his hand out from under mine and takes my chin in his palm. His eyes flutter open and meet mine. "We're going to have to talk about this." He claims me with a kiss, one that takes my breath again and promises he means business. "But first, let me finish fucking you and make you come on my cock."

Oh, God.

A shiver rolls through me, and I clench around him again.

I've never been one for dirty talk. Maybe it's just because no one has ever really done it with me before, but the growly tone in his voice and the fact that he has absolute command of me at this moment makes me nod. "I am in one hundred percent agreement with that plan."

The coming on his cock part, at least.

Not the talking later thing. All the other stuff will have to be addressed at some point I don't even want to think about right now. But if I'm coming clean, so is he. It's only fair. The two of us need to lay everything out on the table...somewhere down the road.

He resumes his movements and kisses his way up my neck to my ear to suck behind it at that spot that sends a jolt straight to my clit. That, combined with the roll and crush of his hips, the friction of his pelvis against my throbbing bud, is enough to finally send me over the edge.

I jerk against the door, my pussy rippling and clutching at him inside me as my orgasm obliterates any sense of reality. Only one thing exists in this brilliant moment of ecstasy that's only broken by a guttural growl as Jameson pushes in one final time and comes—my complete surrender.

He presses me into the door, keeping us both up with the weight of his body. His face buried against my neck brings hot pants of breath across my skin. As much as I'd love to bask in this for a few moments, my entire body tenses at what's coming.

Jameson told me we were going to talk. And he always follows through on his promises. He pulls back his head, and his lips find mine again in a slow, languid kiss, one that sends a little aftershock through me.

When he finally drags his mouth from mine, he grins and grasps my thighs in a bruising grip. "Hold on tight. We're going to the bedroom."

A giggle I haven't heard come from me in years bubbles up, and I press my face against his neck and cling to him as he walks us down a short hallway.

He pauses at the edge of the bed and urges me to raise

my head to meet his gaze. One hand rises to brush my hair back from my face, and he tilts my chin, forcing me to keep my eyes locked on him. "I'm so damn glad you said yes."

"So am I."

Though now that we're in here, I know I'm about to face some hard questions I may not be willing or able to answer, and I hope that doesn't undo everything we just did here and send us back to where we were.

Because despite everything...I like *here*. I like it a *lot*.

17

IZZY

The mattress is far more comfortable than being pressed up against the hard door, but moving in here only ratchets up the tension building inside me and between us.

Jameson said he wants to talk. And that will definitely include him wanting to know why I stop his wandering hands during sex when all I really want is his touch over every damn inch of my body.

I don't think I can...

I'm not ready to burst this pleasant little bubble with my own bullshit quite yet. Not when lying here next to him feels more like home than my own bed does.

Will it still when I tell him?

We lie panting next to each other for a moment, both of us still coming down from the high of what happened when I arrived. The peace won't last, though. Not unless I manage to find a way to distract him from his intended goal.

I roll toward him and straddle his waist, pushing up his

shirt until he leans up to let me pull it free and toss it onto the floor.

God, he's beautiful.

All the sharp angles and lines of hard, honed muscle. But my fingertips automatically go to the bruises at his side and across part of his ribcage. "What are these from? Same place you got the shiner?"

He winces slightly. "Shit. I had hoped you'd forgotten about that."

I laugh and drop my head down to place a kiss against one of the bruises. "Kind of hard to forget about it on a man who always looks so dashing and perfect."

His dark eyebrows rise. "Dashing and perfect, huh?"

"Don't let it go to your head."

Though I fear it's far too late for that.

He chuckles and drags me down against him, until our entire bodies align, his semi-hard cock now nestled right between my legs. "Don't worry about the bruises. Just a little extracurricular activity to relieve a little stress."

"You aren't doing underground fighting or something stupid like that, are you? Is that why you disappear on Wednesday nights?"

Jameson has never struck me as the kind to get into a physical altercation, but he sure never backs down from any verbal sparring, so my mind immediately goes to some sort of cage match where Jameson and some other barbaric monster throw punches at each other, out for blood.

Damn, that shouldn't be so hot.

Laughing, he reaches down between us to rub his thumb over my clit. "I'm a lover, not a fighter. At least, not *that* kind of fighting."

His distraction won't work on me, even with his ministrations making me squirm. "Those are some nasty bruises, though." I brush my fingers over the darkening around his eye. "And this one definitely looks like it came from a fist."

Jameson captures my hand and presses a kiss to the palm. "I thought we were going to talk about you, not me."

I narrow my eyes on him. "I'm worried about you."

He releases a deep sigh and leans up to kiss me. "I'm fine, Iz. I'm just playing hockey."

"What?" I jerk back. "But I got the impression at dinner that you never played."

His face hardens slightly, and he tenses under me and pulls his hand free. "I hadn't since I was very young...until fairly recently."

"Why, though? It seemed like a bit of a sore subject with Bash and Rachel."

He twists his lips, and I'm not entirely sure he's going to answer me. I wouldn't blame him if he didn't since I sure as hell am not looking forward to having to come clean about what I've been hiding, either.

But he eventually relents and shifts under me slightly. "It was always my dad's thing with Bash. It was how they bonded. And it was also what made him such a shitty father. He pushed so hard to be perfect and wanted his boys to do the same. I never wanted to be a part of that because I saw what he did to Bash and didn't want to bring down even more shit on myself." He releases a deep sigh, his chest heaving under me. "But after he died, I just..."

His words trail off, leaving silence hanging in the air between us. Though even without saying it, I can see exactly where he's going with this.

"You were drawn to the ice because it held some sort of connection to him."

"Shit." He scrubs his hands over his face and groans. "I don't know. I just saw something on someone's social media about a men's league and felt this need to go play, at least once, even though I haven't been out on the ice in over twenty years."

I lower myself back down and press a kiss to his neck. "It could be about your dad, or maybe it wasn't really about him at all."

"What do you mean?"

"Well, he died, and you were left with just Bash and Rachel. Maybe it's more about wanting to connect with something you know Bash loves and getting closer to your big brother than about wanting to connect with a father who was shitty to you."

He stills under me and uses his hand to urge my head up so his eyes connect with mine. "How did you get so insightful?"

I laugh. "Grams was a font of wisdom. I must have absorbed some of it at some point."

"She raised you alone?"

It isn't exactly anything I want to discuss right now, but it beats talking about other things.

Distract. Distract. Distract.

I lower my head to his chest, pressing my ear over his heart to listen to the steady rhythm for a moment. "Yeah. My mom died when I was six. I never knew my dad. Grams was it for me most of my life."

Jameson runs his hand up and down my arm, sending little goose bumps skittering over my skin. "I'm sorry."

"There's nothing to be sorry about. She was great. I had a really happy life with her. Just because you have two parents raising you doesn't mean it's the perfect family, right?"

I peek up at him, and his amber eyes darken to almost a chocolate brown.

"Yeah, you're right. Things definitely weren't perfect in my house."

"But you all survived and thrived."

He nods and presses a kiss to my forehead. "Yeah, we did. Though we all had a lot more bruises than this as kids."

"It was that bad?"

A long sigh slips from his lips, and he squeezes me. "It was bad. Bash took the brunt of it because he was the oldest and spent the most time with Dad. If he fucked up something during a practice or a game, we all knew what that meant. We tried to shield Rachel since she was a girl, and she and Bash tried to shield me because I was the youngest. Mom tried to shield all of us. It was kind of a vicious cycle."

I never had to experience anything like that, but I understand vicious cycles all too well. It feels like I've been caught in one since the day I was born. "You broke it, though. You got away from him. And you found something you love. Concentrate on that."

Jameson shrugs. "I try to. I really do. I just want to get *FURY* open already. It seems like it's taken a lifetime to get here."

"You're close, though, aren't you?"

He nods and continues to stroke his hand down my arm. "Very. What about you? You've been doing everything yourself."

And that's only the half of it.

"I won't lie. It's been rough. My finances won't allow me to have my staff with me twenty-four-seven helping get things ready, so I'm doing it almost all myself except the construction stuff, obviously. But I'm determined to get it together, and I finally picked an opening date."

"You did? That's awesome. When?"

I grin against his warm skin underneath my cheek, the idea of finally having *Grandma's Kitchen* open and running filling me with a warmth and pride I haven't experienced in a long time. "Two weeks from Saturday. It's my grandma's birthday."

JAMESON

All the air instantly rips from my lungs, and I cough and try to suck in another breath, but her weight on top of me and the panic setting in won't seem to let me. "Um, did you say two weeks from Saturday?"

She nods and snuggles into me deeper, her arms wrapping around me tightly, like she's searching for something stable to cling to and I'm it. "Yeah. I think Grams would have loved having the opening on her birthday. She would have been ninety-four this year. It just seemed fitting since I'm mostly cooking her recipes."

Of all the days on the damn calendar...

It's not her fault her grandmother's birthday falls on the date Grant and I chose for the opening of *FURY*, not her fault we both chose to open restaurants next door at the same time, but it's created one hell of a quagmire.

There has to be a way to avoid any bloodshed on this, though, some way around this that doesn't lead to either of us hating the other.

I clear my throat and try to sound casual with my question. "Are you sure you're going to be ready? Will you have enough time?"

Maybe it's a dick move to try to nudge her in the direction of postponing, but it beats the alternative. If we open the same night as she does, her little restaurant will be crushed by the weight of Grant's money, power, and influence coming down on *FURY*.

I don't want her to suffer the embarrassment of seeing a line out our door, news media and celebrities, while she may only manage to get a handful of customers. Not because her food isn't excellent. What I've smelled coming out of her kitchen would make even the most discerning palate dance. And not because she doesn't absolutely deserve to have success. But simply because *FURY* will be the draw.

Celebrity chef teams with one of New York's most powerful businessmen—Grant and I are a dream team. Ever since we announced the new venture in *FURY*, we've both been hounded for information and interviews. While Isabella has essentially no one behind her except her friend, Ashley.

Hearing her talk about the way she grew up with her Grams and knowing she had to set up her place all alone while I had as much help as I needed makes guilt over all the shit I did to her rise like acid up my throat.

Whatever calm I felt for those moments out in the living room with her has now fled the building, replaced by a deep, foreboding sense of dread.

She pushes up and offers me a half-smile that doesn't quite hide the sadness. "I have to be ready. No other option."

No other option.

That can't be true. There has to be a way to make this all work, though no solution is presenting itself to me right now. It's hard to concentrate on anything else when a beautiful woman is draped over you and your hard cock is brushing against her wet cunt every time she moves.

She yawns and stretches, the hem of her shirt rising slightly above her hips before she yanks it back into place. I promised her we would talk after we got done in the living room, and I've let her shift the conversation in the opposite direction.

Was that intentional on her part?

Isabella isn't a deceptive person, but she's been evasive about this. I grasp her chin and force her to meet my gaze.

"You ready to tell me why you won't let me take off your shirt?"

A thousand possibilities have swirled through my head —none of them warranting the reaction she seems to have whenever I try to remove it.

She doesn't respond, just chews on her bottom lip like if she doesn't answer, I'll just let it go.

I raise an eyebrow at her. "Scars? Stretch marks? Ugly tattoo of another dude's name?"

She scowls and rolls off onto the mattress beside me, sending a chill through my now-exposed body. Wanting to get away from me physically isn't a good sign. I was joking about it, but whatever it is clearly upsets her more than I thought.

I roll onto my side and pull her back against me. "Sorry. I didn't mean to make a joke about something that seems to really upset you. I just don't understand. There's literally *nothing* you can be hiding that would send me running or make me think you're any less fucking beautiful than I already do." I press a kiss to the back of her neck, and she relaxes back against me slightly. "Seriously, Iz. I haven't been able to stop thinking about you since that day in the rain. Even when we were arguing, all I wanted to do was pull you into my arms and kiss you to shut you the hell up."

Her body vibrates with laughter, and she turns slightly to look back at me. "The wanting to shut me the hell up part I believe."

I feather my lips over hers and feel her melt into me. "Believe all of it. Nothing you're hiding can be that bad."

She shakes her head, and tears shimmer in her eyes, a real dampener on the mood when my cock is still hard and pressing into her ass. "You can't say that when you don't know."

"So, tell me."

Her eyes drift closed, and when she reopens them, the fear there makes my chest tighten. "Can we just...not tonight. I promise I will. Some time. Soon. Just not now."

I want to argue with her, to push her to tell me whatever she's holding back, to get her to open up to me the way she just made me open to her, but I don't want to see this look in her eyes anymore. The pain and the fear. She's already had to fight with me for what feels like forever over the restaurant bullshit. I definitely don't want her to be fighting with me now over something that's ultimately so inconsequential to how I feel about her.

If she needs more time, I'll give her more time. "Okay. But soon, Iz."

She nods, and I lower my head and kiss her deeply, rolling on top of her. A moan slips from her mouth into mine, and she opens her lips and her legs for me, letting my tongue and cock settle right where they belong.

For now.

Hopefully, for the foreseeable future, too.

This thing between us is so much more than the hate fuck it started out as. It's become something new and addictive. I don't want to live without this or her. But this opening thing could be what drives us apart.

If I let it.

18

JAMESON

Grant's eyes harden more the longer he looks at me. "What do you mean *move* the opening date?"

Since the moment I arrived at his office unannounced this morning, he's been on edge. Surprise visits from business partners will do that, apparently.

I shift uncomfortably in my chair under his scrutiny. There's a reason Grant Mason has gotten so far in life, and it isn't because he's a pushover. The man is a force to be reckoned with and won't just roll over without knowing exactly why I'm asking for something and why it's completely necessary.

Like moving the date of the opening that he's been waiting not-so-patiently for, costing him not only time but also money.

He raises a brow at me. "Is there something wrong? Did the inspector not approve us?"

Christ, I wish it were that simple.

I could handle Grant's anger over having to change the date if it were because the contractor fucked up something and we couldn't get approval, but this...the reason I'm actually asking for it...this could spell a major problem for our working partnership.

"No. The inspector had a cancellation and was able to come today. We got the approvals this afternoon."

"So...the staff isn't available? I thought you said you got everyone hired we would need."

"I did. One of the servers knew a sommelier who just moved back to town, so we're good there."

Grant steeples his fingers under his chin and raises an eyebrow at me. "So, what's the problem? What's the hold-up? Why the hell would we want to postpone the opening when we've already made a press release that's been sent to every news outlet in the area and will be announced today, and I've already paid to rush expensive formal invitations and have them sent to half of fucking Manhattan?"

Shit. Shit. Shit.

There goes any hope of catching Grant before he set things in motion. It's amazing what the man can accomplish in only twenty-four hours. Though, with his connections, it shouldn't be surprising.

I rub the back of my neck and glance at my shoes to avoid his annoyed gaze. There isn't any way to say this that isn't going to draw his ire, so I just need to go for it. Ripping off the Band-Aid is going to hurt like a motherfucker, but here it goes.

Tapping my foot on his expensive tile floors, I keep my focus on his tie rather than meeting his angry glare. "Isabella already chose her opening date."

"And?"

"It's the same night."

Grant tenses, his whole demeanor hardening almost instantly. "You told me she wasn't going to be a problem."

I finally lift my head to meet his gaze. "She's not."

"I would beg to differ when you're sitting here, asking me to change the opening date of our damn restaurant because she decided to schedule hers to compete with ours."

"No." I shift forward in my chair and throw up a hand. "It's not like that. It wasn't intentional."

He snorts and shakes his head, releasing a heavy sigh. "Jesus...you're really in deep with this girl, aren't you? You really believe she wouldn't do this to piggyback off our opening?"

"Not when I know it's her dead grandmother's birthday."

She chose that date because it's important to her, because her grandmother was the single most influential person in her life. She wants to honor her. It has nothing to do with our place. I never questioned that for a moment.

But Grant doesn't know her the way I do. He's a shrewd businessman who is always on guard and looking for people to stab him in the back. It's good to be careful in business, to keep your eyes open for snakes in the grass. This isn't that, though. Isabella is far from a snake, and she isn't trying to sneak up on us to strike.

He eyes me for a moment and raps his knuckles against his desk. "Even if that's the case and it's completely coincidental, this won't fly. You need to get her to change her opening."

"What?" I push up out of my chair and press my palms flat against the top of his desk, leaning forward toward him. "You can't be serious."

He reclines back in his chair. "I warned you that she would be a problem, Jameson. I told you not to let her become one. But you apparently ignored me—my guess is more than once considering the way you're defending her right now. If you can't get her to move her opening date, I'll have to make a call to a friend of mine down at City

Hall and get her license pulled so she can't move forward yet."

"You can't do that."

"I can, and I will. This is a business for me, Jameson, and you need to treat it that way, too."

The fact that he can question my commitment to this makes anger flare in my veins. Fisting my hands, I issue a low growl and slam one on the desk. "You don't have to be so heartless."

"It's kind of what I'm known for. Isn't that one of the reasons you wanted me as a partner?"

"Well, yeah, but—"

He holds up a hand. "But nothing. You have to separate business from pleasure. You can't let a little twinge of guilt stop you from advancing toward our ultimate goal."

Jesus, he can be cold...

"That's a hard way to live your life." It also contradicts so much I've seen when he's with Sylvie. It's like he's a different person here in his office than he is when his wife is around. She somehow helps calm the ruthless beast in him.

"I thought we were on the same page when we started this endeavor, Jameson."

"We *were*. We *are*."

"You just let a woman get you all fucked up."

"Shit." I shove off his desk and jerk my hands back through my hair, ignoring the soreness in my body from both the hockey game and what I did with Isabella last night.

That woman *does* have me fucked up.

She's thrown me off my game since that first day she yelled at me in the rain.

I thought I could handle her, manage her the same way I have all the other women who have come in and out of my life. I believed I could give in to the attraction to her and then go on with my life like I always had.

Fuck was I wrong.

Grant rises from his chair and adjusts his watch, visible with his rolled-up sleeves. "It's not that I'm not sympathetic, Jameson. Because believe me," he chuckles, "I've been there. But it doesn't mean I'm going to change my stance on this. We cannot let her open on the same day we do. Get her to change it. There isn't any other option."

Shit.

IZZY

Jameson opens the door slowly, with far less enthusiasm than I had anticipated given the way we left things this morning. The kiss he gave me before I had to leave and rush home almost made me stay. But I don't have that luxury. I shouldn't have even slept here last night, shouldn't have put off what my body needs to stay healthy until the sun came up, but being in his arms felt too good to leave.

And he looks as bad as I feel today.

Dark circles ring his eyes, and his disheveled hair looks like he's been running his hands through it constantly.

I know why I feel like crap, but Jameson doesn't usually seem so out of sorts. We were both running around like mad all day. I didn't even see him during the hour or two that I was actually at the restaurant today, so maybe he's just exhausted.

"You okay?" I push up onto my tiptoes to give him a kiss which he returns, but his hands remain at his sides rather than enveloping me the way they normally do when he kisses me.

Something's wrong.

This isn't just him being tired after last night.

I pull back from him and search his eyes for the answer. But they offer nothing but unease. The usual warmth there seems almost cold, sending a chill over my skin. "What's wrong?"

He ushers me inside with a hand at my lower back and closes the door behind us. For some reason, the click of it securing seems to vibrate through me and bring a cold sweat, like it's some harbinger of something bad about to come.

I set my bag onto the couch and turn to face him. Jameson isn't the type to outwardly show his distress over anything. Last night was the first time I've ever seen him not acting like a total smartass and smug as hell.

Whatever it is, it's eating away at him bad enough to make him look like utter shit and let down the wall of confidence he usually holds so steady.

He sighs and rubs the back of his neck. "Nothing's *wrong*, but there's something we need to talk about."

A tiny bit of relief hits me, and the excitement I had when I first knocked on his door returns. "Oh, I have something I have to talk to you about, too."

Even though running around all day has left me worn out, these are well worth it.

I rummage in my bag and pull out the signs I had printed for the opening. "I probably should've run these by you before I had them printed just to get a second opinion, but aren't they adorable? I'm going to start plastering them around Brooklyn tomorrow."

Unfortunately, I don't have a huge budget to advertise the opening, but grassroots marketing still works. Posting on social media, calling anyone I can to invite them to come, and putting these up on light poles and bulletin boards in the area should be good enough to have the restaurant packed opening night.

His eyes scan the sign, and he swallows thickly. "Yeah. They're great. Were they expensive?"

I sigh and examine them again. "Definitely more than I wanted to spend. But well worth it because they turned out awesome, and I think they're very eye-catching."

"Uh-huh." He averts his gaze and seems more interested in anything than me.

"Why are you being so weird?"

This isn't at all what I expected when I arrived here tonight. I thought all of the weirdness between us was in the past. After what happened last night, after our talk, it felt like we had finally connected in a deeper way. I even considered telling him everything when I woke up this morning, but I didn't want to ruin the good mood with the harsh realities of my life, so I held off even though I know I can't delay much longer.

Now, the good vibes we had appear to have been ruined by something else.

Unless he found out...

"You're kinda freaking me out, Jameson. What's going on?"

He finally locks his focus on me again, a new determination hardening his typically warm and inviting bourbon eyes. "You need to move your opening out by at least a week."

"Excuse me?" A heat flares over my skin, tightening in and making me feel a little clammy. The room starts to spin slightly like I'm stuck on some sort of awful amusement park ride. "I must've misheard you."

"I'm sorry, Izzy." He shrugs, the motion slow and deliberate. "You couldn't have known, but it's the same night as my opening."

"Shit." A strange mix of ice and warmth rushes through my veins, sending goose bumps over my damp skin. My legs wobble, and I sway slightly but manage to brace my leg against the couch to find my balance. "You want me to cancel my opening that I scheduled on my grandmother's birthday because yours is more important? Because you don't want me to what...steal your thunder?"

He takes a step forward with his hands raised. "No, Izzy, it's not like that."

"It sure as hell seems like it is."

How can he even ask this? Did nothing we shared last night mean anything? Was he even listening?

"We spent a lot of money doing a press release and advertising. We have commercials already being recorded that are going to be aired. We've invited a lot of really important people. We can't move it."

It shouldn't surprise me that Grant and Jameson would be going balls-out for their opening. They have the capability to launch with tremendous fanfare. And of course, they had to choose the same day. But it doesn't have to be the end of the world like he's making it out to be.

"Why should I have to move mine? Why can't they both be the same night?"

He grinds his jaw together and glances out the window. "Because it's not good business. For either of us. We need different days so that we'll both be able to really direct focus on our individual places. This is as much for you as it is for me."

"Bullshit." I jam the posters back into the bag and squeeze my eyes shut against the onset of the world spinning around me.

Crap.

With as burned out and crappy as I've been feeling

lately, having my blood pressure spike this way definitely isn't helping things.

"No." I shake my head and glance at him as I grab my bag off the couch and prepare myself to leave. It's clear what his priorities are, and I am not one of them. "I'm not moving my date. Move yours or deal with it."

"Izzy, please."

"Don't *Izzy* me. You knew what you were asking for, and you did it anyway. You knew it was my grandmother's birthday, how important this is to me, yet I bet you didn't even for once consider moving your opening, did you?"

"Of course, I did. I suggested it to Grant. But he said no."

"Oh, now you're blaming Grant."

"You don't get it, do you?" His hands fist at his sides. "He owns fifty-one percent. This might be my restaurant, but really, it's *his*." He points a finger toward the door like Grant is standing right there. "I don't have the ultimate say on anything. No matter what Grant might say about me making decisions, at the end of the day, it's *his* choice. I *don't* have the power."

"You do on this." I clench my fists at my side, mimicking his stance. "You're the one who has to go there and cook, right? So...don't."

His jaw drops, his sparkling amber eyes wide. "You want me to tank my own opening?"

When he says it that way, it does sound pretty stupid. And ridiculous of me to ask. But what else can I do?

Frustration steals any response I might make to his question. "I don't know what I want, Jameson, other than out of here right now."

I take a step to brush past him, and my legs wobble. His strong arm wraps around me, keeping me from falling. I try to elbow my way out of his hold, but he grabs my face and tilts it up toward him.

"Don't leave like this." His eyes widen slightly, and he shifts his hand over my forehead. "Shit, Iz. You're burning up. You have a fever."

"I do?" It would certainly explain why I've been feeling like shit all day even though I was in an amazing mood. I brushed it off as just it being so hot and humid today and running around like a madwoman to get things ready, but apparently, I was wrong. "I'm fine. I just need to get home and—"

The words die on my lips as another wave of dizziness makes me sag into Jameson's arms.

"Shit. I'm calling an ambulance..."

19

JAMESON

The bitter bite of antiseptic barely covers the scent of illness and death. It's one of the worst things about hospitals, and it brings up memories I wish I could forget. Mom in a bed, clinging to life for far longer than she should have. Bash, Rach, and me around her, spending her final moments with her while Dad was nowhere to be found.

It still makes rage flood my veins to know Rach and Bash ran to his bedside when he was at the end. He didn't deserve it. Didn't deserve to have any kind of compassion or forgiveness from them. Didn't deserve to have them sit at his bedside like this.

So completely helpless.

Isabella looks so frail. If the machines weren't beeping with her various stats, I might actually think she wasn't even here anymore. The rapid decline in her appearance since she collapsed in my arms has brought a heavy sense of dread to sit squarely on my chest.

I squeeze her hand in mine and shake my head to try to

clear away the cobwebs filling it after so long without sleep. She should be awake by now. And I'd give anything to have her open her eyes, even if it's to glare at me. Anything to hear her voice, even if it's to continue to accuse me of being a selfish jerk and scream in my face.

Maybe I am.

Even mentioning the possibility of her moving her opening date was a dick move.

A huge dick move.

If she had asked me to do that same thing under the circumstances, I would have told her to fuck off and assumed she didn't give a shit about me. But that couldn't be further from the truth.

God, I hope she doesn't believe that.

I squeeze her hand again and sigh. "Wake up, Iz. Come on."

The longer I wait, the more hopeless the situation feels. But after sitting here for hours and hours with no response from her, her fingers wrap around mine and finally squeeze back.

I jerk my head up and meet her confused gaze. Green eyes flick back and forth, unfocused and hazy. I give her a second to acclimate herself to the sights and sounds of the room.

She swallows thickly. "Did I pass out?"

I nod and bite back the bitterness that wants to come out with my question. "Why didn't you tell me?"

She sighs, and a single tear trickles down her cheek to the shitty hospital pillow. "Because I didn't want you to pity me or think I'm a damn invalid."

Pity her?

Pity definitely isn't the word for what I'm feeling right now, and I open my mouth to argue, but she shakes her head, more tears falling.

"Don't. Don't pity me or try to deny it. I see it in your eyes."

"That's concern, Iz, not pity." I use my free hand to pull back the sheet covering her and expose the tube coming from her abdomen. "Is this what you were trying to hide from me?"

If she had let me take her shirt off or even lift it slightly, I would have felt it for sure, and I definitely would have had questions. Because until the doctor and Ashley told me what was going on, I was fucking clueless.

She squeezes her eyes shut again. "I didn't want you to know. I didn't want anyone to know. I've always worn a body shaper to keep it concealed under clothing, and so it doesn't get caught on anything. I didn't want to have to answer a thousand questions that would have made you see me differently."

"It wouldn't have made me see you any differently."

"Bullshit." Her eyes flutter open, and she motions down to the tube. "*This* is not sexy. And as soon as you saw it, anything we were doing would have ground to a halt. I just wanted to be a girl who was attracted to a guy and got to have great sex."

I waggle my eyebrows playfully. "Great, huh?"

She chuckles and winces. "Don't let it go to your head. I'm surprised they even let you in here."

A smirk pulls at my lips, and I brush my thumb over the top of her hand. "I told them I was your fiancé. It helped that the admitting nurse is a big fan of *Prime Chef*."

The tiniest of smiles hits her mouth but doesn't quite reach her eyes.

"But the doctor has been a little tightlipped about your condition. When I asked what was wrong, I think he was surprised I didn't know since it wouldn't exactly be easy to hide that you're in kidney failure from someone you're about to marry."

She flinches slightly at my words, but I can't fight back the anger that rises in me. It's hard not to get mad when I think about what's been going on for weeks and weeks.

"What were you thinking, Iz? You've been working insane late hours and pushing yourself nonstop for weeks. I'm fucking exhausted doing the same thing with way more help than you do. And I'm not *sick*."

Her tears fall in earnest now, and she takes another shaky breath. "This isn't something new, Jameson. My mother died of the same thing when she was even younger than me. I knew what was coming. And when I finally hit stage five and had to go on daily dialysis, I knew it was only a matter of time before that wouldn't be enough."

"Why haven't you had a transplant?"

"Because it wasn't bad enough yet, and partially because I'm type O negative."

"I don't understand."

"I can only get a kidney from someone else who's type O negative, and because type O is the universal donor, their kidneys often go to patients of other blood types who are more urgent cases. I've been on the transplant list for over two years but never high enough to get one."

"How is that possible?" I shake my head. "They just let you slowly die for years?"

She shrugs slightly. "There are only so many kidneys available. They have to look for matches and treat emergent cases with priority."

"That's bullshit."

"Yeah, well..." She shrugs again. "It's my life. But I promised Grams and myself that I wasn't going to stop living and just wait to die. I told her I was going to get my restaurant opened, no matter what. Otherwise, I would have been waiting forever and maybe never done it."

I clench my hand around hers a little too tightly, and she winces and pulls hers away.

"Shit." I scrub my palms over my face. "I'm sorry. This whole thing is just—"

"Too much to handle?"

I drop my hands to look at her. "What? No. Why would you..."

But I don't finish my sentence because the woman staring back at me isn't the same one I've gotten to know over weeks and weeks of bickering and flirting. This isn't that feisty woman who argued with me on the street over a parking spot or who stormed into my restaurant and literally poked her finger in my chest to tell me off over stealing employees. This isn't the woman who fucked with my menu or put salt in my sugar jar to sabotage me as payback for everything I did to her.

This woman is afraid. And she has every right to be, given what's happening to her.

I can't pretend to understand anything the doctor said when I first brought her in. I can't even begin to comprehend the way the body works or what it takes to accomplish the kind of thing we're talking about with Izzy's health.

All I do know is that death is a very real possibility for her. And here I was worried about a goddamn opening.

"Is Ashley here?"

I shake my head. "She had to go to work. She tried to switch her shift but wasn't able to. She's coming back as soon as she's done, but I'll go call her and tell her you're awake."

She nods while keeping her half-lidded gaze on me. "Thank you."

"For what?"

This woman doesn't have anything to thank me for. If I hadn't been pushing her, pushing this competition between us, none of this would've happened. She was healthy before —at least healthy enough she was living a normal life and was confident she could open a restaurant on her own.

Now, she's lying here, facing down the Grim Reaper all because of what a fucking dick I am.

Her eyes drift closed, and she relaxes into the bed. Just talking to me for five minutes was enough to exhaust her again. And even though she brushed off my touch before, I take her hand in mine and kiss it.

Something tells me it might be my last one.

———

IZZY

The door to the room opening stirs me from a light sleep, and I blink myself awake just as Thaddeus enters, a tablet in his hand and shrewd eyes narrowed on me over the brim of his dark glasses.

"Isabella, it's nice to see you're awake. Though, I wish I didn't have to see you under these circumstances. How are you feeling?"

"Hi, Thaddeus."

When you're on a first-name basis with your nephrologist, it's not a good sign for your health, yet I can't think of him as Dr. Oakley. Not when he treated Mom for years and years and me since childhood. Not when he used to come to dinner at Grams' house every Sunday night and became almost a part of the family.

I swallow and glance at Jameson, where he sits anxiously in the chair next to my bed.

He's still here.

It could have been minutes or hours ago that I fell back asleep, and yet, he stayed by my side. It makes the truth of the answer to Thaddeus' question hurt too much to voice. "I've been better."

Thaddeus taps at something on the tablet. "I would imagine so." He glances over at Jameson, then back to me. "I was surprised to hear about your engagement, considering you didn't mention anything at your last appointment."

Shit.

I forgot Jameson used that to get in here and Thaddeus would find out.

Jameson pushes to his feet and clears his throat. "Yeah, sorry about that. I just didn't want to get kicked out."

Thaddeus gives him an annoyed look, then shifts his questioning gaze to me. I know what it means. He wants to know whether to continue with Jameson in the room.

I'm not ready for him to hear all the gory details. I may never be. "Jameson, why don't you go home for the night. It's late."

He looks like he's about to argue with me, but the withering glare Thaddeus gives him makes him shrink back slightly.

"Um, okay. I'll come back tomorrow." Jameson locks his gaze on me and waits, but when I don't have anything else to offer, he turns and leaves the room, closing the door behind him.

Watching him walk away makes tears burn in my eyes again, but it's something I'm going to have to get used to. The very reason I didn't want to get involved with anyone in the first place.

Thaddeus waits until the door clicks shut before turning back to me. "He doesn't know anything, does he?"

I sigh and drop my head back to stare at the white ceiling tiles. "Very little. The basics."

Thaddeus wanders over and takes the seat Jameson just vacated. A little informal for a doctor, but given our lengthy history, if he acted any other way, it would just be weird. "It's bad, Izzy. You let it get bad."

"I didn't know. I—"

He frowns at me and raises his tablet for me to see. "Your heart rhythm was very abnormal when you arrived, which, coupled with the fact that you have an infection of the peritoneum, is most likely why you passed out. We gave you medications to treat it and your potassium levels temporarily, plus antibiotics for the infection, but the only long-term solution is beginning hemodialysis tonight. The peritoneal dialysis you've been doing at home stopped working. My guess is several days or even a week ago."

The angry edge to his voice has me cringing and the tears spilling over. "I'm sorry."

He pulls off his glasses and rubs his eyes. "Don't apologize to me, Iz, unless you did this intentionally because you've suddenly developed some death wish? Do I need to worry about depression?"

"God, no." It hadn't even crossed my mind that he might suspect that. "Not intentionally, but there's a chance I may have done some things that contributed."

"Like trying to open a restaurant by yourself and pushing yourself too hard?"

Exactly what he—and Ashley—warned me about over and over again before I even undertook this venture.

They begged me to wait until after I got a transplant. Until I was stronger and didn't have so many other things to be concerned about. But I wasn't having any of that. Grams' death and my promise to her before it meant I had to move ahead and not wait for my life to pass me by.

"Yeah, like that. And there may have been a few missed sessions. I may have missed meds once or twice."

Thaddeus releases a heavy sigh that bears the weight of the history between us. "You know what this means, Iz. We've already moved you over to hemodialysis, and you'll be coming in three times a week at least for treatment until we can get you a transplant match. In the meantime, you'll likely be weak and unable to perform some of your daily functions as normal."

I do know what it means, but I have to ask anyway. "There's no way I can go back to work, is there?"

"I wouldn't recommend it, and frankly, I think it would be stupid to even try. You need to concentrate on staying as healthy as possible until we can get you a kidney."

He would never say that to another patient that way, but we've always spoken frankly with each other. It's one of the reasons Mom loved him as a doctor and why I do, too.

I nod slowly and wipe at the tears on my cheeks. "That's what I thought."

His hand lands on my leg, and he squeezes gently. "I'm sorry, kiddo. Really, I am." He pushes to his feet. "We're going to keep you here a couple days, maybe a week, until we can get some good baseline levels before we send you home. You'll need surgery to put the permanent fistula in your arm in a few weeks. Until then, we'll use the temporary catheter we placed in your chest, and we'll get the abdominal one removed since you don't need it anymore."

"Okay."

There's nothing else to say.

It is what it is.

Throwing a tantrum about how unfair life is won't get me anywhere. It won't bring Mom back. It won't cure this stupid disease or get me a new kidney. All it will do is send my heart rate skyrocketing again and make me feel like even more shit.

Thaddeus pauses at the door and turns back to me.

"What about your 'fiancé' who was here? Do you want me to keep him informed if he asks?"

Regret twists my stomach, and I shake my head. "No. Anything he needs to know can come from me."

It *needs* to come from me.

"He seems...nice."

I laugh despite the lack of humor in this entire situation. "I think that may be the first time in history anyone has ever referred to Jameson Fury as 'nice.'"

He shrugs. "He's been here with you since the moment he brought you in. That says a lot."

Unfortunately, it says a lot of things that are tearing me apart inside.

All I can do is watch Thaddeus walk out of the room with a parting sympathetic smile and settle in for what will undoubtedly be a long and painful road.

20

JAMESON

My hand shakes as I pick up the phone to call Bash. The adrenaline I've been operating on since Isabella collapsed has finally run out, and now, my entire body is revolting and screaming at me to stop and go to bed.

It's so tempting to just give in, to let myself crash and sleep and forget the awful reality of what's happening...but I can't. Not knowing Izzy is lying there all alone in that awful hospital room. The last thing I wanted to do was leave her there, but the look the doctor gave me and what Isabella said made it pretty clear she didn't want me there for whatever conversation they were about to have.

That hurt almost as much as the fight I got into during my last game that earned me these bruises and this black eye. But even though I want to crash, for some reason, I just have to talk to Bash. Something tells me he'll understand.

He answers almost immediately. "Jamo, what's up? It's late there."

I pinch the bridge of my nose and suck in a deep breath.

I wasn't even sure I was going to call him, but as soon as I got home, it was the first thing I did—the only thing that felt *right*. "Isabella is sick."

"Huh?" Bash jostles the phone, and the background noise that floods around him dissipates before he comes back on the line. "Did you say Isabella is sick? What's wrong?"

What isn't wrong?

It feels like I got a glimpse of something beautiful only to have it violently ripped away from me the next minute.

"She isn't just sick, Bash." I have to fight back a sob before I can continue. "It's really bad."

"Shit."

"Apparently, she has some form of kidney disease that's been killing her for a long time. Only it just got a lot worse. She collapsed and is in the hospital."

"Oh, hell. Is she okay? I mean, obviously, she's not okay, but is she going to be?"

I lean back on the couch and grab the bottle of Jack Daniels off the side table. "I don't know." My gaze drifts to the bag that fell to the ground when she crumpled into my arms. I take a huge drink from the bottle and wince, push myself up from the couch, and wander over to pick up her bag before sitting back down. "She needs a transplant."

"And if she gets one, she will be okay?"

"I don't really know. I guess. Maybe?" I pull one of her signs from the bag.

Grandma's Kitchen opening Saturday, September 30th!

Not anymore.

And it might not ever open. Not if she can't find a donor.

Tears blur the words, and I rub them from my eyes. "It

226

sounds like finding a kidney for her isn't going to be that easy due to a lot of other factors."

Bash sighs. "Shit, man. I don't know what to say. I mean, I knew something was going on between the two of you. There was definitely some sexual tension there. But the way you're talking, it sounds like it was a lot more than I thought."

Fuck.

I take another deep pull from the bottle and wince again at the burn going down my throat. "I didn't think anything *was* going on between us. But I was wrong. And now...I don't know what to do."

"The only thing you can do. Be there for her. As much as you can."

"That's easy for you to say. You didn't have to see her like that. You didn't hear her basically order me away."

He sighs again, and a door slams somewhere in the background. Wherever he is, he must be trying to find somewhere more private. "No, I don't. But I did have to sit in the hospital after Greer's accident, praying she'd be okay. And I sat beside a hospital bed with you and Rachel with Mom. And then with Dad..."

This time, I practically chug the bottle. If we are going down this road, I'm going to need some liquid courage. "How did you do it?"

"Do what?"

He knows what I mean, but he wants me to say the words. After two decades of avoiding talking about Dad and what happened, he's going to drag as much out of me as he can now that he's managed to get me talking.

I had always assumed it would be Rachel who would finally break the dam since she's the one who bonded with Dad later in life, but somehow, Bash got over the worst of it.

"How did you go and see that man who called himself

our father? How did you forgive him when I couldn't even bring myself to talk to him, let alone get on a plane when he was dying?"

Just the thought of it makes the bourbon I slammed churn viciously in my stomach. Back when I got that call from Rach that he was sick, I wasn't in any place to even consider talking to him, and there was no way I was forgiving him for what he did to all of us. And when he was ready to finally die, it still wasn't enough to get me back to Michigan. Yet, seeing Izzy like that has somehow broken through the wall I've kept up around my feelings for Dad.

I want to rage about it. I want to call out Bash and Rach for giving that fucker the time of day.

"It wasn't fucking easy, Jameson. Believe me. I didn't want to be there. I thought Rach was crazy for going. It's not like the man deserved it. But at the end of the day, I realized that by holding on to all the shit he did to us—all the anger and animosity and hatred—I was only poisoning myself. He was a human being who made a lot of really shitty choices, ones that affected all of us negatively. But he was still a human being. He didn't deserve to be alone when he died."

"Fuck..." I fight the roll of my stomach and threat of the booze to make its way back up. "What if she dies?"

"You can't think like that. Don't assume the worst. If you don't have hope, you don't have anything."

"Jesus, when did you become such a fucking poet?"

He laughs. "I don't know, man. Maybe Greer brings it out in me."

I snort and roll the bottle between my hands. "Or maybe you're just a big pussy at heart."

"I'd like to hear you say that to me face to face. Or better yet, out on the ice."

I freeze, though it isn't from the threat from one of the biggest bad boys the NHL has ever seen. It might finally be time to face the music. I have two options now—end the call or come clean. But given what is happening with Isabella, it doesn't feel right to keep it from Bash or Rach anymore.

"I could take you on the ice, Bash."

He releases another deep laugh. "Bullshit. You haven't played hockey since you were in grade school."

"That's not true."

Silence creeps from the other end for a moment. "What do you mean?"

I drag in a deep breath and prepare to confess my weakness. The thing I've been hiding, though, I haven't really been able to come up with a good reason why other than I'm a pussy who doesn't want to have to examine my own reasons for doing it in the first place. "I've been playing in an amateur league here for the last eighteen months."

"What? Why didn't you say anything? I thought you hated hockey."

"I never hated hockey. I hated that Dad loved it more than he loved us."

"Shit, Jamo. I mean, we all felt that way...is that where the black eye came from?"

I snort and shake my head. "Yeah. I figured you wouldn't buy that lame story, but I had to come up with something. I got into a little tussle during one of the games."

"At least you're keeping the family tradition alive in that respect."

"Yeah. It's the others I worry about, though." Dad was incapable of truly loving anyone, not even himself. Certainly not Mom, Bash, Rachel, or me. And I'm terrified I won't be able to, either. "How did you know you loved Greer?"

"Oh, Jesus. We're really getting deep tonight, aren't we?" He releases a laugh that holds no humor. "I can't tell you that, Jameson. It was just a feeling. One day, I just knew. If Isabella is the right one for you, you'll know it."

"And if she isn't?"

"The fact that you're this distraught over her being sick is the answer you're looking for."

I think it is, too. I just never thought it would be that simple when nothing else in my life seems to be.

IZZY

Technology may have advanced by leaps and bounds over the last several decades, but hospitals always feel the same.

Dreary.

Depressing.

The last place you want to spend any time.

Even after years of coming here for testing and treatments, getting to know the nurses and my doctors on a personal level, it never gets less miserable. But maybe that has something to do with the fact that I keep getting sicker, too.

I never thought I'd get to this point—and certainly not this young. Even knowing the path my disease typically takes, I convinced myself that since it has been so long and I was doing okay, I would continue to—maybe indefinitely.

Perhaps that was playing ostrich and just putting my head in the sand, but I refused to give in to this until it made it impossible for me not to.

And that time seems to have come.

The battery of tests Thaddeus has put me under over the last twenty-four hours since I woke only confirm what we both already knew. We've reached the point where things are dire. It's no longer a matter of keeping my kidneys working even at little function. They've essentially died, and only hemodialysis is going to keep the toxins in my body from killing me.

Though where I am was inevitable, I've been fighting the urge to have a full-on breakdown all day. Even Ashley here telling me it's okay and trying to distract me has barely kept me sane. Yet, I refuse to lose my shit. Not when I told Grams I'd always be strong and would always fight.

Ashley taps my shoulder and motions toward the television screen. "Did you see that? The blue frog was Jermaine Johnson."

"No way. Sorry, I missed it." I can't even enjoy mindless shows like Webflix's *Mystery Singer* like I should be able to. And not just because of the bad news Thaddeus delivered, but because I know what else is coming and what I have to do.

Waking up yesterday to find Jameson beside my bed was equal parts infuriating and heartbreaking. He was the last person I wanted here and the only person I wanted to see. That conflict warring inside me has been almost as painful as knowing I'm not going to be able to open *Grandma's Kitchen.*

And almost as if he can tell I'm thinking about him, he appears in the doorway of my room, a bouquet of posies in his hand. He offers me a little half-smile, and when Ashley follows my gaze, she leaps up out of her seat and over to him. She leans in to whisper something, and he nods before she gives me a little wave and disappears down the hallway.

Knowing her, she won't go far. She knows better than to leave me alone with Jameson for any real length of time. Knows what it could do to me.

He enters slowly, glances at the television, and points to it with his free hand. "You like the show?"

"It's better than *Prime Chef.*"

Jameson laughs even though it doesn't quite reach his eyes. "You know, if anyone else said that, I'd probably be pissed, but from you, I almost anticipated it."

"I guess I'm predictable, huh?"

He lowers himself into the chair next to the bed and sets the flowers on the small table to my right. "No, Izzy, you are far from predictable." His concerned gaze sweeps over me. "How are you feeling?"

"As good as can be expected, I guess."

It's the same awkward question patients always get asked in these situations, and there really isn't any good way to answer it. Nothing has changed since he left yesterday, except I've had a few more drugs pumped into me that have artificially made me feel a little better for a very short period of time.

He nods and glances around the room while he rubs at the back of his neck. "There anything else I can bring you that would make you more comfortable? I was going to cook for you, but I wasn't sure what you were allowed to eat."

Dammit. Why does he have to be sweet?

It was so much easier when he was an asshole.

I shake my head. "No. Ashley already went to my place and got me everything I need."

He clasps his hands on his lap and rocks forward slightly.

God, he's so uncomfortable.

The confident, shameless Jameson Fury is gone, erased by the stupid disease ravaging my body. A tear trickles down his cheek, and he reaches up to swipe it off.

Shit. Did I really just see that?

A vise wraps itself around my ribcage and squeezes. The pain the rest of my body has been experiencing is nothing compared to what I know is about to come. Because I hate seeing him like this. This isn't him. This isn't who he is meant to be. It's not who I *want* him to be. This shell of a person who stays because of some kind of obligation or pity.

I can't allow that.

"Thank you for the flowers, Jameson. They're beautiful."

He offers me a tentative smile and motions toward them. "I asked Rachel what kind to get you. They were her suggestion. She says hi, by the way. Everyone does. And that they're thinking about you."

"That's nice."

And completely unnecessary.

The whole Fury family is now caught up in my drama all because the two of us couldn't keep our hands off each other.

He releases a sigh. "So, what's next?"

"What do you mean?"

"Well, are you going to get to go home, or do you stay here now until they have a kidney for you?"

God, he's cute. So adorable wanting to understand.

"I stay until they get me a little bit healthier, but I go home until I have a kidney and come back for dialysis three times a week. I'll be exhausted and weak and still spend a lot of my time in the hospital."

This is so much harder than I had prepared myself for.

I take as deep a breath as I can manage and hold his gaze. "But you don't have to."

He stills and narrows his eyes on me. "What do you mean?"

"You don't need to be here, Jameson. I didn't ask you to—"

"I know you didn't ask me to be here, Izzy. I *want* to be here."

His words and the emotion lacing them bring the prick of tears to my eyes. The pain he feels is palpable. And here I thought I was the one suffering.

I blink away the threatening tears and refocus on my mission. "There isn't any reason for you to be here, Jameson. Thank you for bringing me to the hospital. Really. I appreciate it. If it happened when I would have been home alone, I might not be here. But there's no reason for you to stay."

"No reason for me to stay?" He clenches his jaw so tightly, a muscle there tics. "Are you serious right now?"

"I am." Staring into his rich bourbon eyes, glimmering with tears for me, makes this even harder than I could have predicted. "We had some fun. And great sex." I force a smile. "But we both know this was never going to be anything more than that. Having fun." I sweep my hands over myself. "And I'm done having fun for the foreseeable future. You have a business to go run. A restaurant to open. Adoring fans who are waiting for you. So, go. There isn't anything for you here."

My words hang between us like atom bombs threatening to decimate everything in their path. In this case, any affection Jameson might have for me. Then they seem to hit him —one by one. Word by painful word.

He opens his mouth and closes it again.

It gives me an opening to lay the final blow, the one below the belt sure to knock him down for the count. "Hell. You're probably happy you finally got rid of the competition."

"Jesus Christ, Izzy...is that what you really think? That's what you really think of *me*? That I would be happy about this? You being sick?" He shoves out of his chair and leans over me, anger flaring deep in his eyes that held so much concern only moments ago. "That's how little you think of me?"

OF COURSE NOT!

I want to scream the words. I want to tell him how much

234

I want him to stay. I want to have him climb into this bed with me and pull me into his strong, warm arms.

But I can't.

Because I would never burden him with this. With having to sit here and watch me die slowly if I don't get a kidney. Or the weeks and months of recovery it's going to take to get back to a semi-normal life, even if, by some miracle, I do get one.

All the pills and tests and doctor's appointments and everything else I will have to go through.

The emotional expense—I won't make him pay it.

"I do think that, Jameson. And I think it's time for you to leave."

He rears back like I just slapped him, his mouth hanging open and looking completely lost. It hurt him, but the shameless, confident *Prime Chef* winner like him doesn't get knocked down for long. Look at the way he came storming back from what I did to his menu. He'll move on—likely sooner rather than later. And I'll just be a distant memory of a few good nights.

I have to believe that. If I don't, I might reach out for him.

But he turns on his heel and storms out of the room like he can't get away from me fast enough, eliminating that possibility.

It's exactly what I wanted. What I knew I had to do from the moment I woke up in this bed and realized what was happening and that Jameson was here. That doesn't mean it wasn't one of the most painful things I've ever had to do in my entire life.

This alone may kill me even if my damn kidneys don't.

21

EIGHT WEEKS LATER

IZZY

I glance at Ashley in the driver's seat. "Do we really need to do this today?"

She nods enthusiastically before returning her eyes to the road. "Yes. We really do. I told you Rochelle wants to start listing the place again and that we need to come to get a few things out of there before she can do that. You know...personal items."

Personal items?

I don't know what "personal items" I possibly could have left there that are of any importance. If they were, I would've needed them over the last two months and they would already be gone, but if that's the hang up on getting the place leased out to someone else, then I guess it needs to happen.

God knows I won't be using it and can't afford to pay the rent anymore.

The closer we get to the restaurant, the more my stomach turns and my hands get clammy. I wipe them against my jeans.

Ashley catches the move. "Why are you so nervous? I told you...I doubt he'll even be there. It's why we're coming so early."

I peer out the window at the rising fall sun trickling onto the street through the buildings. "I'm just not ready. I don't know if I can handle seeing him right now."

Things have been difficult enough with my recovery without throwing Jameson into the mix. I thought being sick and waiting for a kidney was the hard part, but then once they found a match, it was like an entirely new battle erupted.

First, the infection that almost killed me, then antirejection meds that made me sicker than a dog. It feels like I've been fighting a war for months after finally ending the one with Jameson. And I guess, in a way, I have been—a war for my life.

I can't deal with another war in my heart, too.

Ashley reaches out and squeezes my wrist. "But things are getting better now, hon. It's time to wrap up this chapter and start a new one, right?"

Her words make sense, but it's so much easier said than done.

No amount of time or pain medication can erase the look on Jameson's face when I said those final words to him. When I took the very thing that had once stood between us and used it to crush him. But they had their desired effect. He has stayed away, and I've managed to avoid seeing any sort of press about *FURY* during my recovery.

Mostly because I stayed off social media and refused to watch the news out of fear I might see him on a morning show or in a random photo and have a meltdown.

Books and binging Webflix are my new way of life. But soon enough, I'm going to have to figure out what I'm going to do going forward.

The sheer cost of my transplant means I can no longer afford to open the restaurant even though I prepaid a year of the lease. There's just too much overhead expense and not enough time to recoup my start-up costs and make any sort of a profit.

Which leads to a very uncomfortable question I've been avoiding asking Ashley since she convinced me to come with her today. We turn onto the street the restaurant sits on, and my heart thunders against my rib cage violently.

I stare at the familiar buildings passing by. "Will you do something for me?"

She glances my way. "Of course."

"If he *is* there, will you go ask him if he still wants to buy my range? I could really use the money."

I feel like such an idiot not doing it months ago when he offered, but I was being petty and the world looked a lot different back then. My priorities were different. One-upping Jameson and having something to lord over him meant more to me than having the money that could make such a huge difference now.

Ashley shakes her head. "No. You can ask yourself."

She points through the windshield at the front of the restaurants where a familiar lounge chair sits across the two parking spots in the front with none other than Chef Fury reclining on it, looking every bit as delectable as he did that hot summer morning even though it's now fall and he's in jeans and a long-sleeved T-shirt.

Shit.

"Keep driving."

I reach out to grab the wheel—probably not the brightest move—but Ashley is too fast, and she maneuvers as close as she can to Jameson and throws the car in the park.

"No. You're going to get out."

"No, I'm not." I flick the lock on my door, securing myself inside.

She chuckles. "Did you seriously just lock your door like that's actually going to do anything?"

With one finger, she presses a button on her armrest that unlocks all the doors in the car.

I gasp and scowl at her. "You bitch! You set me up."

She shrugs and tries to look innocent. "I have no idea what you talking about. I didn't know Jameson would be here today."

Jameson.

Somehow, I'd momentarily forgotten the man who was the center of all my dreams and nightmares while I was recovering is right outside this car. My focus drifts away from Ashley and toward the cause of my panic.

His eyes connect with mine through the windshield, the sweet amber swirling with as many emotions as the last time I saw him, and he pushes up from the chair slowly and deliberately.

He makes his way to the passenger side of the car and pops the door. I cross my arms over myself protectively, ignoring the slight pull at my side, lingering pain from the transplant that is gradually improving, and refuse to look at him.

"No." I shake my head. "I can't." I raise a hand in his direction. "I can't handle this today. Just no."

Instead of closing the door and letting me go on with life, he extends a large hand out in front of me, ensuring it will be in my line of vision even though I won't turn my head toward him.

That hand...

Heat floods my core just thinking about what he did with his hands. The beautiful food he created. How he touched so much more than just my body. How he reached inside to my soul and made me feel so...complete.

And I destroyed him. I used the words I knew would hurt him the worst to push him away.

I bury my face in my hands and shake my head. "I can't. I just...can't."

"Please, Isabella, just give me five minutes. And then, if you want, Ashley will bring you home." His voice doesn't waver or reveal anything.

Is he still mad? Does he hate me?

I force my head up and glance at her. A naughty grin tugs the corner of her lips as she doesn't even bother to hide her amusement at the situation.

Yeah, real fucking funny. I'll get her back for this.

One thing the Jameson situation has taught me is that I am capable of coming up with some pretty good tricks of my own. She'll pay for her betrayal once I'm done dealing with whatever Jameson wants.

You can do this, Iz. Five minutes...

With the man who almost broke you...

Because letting him in and letting myself believe in something I could never have almost *did* break me. But now, I've survived a kidney transplant. I can survive Jameson Fury for five fucking minutes.

I hope.

After a deep breath and intake of courage, I reach out and place my hand in his. His strong, warm palm wraps around mine, and he gives me a gentle tug. I unbuckle my seatbelt with my free hand and let him pull me from the car slowly.

Jameson's being so careful, so gentle with me. The very thing I hate so much, even if it might be a little bit warranted due to the pain I'm still in.

He pulls me from the car until I'm standing, facing him on the street; the only thing between us is the chilly fall air and the harsh words that were spoken. His hands reaches out to brush a stray hair behind my ear, and I have to physically fight the desire to lean into his warm palm and embrace his touch.

Instead, I take a fortifying breath. A familiar scent mingles with the one that's all Jameson.

Food.

Something I've eaten before.

Something that makes my mouth water and my stomach rumble.

"What's that?" I glance over his shoulder at our restaurants—at least until my half gets leased to someone else. His sign isn't lit. Besides, he never struck me as a breakfast-joint-type chef. "Are you open?"

He shakes his head. "No. But I have something to show you." His grip on my hand tightens, and he tugs me forward, but not toward his door, toward mine. "Come on."

"What are you doing? Where are we going?"

He glances back at me with humor dancing in his eyes. Whatever animosity he had for me that day when I said those terrible words and forced him out of my life seems to have dissipated over time. Either that or he's a hell of a good actor.

I let him open the door to my place and drag me into the unknown.

———

JAMESON

Izzy follows me into the restaurant tentatively, as if she's waiting for some massive prank like a bucket of water to fall on her head.

She doesn't trust me.

Maybe she shouldn't after all the things I did to her. But she will. I just have to give her some time to understand everything that's happening and where I stand in all of this.

She freezes just inside the door, her gaze bouncing around the restaurant and the staff bustling around getting things organized. Lifting her head, she sniffs the air, heavy with the smells of some of the things I have them working on. With her jaw hanging open, she whips back and looks at me, her eyebrows raised. "What the hell is going on?"

"They're getting ready for your opening next Friday."

"What?" She takes another step and then shakes her head. "No. I can't. I don't have the money to open anymore. And I'm in no physical shape to do it even if I financially could."

I take a step closer to her, needing to be near her even when I know I have to give her time to take in everything. "You'll have help. Ashley quit her job and is going to come work for you."

"What? She can't. She's been there for years, working her way up. She's a shoo-in for chef de cuisine when Emilio retires in the next year or two."

I shake my head and capture her arms in my hands to hold her steady because it looks like she's about to pass out. Maybe I should've thought through this reveal a little better, but once I knew everything was ready to move forward, Ashley assured me it would be okay—that Isabella was ready for this.

Maybe she was wrong.

Izzy's mouth opens and closes, and she sucks in a shaky breath. "I'm not ready. I can't be ready in ten days. I haven't finalized the menu. I haven't done any advertising. Dammit, I don't have the *money* to do *any* of it, Jameson."

I take another step closer to her until my chest is almost brushing against hers. Being like this again, close enough to feel her shaky breath and smell that sweet scent I've been dreaming about, makes the last few months completely worth it. "Yes, you do."

"No." She shakes her head, a mixture of panic and despair overtaking her beautiful features. "You don't understand. My medical bills—"

"Are taken care of."

"What?" Her eyebrows fly up. "How is that possible?"

"A generous benefactor."

"Who the hell has that kind of money?" She freezes, and her eyes widen slightly. "Grant and Sylvie?"

I nod and offer a shrug. "They insisted."

"Oh, my God. I can't accept that."

"You can, and you will. Grant felt terrible about asking you to move the opening date."

She scowls at me. "No, he didn't."

I chuckle. It's good to see her attitude and ability to call me on my bullshit hasn't changed just because we were apart. "You're right; he didn't, but when Sylvie found out, she was furious. And trust me, you don't want to see that woman angry. She had a talk with Grant, and we got things sorted out."

"What things?"

"Well..." I scan the restaurant and the bustle around us that I wasn't so sure would ever get to this point. "As I mentioned, they're taking care of your medical bills, and they're also paying the rent here for another six months on top of what you already paid so you have plenty of time to not have to worry about making some massive profit."

"No, no, no." She pulls out of my hold and raises her hands. "I don't want any handouts. I can't take their money."

"What about my money?"

"Excuse me?"

I raise an eyebrow at her. "Would you take *my* money?"

She scowls at me again and crosses her arms over her chest. "You don't have any money. It's why you needed Grant as a partner in the first place."

I grin at her. "That's true. But over the last couple of months, I've been hired to be the face of a few culinary brands. It turns out being a celebrity chef pays pretty well if you get the right contracts. I'm going to be filming a few commercials and appearing in some print ads soon."

"You're serious."

"I am. I want your restaurant to succeed, and I don't want this little hiccup to stop you."

She chuckles softly. "You call having a kidney transplant a little hiccup?"

A laugh slips from my lips, and I press my hand to my side against the twinge there. "You know what I meant. You're too good, too driven to let this alter your course. I won't let you fail."

She watches me with skepticism in her gaze. "Why? It's none of your business."

Here she goes again. Trying to push me away.

It wasn't wholly unexpected, but it still hurts more than I'd like to admit. To have her standing here so close to me yet trying so hard to keep me at arm's length is a major slam to the ego.

"Ashley kept me updated about what happened with your infections in your recovery. I was worried."

"So, you were stalking me?"

I shrug and smile at her. "More or less. Why, are you going to take out a restraining order against me now?"

She glances behind her at the restaurant where the employees I've scraped together from my place and a few new ones hover and watch us anxiously from near the kitchen. "I might. All this is a little crazy. I don't think you're mentally stable."

"You've always known I'm not mentally stable."

"That's true. But I can't do this, Jameson. I can't take your money."

I open my mouth to argue, but she holds up a hand.

"But..." She releases a resigned breath. "I *will* take Grant and Sylvie's just because he was a dick. *Only* as a loan. One that I will repay."

It's better than nothing.

For a second there, I thought I was going to have to really fight to get her to accept the offer.

"I'm sure I can get you a decent interest rate."

She grins at me. "I'm sure you can." Her smile falters, and she shifts uneasily from foot to foot. "But I don't get it. Why are you doing all this, especially after what happened between us? It's been months...."

"You made it pretty clear you didn't want to hear from me. I didn't want to contact you and interfere if you didn't want me there."

"No, you didn't contact me because you were *pissed*."

I close the tiny distance between us and press my body against hers, capturing her face between my palms. "I'm doing this because I want you to succeed. This is your dream, and you deserve to have it." I open my mouth to say the words I've been holding back for months but snap it closed again. "And you're right. I was angry about what you said that day in the hospital. Because it couldn't have been further from the truth. But I got over it quickly and realized I cared more than I was angry."

246

"Really?"

I press my forehead against hers and sigh. "Really."

Tears trickle down her cheeks, but it takes a moment before she reacts. She throws her arms around my waist and squeezes.

Fuck.

I wince and tighten up my body against the sharp stab of pain.

She jerks back, eyes wide. "Are you okay?"

Nodding, I rub at the spot. "I'm just fine now that you are."

Her gaze dips down to my side. "Another hockey injury?"

I shrug. "Something like that. Now let me show you what else I have set up. But first, there's something I've been dying to do..."

It feels like it's been forever since I held in her my arms, felt her against me, smelled her heavenly scent. This is a moment to seize, not let pass by in a rush to move forward with my other plans.

I lean in and press my lips to hers gently, taking the kiss I've been dreaming about for the last eight weeks and savoring the taste of the woman who holds my heart. Pouring everything into it. Everything we've been through. All the hatred and attraction and tension and loss all rolled into one action.

When I finally drag my head away, she's breathless, and a flush fills her cheeks. "Wow..."

"Wow, what?"

One of her shoulders rises and falls. "I wasn't expecting

that. I guess I just assumed you were angry and wanted nothing to do with me and would never want to be near me again."

The irony of her statement makes me bark out a laugh which sends a twinge of pain to my side again. I drop my hands from her and instinctively grab it.

She narrows her eyes on my hand for the second time. When her gaze reconnects with mine, I can see all the dominoes fall into place in her head. "Oh, no, Jameson. You didn't...."

22

JAMESON

I knew I wouldn't be able to hide it from her for long, and it had never been my intention to. If she had wanted to see me, if she had *asked* Ashley to get in contact with me at any point, I would have been there as soon as was humanly possible.

But what I said to her was true—I never wanted to interfere if she didn't want me there. Plus, I was never quite sure how to say, "Hey, by the way, I gave you my kidney."

Now that she's figured it out on her own—a little earlier than I had thought she would—it kind of saves me from having to figure out how to broach the subject.

As soon as I winced and grabbed my side, I knew she would understand. She would instantly recognize the tell-tale location of my pain because she's undoubtedly still feeling it, too. Two months out, I'm mostly healed, but certain things still send those little reminders that my body isn't complete anymore.

I lock eyes with her confused ones and nod. "I did."

She jerks out of my hold, grasps the hem of my shirt,

and tugs it up. The fresh scar across my side stands pink against my skin under the florescent lighting of the restaurant. "You..." She glances up and back down and tenderly brushes her fingers across the scar. "But how?"

I grab my shirt from her hand and yank it back down. "You are right about what you said before. I was pissed at what you said that day. More than pissed, actually. It felt like you had stabbed me in the fucking heart. Especially because I had come that day to tell you that I was falling in love with you."

A gasp spills from her lips, and she presses her hand over her mouth.

"I was coming to tell you that I would be with you no matter what happened. That I would support you. I was prepared to never leave your damn side until they found you a fucking donor and I could bring you home. But then, you tossed me away like I was week-old leftovers and accused me of *wanting* you to be sick."

Even saying the words now brings back all those old feelings and raises the temperature of my blood. I forgave her a long time ago for what she did and said, but the hurt is still there and maybe always will be.

Tears fall from her eyes now, and she shakes her head. "I'm so sorry—"

I hold up a hand to stop her. "I don't need you to apologize. Really. You don't have to. Because like I said, I was pissed...until I talked to Rachel again."

"Rachel?"

"She told me what a fucking moron I was. Something she likes to remind me of often, by the way. She said you were clearly pushing me away because of what you were going through and that you definitely didn't mean anything you said."

A tiny smile plays on her lips. "Well, I did mean some of it."

I lean in and kiss her forehead. "I know you did."

"But not that really bad stuff." She sniffles and clings to my shirt. "You have no idea how much it hurt for me to say those things to you. To push you away."

"If it was anything like how much it hurt me to hear it, then I do."

It had been an awful few days after, drowning my sorrows in booze and carbs and avoiding calls from a frantic Grant worried about our impending opening I didn't give a fuck about anymore. All I wanted to do was cry and curse the woman who had broken me.

"But the kidney?"

"Well, Rachel being Rachel asked me what your blood type was. And when I told her, I practically went deaf with her screaming through the phone. Because it turns out all three of us are also *O negative*."

"Really?"

I nod. "I never knew my own blood type. Probably pretty stupid on my part not to. But Rach knew from dealing with the hospitals when Mom and Dad were sick. Turns out they were both O, so we had to be. Anyway, once I knew I was the right blood type, it wasn't even a question I was going to find out if I could donate."

Tears flow down her cheeks, and I reach out and brush them away with my thumbs. The last thing I ever want to see again is tears from this woman.

She hiccups through a sob. "But why didn't you tell me?"

I release a big sigh and prepare myself to say the words I've been holding in for weeks. "Because even though I believed what Rachel told me. Even though I wanted to believe you didn't mean what you said to me, even if you had meant every single word, it wouldn't have mattered. I would've donated anyway. Even if you never wanted to see me again, even if you thought I was the biggest asshole in the world." I grin at her. "Which, deep down, I know you still do. It wouldn't have mattered." It couldn't have mattered. "I didn't want to tell you and have you feel obligated to be with me or forgive me the same way you didn't want me to feel obligated to stay with you."

"Oh, Jameson." She leans in and presses a kiss to my lips. This one is sweet and slow and full of all the love I feel for her reflected back at me. She pulls away slightly and brushes her fingertips over my heart. "I love you. I did even when I fucking hated you."

I grin at her and squeeze her as tightly as I dare to not cause her or myself any discomfort. "Ditto."

"But God...all of this is too much. My medical bills, the rent, and now a fucking kidney."

It is a lot. But not really. Not when you love someone.

What I said was true. Once I knew it was a possibility that I could be the one to save Isabella's life, nothing else mattered. The pain was irrelevant. The fact that *FURY* was going to have to be put on hold was pushed so far to the back of my mind that it wasn't even a consideration.

My priorities changed so fast, it almost gave me whiplash.

I chuckle and press a playful kiss to her lips. "I guess you're going to have to think of something *really big* you can offer in return."

She joins my laugh, the carefree humor on her face such a welcome change from the last time I saw her. "I guess so, but I'm not sure what I have to offer."

"Oh, I have something in mind."

———

IZZY

Given all the shocking information I'm trying to process at this moment and everything that is being revealed, Jameson having something in mind is a little disconcerting. The man is obviously insane.

"Should I be worried?"

He pulls away from me, grabs my hand, and drags me toward the wall that separates our two places. "Well, because of my surgery and recovery, we had to push back the opening date of *FURY*."

My heart sinks into my stomach. "Oh, shit. I hadn't even thought of that. I'm so sorry. Grant must be pissed."

Jameson chuckles and wraps his arm around my shoulders. "Don't worry about Grant. Sylvie handled him. Anyway, I didn't want to interfere with your opening. So, we haven't picked a date yet. But..."

He glances at me, waiting to gauge my reaction, but I have no idea where he's going with this.

"But what?"

"But I'm wondering if we're missing a huge opportunity here."

"An opportunity for what?"

"We already share body parts. Maybe we should share a restaurant space."

I practically choke on my own breath and turn to face him. "You're joking."

He shrugs slightly. "I'm not. I've been thinking about it a lot. The two of us together would be unstoppable."

Clearly insane.

What he's suggesting makes absolutely no sense. None at all. From day one, the differences between us have been glaringly obvious. "But we have totally different styles.

Totally different foods." I motion around the restaurant. "Totally different décor."

"You bring something incredible to the table I don't have. Something you can offer that I've never been able to and probably never can."

Absolutely nothing comes to mind. "What's that?"

He presses his hand over my chest. "Heart."

My tears blur the room around us, and I choke back a sob.

In the past, I've been accused of being overly emotional at times. Grams used to always say I wore my heart on my sleeve and that's why I got hurt so easily. Maybe that's true, or maybe I just had shitty luck with friends and in relationships. Either way, it always left me feeling like it was some sort of insult to think with my heart instead of my head.

But that single word from Jameson has changed my entire perspective on it. The way it hung on his lips, mixed with a hint of regret and longing for it.

"You have heart, too, Jameson."

He shakes his head. "Not like you do." His fingers curl slightly into my chest, emphasizing his point. "You have more heart than anyone I know, and you have your Grandmother's recipes, which overflow with it. Can you imagine what I could do with them if I got my hands on them and what you could do with mine?"

I raise a suspicious eyebrow at him. "You think I'd let you mess with Grams' recipes?"

He waggles his eyebrows right back at me. "I think *we* can mess with them together. It could be a fun idea. One new menu with two different dining experiences. Or maybe we keep our separate menus and offer two different options for people when they walk in the door. We can figure it out." He shrugs and grins. "Maybe we call the place *Grandma's Fury* since she'd be so pissed about it."

A laugh bubbles up my throat, and I drop my head back and release it into the space, ignoring the tiny pinch of pain it brings. "Shit. Grams would love that name. But I'm not so sure it's a good idea. Would we even have time to do something like that if you've already started plans for opening next Friday over here?"

He nods. "I talked to my contractor, and he assured me he could get all the approvals we need and an opening between our two spaces done in the next few days. Grant is willing to flat out purchase this building from the current owner to give us free rein with any changes and resolve any rent issues. And I ensured we both have full staffs. It would just be the question of the menus." He narrows his eyes on me. "Which I don't particularly trust you to handle, so I'll be taking any final ones to the printer."

I chuckle. "Fair enough. What about Grant and Sylvie?"

"I bounced the idea off them, and they love it."

I scowl at him. "I have a hard time believing Grant loves it."

"After I told him how incredible your chili was and how much confidence I have in your ability, he came around to the idea. I also threatened to walk if he wouldn't at least consider it. And then when I explained that we wouldn't be a pigeonholed restaurant, and we could offer fine dining items as well as things that are a little more approachable for the neighborhood—people could come in with their kids or with clients—he came around."

When he explains it that way, the idea does have promise. Though I never anticipated running a restaurant with a partner, there isn't anyone I would want to do it more with than Jameson. Plus, we'd have Grant and Sylvie backing us.

"You really think we can pull it off in such a short amount of time, or would we have to push back the date?"

"As long as the inspector can get us approved, my

contractor says he can get it done. And Grant can have the paperwork handled by his attorney the same day we decide on final terms for everything." He looks around again. "We'll be busting our asses the next two weeks, but I think we can do it. I think we *should* do it."

"Wow." I run a shaking hand back through my hair and glance around the restaurant I thought I was coming to say goodbye to. "This is definitely not how I had expected my day to go."

"I bet not."

"I'm just a little...overwhelmed right now."

He grabs my shoulders, holding me steady in front of him and locking gazes. "You don't have to do everything by yourself anymore, Iz. You have me. You have Ashley. We have rich financial backers who have faith in both of us. There's no way we can fail."

Oh, God, Grams would have a field day with this.

She would probably be jumping up and down, screaming at me to run from the offer, to stand my ground and do my own thing and not let a man change my mind. But this man is a part of me. And not just physically now.

He may have given me his kidney, but I gave him my heart long before that, and despite all the reasons not to, I trust him to take care of it.

I wrap my arms around him and kiss him with all the emotion I've held bottled up inside me the last two months. "I've missed you so much. Your shameless arrogance. That smirk you give when you know you're right. Even the way my blood pressure rises when you piss me off." I grin against his lips. "You have a deal, Jameson. *Grandma's Fury* is a go."

He grins at me and waggles his eyebrows. "What about us? I've been medically cleared for physical activity. What about you?"

I lean in to brush my lips against his ear. "I was cleared

on Friday. Do you think we can get rid of the staff for the rest of the day so we have some time alone?"

He pulls back and grins at me. "That can be arranged."

"Good. Because I've been having fantasies about a certain béarnaise sauce."

EPILOGUE
THREE YEARS LATER

IZZY

Jameson slides up behind me and wraps his arms around me tightly, nuzzling his face into the back of my neck. He leans in toward my ear so I'll hear him above the bustle and noise around us in the restaurant and kisses me there. "Is this the happiest day of your life?"

Standing here, staring at what's hung on the wall right by the hostess stand, I almost answer *yes*, but instead, I turn my head slightly toward him and grin. This is too good of an opportunity to pass up. "No, I'm pretty sure that was watching you react to the menu changes I made on live television."

The chuckle that radiates through his chest and into my back makes me laugh even harder. He squeezes me gently. "Ouch. I guess I know what your priorities are. Taking me down a peg tops receiving a Michelin star."

I reach up with one hand and rub it against the rough stubble on his cheek. The man has been working so hard lately that I can't even remember the last time he bothered to shave.

Although, it would've been nice for him to clean up a little tonight, knowing we're here celebrating and that photos are undoubtedly going to make it into some very big magazines and newspapers.

"What about you?"

He drags his head back slightly, with an eyebrow arched. "What about me what?"

"Is this the happiest day of your life?" I motion to the framed page giving us the star and calling *Grandma's Fury* "a culinary wonderland of delight for people looking for unique and incredible flavors or just a taste of downhome cooking." It truly is a brilliant description of what we do, and being recognized for it by one of the most prestigious culinary awards in the world is something I never even dreamed about. But Jameson has. "This is what you work your whole life for."

He shrugs nonchalantly, but I know what this means to him. This is the culmination of everything we've *both* worked so hard for. Years of long hours and little sleep. Days we wanted to throw in the towel. Arguments over dishes and pretty much everything else...that often ended in incredible make-up sex.

It was all worth it.

Jameson kisses my neck again in a way that definitely isn't appropriate when we're standing in front of all these customers. "You think we can kick everyone out of the kitchen for a little while?"

I chuckle and grind my ass back against his crotch where his cock is already stirring to life. "Put that thing away. It's already gotten us into enough trouble."

"Hey!" Rachel's voice cuts through the noise around us.

"If you two are done dry-humping each other, we're ready to make a toast."

We both turned to look at Rachel, and she motions us over to where she stands with Grant, Sylvie, Ashley, Flynn, Bash, Greer, and their daughter Annabelle, who all flew in to help us celebrate when we learned we received the star. Jameson releases a heavy sigh and inclines his head toward them.

I drop my head back against his shoulder. "We should probably go over there."

"Yeah, we should. But I'm pretty good right here." He presses himself against me even tighter.

Rachel groans. "Seriously, you two look like you're trying to get her pregnant in public."

We both laugh, and Jameson's hands slide out over my protruding belly lovingly.

I glance back at him. "Too late for that."

Though that wasn't in public. That was very much in private.

Thank God.

Because if anyone had seen what he did with that whipped cream the night I got pregnant, they would not be able to eat any of the desert we're serving tonight.

"Let's go." Jameson grabs my hand and leads me back to everyone who already has their glasses of wine full and ready.

Grant clanks his knife against his glass to quiet everyone down. "Now that the couple of honor has finally graced us with their presence, I'd like to propose a toast—to this wacky idea Jameson had. I'll admit...I thought he was a little insane when he suggested it."

I scowl at Grant, but he just grins back at me. Over the past three years, our financial backer and I have come to an understanding about some of the things he said and did before we merged our endeavors. He's now seen the light—the fact that *Grandma's Fury* is one of the hottest spots in the entire New York metropolitan area doesn't hurt. But I will continue to give him crap about it until the day he dies.

"But I have to say...*Grandma's Fury* has really gone above and beyond anything I ever could have expected. Congratulations! You guys deserve it."

"Hear! Hear!" Everyone raises their glasses and takes a sip—me of my water.

Then, Bash clears his throat, a hint of moisture in his eyes. It's been nice to see him grow closer to Jameson. The fact that they've been able to open up to each other and Rachel so much more about the things they went through as children has helped Jameson deal with all the feelings he's had bottled up for so long, the ones that ate away at him and made him feel the need to put on such an act around everyone. He's still the same shameless chef he always was, but he shows a lot more of what's underneath now, especially with me.

Bash locks gazes with Jameson and raises his glass. "I just want to add that Mom would've been more proud of you and this than of any other thing any of us have accomplished."

It isn't meant to be a dig at himself or even Rachel but a true testament to Jameson's work and his connection to their mother. She gave him his love of food and made the kitchen his safe place in their home, and now, we've created our own home here.

Jameson clears his throat behind me, clearly uncomfortable and fighting back the emotion he's still learning to expose. "I want to thank everyone for their support, whether it be emotional or financial over the years. There were definitely times I didn't think I would get here." He glances at me with a lopsided grin. "And I never imagined it would be with a partner as beautiful and talented as my wife."

Oh, crap. Here come the waterworks.

It's hard enough to keep my emotions under control as it is with all the hormones ravaging my body right now, but when Jameson gets choked up and says things like that, I'm a total goner.

Just like I was from the moment I saw him on the street that first day, drenched and full of arrogance.

I might not have known it then, but there's no denying Jameson Fury owns me—body and soul. He might think he "won" our little feud, but in the end, I was the one who won because I got this and him.

———

JAMESON

I wrap my arm around Isabella and squeeze her gently, needing the contact with her to keep me rooted and prevent me from falling apart like a total fucking pussy in front of everyone. Bash would never let me hear the end of it if I did, especially after all the crap I've given him over the years about what a pushover he is when it comes to Greer and then Annabelle when she came around.

But it's hard not to give in to the rush of emotion at his words about Mom. If she were here, she would be proud, and it would mean so much more than any recognition I could have gotten from Dad if I kept playing hockey as a child and gone on to the NHL like Bash. Because her love and support and pride were one hundred percent about *us* and our accomplishments, not about what they said about her like it was with Dad.

Bash knows that, too. Which is why his words hit me so hard.

That and knowing how much Mom would be thrilled to be here with her granddaughter and to know she has a grandson on the way.

My son...

I glance at Izzy's belly where her hand rests and have to choke back the tears that threaten to steal the words I have to speak to respond to Bash.

We weren't even sure it would be possible after her transplant, and now, we're so close to having him here. The thought of being someone's father when I had such a shitty one of my own makes me break out in cold sweats every fucking day, but I'm determined to give him everything Dad never could give us. He'll never want for anything in his life, and he'll know he's loved every moment of every day.

Looking at Bash and Rachel and knowing they're just as happy as I am makes the tears I've been fighting finally sting my eyes. To avoid being caught crying, I glance at the long table in front of us, the one we all sat at one fateful night a few years ago when things were so different. Staring at the beautiful glass bowls with floating candles Rach picked out as centerpieces before we opened, the flickering flames remind me that the people who aren't here are absolutely watching us right now and know how much we love them.

I clear my throat and force myself to look up at everyone. "I knew tonight wouldn't be easy. Not with all it took for us to get here. Not when there are people we all want here who can't be, but at the end of the day, we've finally hit a milestone most chefs can only dream about. And we did it with a wacky concept that probably shouldn't have worked."

It was a little crazy to bust open the wall between the two spaces, but it allows us to serve both menus on each side easily and permits customers to choose where they

264

prefer to dine—in a more casual, eclectic, laid-back atmosphere at "grandma's" side or a more upscale vibe on the "fury" side.

Grant thought it was complicated, but somehow, it works. We have people coming in for lunch of Grandma's mac and cheese coming back for dinner to have my roasted lamb and truffle potatoes. They love it, and it even makes it easy for parents to have a nice date night without a babysitter. They can bring their kids and order something from the other menu, which makes *everyone* happy.

So many people looked at it and said it wouldn't work—both the restaurant concept and Isabella and me.

The two of us started out on opposite sides—literally—ready to take down the other in order to ensure victory. But in the end, it was only coming together that saved us both. Me from becoming an embittered, angry, selfish asshole and her from literally working herself to death in order to make her grandmother proud.

Now, we both have our dream, and it's one we share. I wouldn't want it any other way.

"So, thank you all for your unwavering love and support." It's all I can say about that. I can't get out any other words without crying, so instead, I take a sip of my wine and raise a glass to the people who *truly* made this happen. "To Grant and Sylvie, who were willing to take this chance on us."

"Hear! Hear!"

The whole table erupts in talking and laughing, and Isabella leans her head against my shoulder. "You okay?"

I nod and swipe away the single stray tear that makes it from my eye. "Yeah? You?"

"The baby liked your speech." She grabs my hand and presses it against her stomach.

Our little man kicks wildly in a way that cannot be

comfortable. I lean down slightly to ensure he can hear me —or at least, that's what all the baby books tell me. "Settle down there. Your mom and I have a long night of cooking ahead."

Isabella grins at me and shakes her head. "He's a Fury. There's no way he's going to listen to authority."

I chuckle and press a kiss to her lips—long, slow, and sweet, just the way she likes it and I've come to love, too. She melts into my embrace, and I pull her as close as our little one will allow.

Having her in my arms now still feels like it did that first night in her kitchen. The one place I am finally free to be me without reservation or apology.

When I pull away, she smiles at me with tears in her eyes.

"We better get back to the kitchen and get cooking before all these tables start getting restless and we lose that star."

I bark out a laugh and drop my forehead against hers. "You're probably right. But I don't know how I'm going to make the béarnaise sauce tonight without thinking about the night that brought us together and ultimately got us here."

She shakes her head. "That night didn't bring us together or get us here."

"Oh, no?"

"No."

"What did?"

"This." She presses her hand over my chest and takes mine and presses it over hers. "Heart."

———

266

I HOPE you enjoyed *Sinfully Shameless Chef* and the rest of The Fury Family Series!

For another steamy and angsty story from Gwyn, check out her USA Today Bestselling stand-alone novel *Billionaire Lumberjack!*

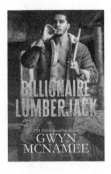

Get your copy: books2read.com/ BillionaireLumberjack

To stay up to date on news, sales, and releases from Gwyn, join her newsletter here: www.gwynmcnamee. com/newsletter

ABOUT THE AUTHOR

Gwyn McNamee is an attorney, writer, wife, and mother (to one human baby and two fur babies). Originally from the Midwest, Gwyn relocated to her husband's home town of Las Vegas in 2015 and is enjoying her respite from the cold and snow. Gwyn loves to write stories with a bit of suspense and action mingled with romance and heat. When she isn't either writing or voraciously devouring any books she can get her hands on, Gwyn is busy adding to her tattoo collection, golfing, and stirring up trouble with her perfect mix of sweetness and sarcasm (usually while wearing heels).

Website: http://www.gwynmcnamee.com/

Facebook: https://www.facebook.com/AuthorGwynMcNamee/

FB Reader Group: https://www.facebook.com/groups/1667380963540655/

Tiktok: https://www.tiktok.com/@authorgwynmcnamee

Newsletter: www.gwynmcnamee.com/newsletter

Instagram: https://www.instagram.com/gwynmcnamee

Bookbub: https://www.bookbub.com/authors/gwynmcnamee